LOVE & VENGEANCE

A LOVE & RUIN STANDALONE NOVEL

J.A. OWENBY

Best Wishes,
J.A. Owenby

LOVE & RUIN EXCLUSIVE BONUS SCENES

Enjoy exclusive Love & Ruin bonus scenes, giveaways, and new release updates! Sign up today at *https://www. authorjaowenby.com/newsletter*

"Gemma, how long have you been keeping this secret?" Pierce's eyes filled with a combination of caution and unease as he digested what I'd shared with him. He rocked back and forth in his leather office chair, and it creaked beneath his weight, breaking the silence between us. Pierce cleared his throat. "When did you receive the letter?"

"Two days ago." I reached into my designer handbag and removed the envelope. Leaning forward, I placed it on his desk. "Here." I brushed strands of my long red hair from my face as I waited.

Pierce's gaze narrowed with concern as he read the contents. "Gemma, he's threatening you and everyone you love. It's obvious his obsession with you hasn't lessened. We have to take this seriously." He glanced at the return address. "The bastard even had someone else mail it for him so the prison wouldn't know what he wrote." He shook his head and muttered a few profanities. "You have to tell Hendrix."

I slipped my trembling hands under my legs in order to still them. "How? How do I tell him that Brandon Montgomery sent me a threatening letter and that he will be a free man?" Bile rose in my throat, and I clutched my chest, attempting to control my thundering heartbeat. Tears clouded my vision as I stared at the floor, then back at the troubled brown eyes of my friend. "He kidnapped and raped an underage girl, then transported her across state lines. Why would he be released early? Who in their right mind would allow it? It doesn't make sense."

Pierce handed the letter back to me, and I shoved it into the zippered pocket of my purse. "What if he's just trying to scare me? I've analyzed the shit out of the situation and struggled with what to do, and I figured my best option was to hire you to consult and gather information."

I glanced nervously around the room, hating the fact I hadn't discussed this with my fiancé yet. I was no stranger to hiding information from him in order to keep him safe, but I felt gutted when I was forced to do it. At least my monster of a father was dead now, which left me with one less enemy. Unfortunately, my father's connection with the Dark Circle Society continued to put me in the spotlight. "I don't feel like we need security at this time, but if he's telling the truth, that will change."

Pierce stood and stared out of the picture window overlooking the wooded acreage. His newly built seven-thousand-square-foot log home sat in the middle of the twenty-acre property. "I can't imagine what this has been like for you." He ran a hand through his short dark hair, his white polo shirt stretching across his broad back, his muscles rippling with every move. He placed his hands on his hips and turned toward me. "You shouldn't keep this from Hendrix. *I* can't keep this from him." He folded his arms over his chest, frustration etching into his expression.

I shook my head adamantly. "That's why we signed a confidentiality agreement. I hired you because I trust you not to tell him. If it's true, then I'll talk to him. Right now, I need your help confirming the information."

"Gemma." His voice was soft, gentle, a complete contrast from what I knew he was capable of. As an ex-marine and the owner of a highly successful security company, Westbrook Security, he was trained to end a life with his bare hands. Over the last few years, he'd also protected me while I was on tour with my band, August Clover. I trusted Pierce as much as I did Hendrix.

"That's why you slid an envelope full of cash across my desk and refused to talk until the agreements were in place? That was a smart play, Gemma."

"I promise I wasn't trying to manipulate you. I need to protect Hendrix. I was well aware of the position I would put you in unless I paid you. You're a man of your word, and I realized that once I was officially your client again ..." I blew out a breath. "I'm sorry, it was the only solution I could come up with. It wasn't as though I could talk to Franklin either. He would have insisted on telling Hendrix."

Pierce sat down again and steepled his hands, appearing deep in thought. "I won't say anything to Hendrix, but as a friend to both of you, I highly recommend you speak to him. Let me look into it. I want to make sure Brandon isn't fucking with you."

"Thank you." My attention darted around the room, and I noted the pictures of Pierce and Sutton that lined the bookshelves. "Hendrix deserves to be happy and enjoy his bachelor party and celebrate with family and friends over the next several weeks. I'll do whatever it takes to make sure nothing screws up our wedding day." I gulped. My throat was suddenly tight with anxiety at the idea that Brandon would be a free man a few days before our nuptials. Shifting in my seat, I rolled my next words around in my head, hoping I would be able to articulate them the way I wanted to. "Pierce, I have one more favor to ask."

He propped his elbows on his cluttered desk, providing me with his undivided attention. "You know I'm here for you, Gemma. What is it?"

Squirming around in the chair like a little kid waiting to be disciplined, I gathered my courage and envisioned Ada Lynn motioning for me to spit it out. Although we weren't related, Ada Lynn had been a grandmother to me. She'd taken care of me through some of my darkest days, then helped me move to Spokane and start my life. I loved and missed her more than I could articulate.

"I was hoping Sutton would also be here, but I'll catch her later." I scooted to the edge of my seat, silently pleading with the universe that Pierce wouldn't say no. "There's something … umm do you?" *Ugh*. My nerves were getting the best of me, and I felt as though I were tripping over my words.

His forehead creased. "What's wrong? Gemma, you can tell me anything."

"I know. Unlike the first day we met." A nervous giggle slipped from my lips. "You were pretty scary at the beginning."

"I was supposed to be. We're friends now, though, so you see the more human side of me."

I nodded and wrung my hands. "Since Ada Lynn is no longer with us, and neither are my parents …" A sharp pang traveled through me, and I struggled to continue. I wondered if I would ever recover from losing Mom and Ada Lynn. My father was a different story. Hell was too good for him. "Franklin is the closest thing I have to a father, and he's on the groom's side. Over the last few years, you've become family to me. You've been right beside me during some dark days, and you've always been there when I needed you. You're like the older brother I never had."

"Thank you, Gemma. You're family to me as well. And you're right —we've been through a lot together."

"I was wondering if you would walk me down the aisle and give me away," I blurted before I chickened out, nervously fiddling with the hem of my Halsey concert T-shirt.

If his answer was no, I would be on my own. My heart ached at the thought. Most little girls dreamed about their dads giving them away, but not me. Not now. If Pierce was concerned it would cause issues, then I would hold my head up and pretend Ada Lynn was on one arm and Mom on the other.

Pierce's expression lit up with his smile. "Hell yeah. I would be honored." He approached me and pulled me out of my chair, then embraced me tightly. "When I look at you, I remember the shy, terrified girl I met for the first time in Louisiana. You've come so far, and I'm grateful I'm a part of your life."

"Thank you," I said. His words had touched my heart more than he would ever understand. We released each other, and I dabbed my eyes with my fingers. "And for the record, the name Charles never fit you. I'm not sure who came up with the idea, but it wasn't flattering." I laughed, recalling the first time we'd been introduced.

Pierce's laughter filled the office, and he sat on the edge of his desk, a lopsided grin easing across his face. "Yeah, the FBI doesn't really give you a choice. When you work for them, you go by whatever name they assign you." His facial features grew serious. "It seems like a lifetime ago that you and Hendrix were in the tornado. It devastated the entire town. Franklin was a fucking mess when Mac called and told him Hendrix was in the hospital."

"I'm not sure what was harder, losing Hendrix to the amnesia or fighting off Carl." The memories of Carl attacking me roared through my mind like a freight train. There wasn't a day that went by that a flashback from my past didn't plague me, but Pierce was right. I wasn't the same person I'd been before I met Hendrix and his sister Mackenzie.

"I'm grateful it's all in the past. You and Hendrix have a wedding to focus on. In the meantime, I'll make a few phone calls and see what I can find out for you."

"Find out about what?" Sutton, Pierce's wife, entered the room, smiling at us. Her long blonde hair flowed past her shoulders, and her blue eyes sparkled.

"Oh, great. You're back!" I gave Sutton a big hug, then sat down again. "Do you have a minute? I need to talk to you."

"I'm all ears." Sutton placed her handbag on Pierce's desk and gave him a quick peck on the lips. She flipped her long blonde hair over her shoulder, her blue eyes sparkling with anticipation. It always amazed me that Sutton could look stunning in a basic top and jeans, but she did.

"I wanted to see if you would be interested in being one of my bridesmaids. You and Claire both, actually. I've just not had a chance to talk to Claire yet."

"Yes! I would love to. Thank you." Sutton nudged Pierce in the side and grinned at him. "I'm going to be in August Clover's wedding. Well, the band isn't getting married, but never in my lifetime would I have suspected I would be a bridesmaid for Gemma Thompson."

Pierce's chuckle rumbled through the room, and he slipped his arm around Sutton's shoulders. "She was bouncing around the kitchen, screaming like a little kid when I called Hendrix last year and asked if you guys would perform at our reception. Even if he'd said no, she got to talk to him on the phone. She was totally fangirling, and it was adorable." Pierce laughed, then quirked an eyebrow at me, and I nodded. He chuckled and kissed Sutton's forehead. "Babe, you're not the only one in the wedding." He winked at her, a mischievous twinkle in his eye.

"What? You mean for Hendrix? Did he ask you to be a groomsman?" Sutton asked, glancing at her husband.

Although there had been some tension between Hendrix and Pierce at the beginning of their relationship, they'd become close friends. Pierce and I had never discussed it, but Hendrix had suspected Pierce's feelings for me were more than professional. Once Sutton waltzed back into Pierce's life, though, it was no longer an issue.

"Gemma asked me to walk her down the aisle and give her away. If Hendrix was going to ask me to be a groomsman, he lost out." A wide grin played across his lips.

Sutton clapped her hands together. "That's perfect! Oh, Gemma, that's wonderful. I'm so glad you said yes, Pierce."

She beamed at us, and I relaxed a little, grinning at my friends. Even though we were all close and practically family, it was a bit awkward asking another woman's husband to give me away. Fortunately, Sutton didn't have a jealous bone in her body. I suspected it was because she could whip his ass if he ever got out of line. Not that it would ever cross Pierce's mind. He was crazy about her. I stifled a giggle that threatened to erupt. Anyone who was as gorgeous and deadly as Sutton deserved my respect. When Pierce had introduced her to our group, she'd fit in immediately.

"Sutton, Mac might need a little bit of help if you're up to it. I don't want the bachelorette party to be at a strip bar." I grimaced at the thought of gyrating crotches in my face.

Sutton laughed lightly. "I'll be happy to help in any way that I can. I know Claire adores you and will be excited as well. Do you have dresses and colors selected yet?"

"No, and since I waited too long to get my shit together, we only have a month to decide on the rest of the details. Poor Mac is a little frantic."

Pierce chuckled. "Franklin mentioned she's bitten off more than she can handle."

Glancing at my Apple Watch, I picked up my purse off the carpeted floor. "I need to meet Mac so I can try on gowns. Thank you both for agreeing to be a part of the wedding." I hugged them goodbye and glanced at Pierce before I left the room. I suspected he would have some information for me by the next day.

Thoughts of Brandon's letter assaulted my mind, and I shoved them back into the dark hole they deserved to be in. "Not now, motherfucker," I muttered as I let myself out of the house and walked to my car. I refused to give him another thought until Pierce had learned more.

I slid into my new Beemer and laid my head on the steering wheel. Inhaling slowly to calm my raging anxiety, I attempted to squash the guilt that was nudging me about keeping a secret from Hendrix. Until Pierce confirmed that Brandon would be released early, there was no reason to alarm him. For the first time since I'd walked into Hendrix's life, he had finally stopped looking over his shoulder, and so had I. Claire, Sutton's sister, deserved the credit for taking down Dillon Montgomery, but it had set us all free. Hendrix and I had thought the nightmare was over, and we'd set a date for our wedding on the coast of Maine. Late September was still warm enough to have the ceremony outside, even though the temperatures at night would dip into the forties. Our vacation home was large enough to house our family and wedding party. At least the media hadn't found out the location. Hendrix and I had taken painstaking measures to keep our plans under wraps.

After starting the car, I tapped out a quick text to my fiancé.

I'm on my way to meet Mac and try on dresses. I love you. Can't wait to see you tonight.

Before I could toss my phone on the seat, it rang. I couldn't help but grin as I pressed the answer button on my steering wheel. "Hey, babe." I pulled out of Pierce and Sutton's driveway and headed toward downtown Spokane.

"Dresses, huh?" Hendrix's voice filled the space as if wrapping me in his arms. Butterflies ran amok in my chest at the thought of him in a tux, with a wedding band on his finger.

"Yeah. I'm excited. The shop actually closed so I could have some privacy and not worry about the media or fans spotting me. Marie, the owner, is super sweet."

"Everyone loves you, Gem. Especially me. I'm counting down the days until I can call you my wife."

"Me too. I have a lot of planning to do before the day arrives. I'm glad we're not touring until afterward. It gives us some time to spend together and with our families."

"Speaking of which, did you ask Pierce?" he asked.

"Yeah. I wish you'd been there. He lit up like a Christmas tree." I couldn't help but laugh, my heart warming again.

"He's a good guy. I figured he would be happy to give you away, but I think you really needed him to do it too. I'm well aware that parts of this wedding will be difficult for you. I have my parents here, but you ..." Hendrix's voice trailed off.

"It's going to be a big day, but I've learned to surround myself with amazing people, which helps so much. It doesn't replace Mom and Ada Lynn, though."

"I know, Gem. I wish I could take away the pain, but know I'm here, and I love you more than life itself."

"I love you too."

"I need to go. I'm meeting Cade and Asa to discuss groomsmen's details," he said.

I could almost envision his sexy smile as he spoke. "Tell them I said hi, and I'll see you at the house this evening."

"Sounds good. I'll talk to you later."

I disconnected the call and focused on the road. I hoped like hell Pierce would have some information soon.

"BESTIE!" Mac yelled and engulfed me in a hug as though she hadn't seen me in weeks. I laughed and joined her on the sidewalk in front of Marie's Wedding Emporium.

Mac's big brown eyes danced with excitement as she adjusted her light pink sweater she'd thrown on over a white tank top. Her brown hair flowed past her shoulders. Although she looked adorable with the braids she used to wear all of the time, it was nice to see her thick strands down more often. I suspected Cade, the love of her life, had something to do with that.

"Hey. Thank you for coming with me. I'm nervous and excited all at the same time." I glanced around, hoping to slip inside the store before a fan spotted me. August Clover's fame had skyrocketed in the last year, and it was rare that I was able to enjoy a day in public without people asking for an autograph. I wasn't complaining, but today was my day, and I needed to be as discreet as possible.

I rapped my knuckles on the glass door. An anxious fluttery feeling descended on me as we waited. Mac slipped her arm through mine and flashed me her toothy grin that I'd grown to love, instantly calming my nerves.

The window shade moved, and kind brown eyes peeked out at us. The entrance whooshed open, and Marie waved us in. Her dark hair was styled in a fashionable bob that fit her narrow face. She smoothed her white blouse with her hand, her manicured nails and diamond ring flashing in the overhead lights. When I'd spoken to her over the phone about how long she'd been in business and the connections she had, I placed her in her mid-thirties. The main reason I chose her, though, was because she was originally from the South, and we connected over our Southern roots. She exuded warmth and friendliness, which was comforting. She'd felt safe.

"Hello, ladies. Oh, I'm so excited you're here! Gemma, I looked at some of the images you selected on Pinterest and I was able to make some phone calls." Excitement flickered through her gaze. "I have four of the six dresses here for you today."

"What? That's amazing. Thank you."

"Oh, hon. I'm just thrilled you chose me out of all the shops to work with. I can't believe I'm assisting *the* Gemma Thompson with her wedding gown!" She covered her mouth with her hands, her eyes widening. "I'm sorry—I totally fangirled."

"No worries. Gemma's used to it." Mac patted Marie on the arm.

"Well, no more of that. Let's get started." Marie guided us through rack after rack of dresses.

Mac lingered behind, eyeing the selection. I wondered if she and Cade were ready to set a date of their own. Marie and I entered a large room in the back of the building, and Mac's hurried footsteps caught up with us. Full-length mirrors spanned an entire wall, along with pristine white chairs and a couch.

Mac let out a low whistle. "This is nice."

"We want each customer to feel valued and appreciated. In my humble opinion, it's what separates us from other shops." She pointed to a stand near the furniture. "I hope you like champagne. It's one of the little perks I love to offer my clients." Marie popped the cork, and we all laughed as the liquid bubbled over the lip of the bottle. She poured each of us a glass, then held hers up for a toast. "To a fairy-tale wedding filled with love and a happily ever after."

"Hell, yes!" Mac raised her glass.

"Cheers to a fairy-tale wedding." I joined my glass with theirs, the light sound of the clinking filling the beautiful room. Brandon's sneer flashed through my mind, and my hand shook slightly. I took a large gulp, hoping the alcohol would settle me down a bit. If I didn't get my shit together, Mac would notice and ply me with a million questions that I couldn't answer yet.

My attention bounced between Marie and Mac; both of them had their attentive gazes trained on me. *Dammit, they saw me shake.*

"I know it's a big decision, but don't you worry about any of the dress details. I'm here to help with every step." Marie gave me a kind smile.

Mac didn't. She pinned me with an intense look, but I ignored it. I was prepared to pass my nerves off as wedding jitters if she made a big deal about it.

I took a deep breath and set my drink down. "I'm ready."

An hour and four gowns later, I was still undecided. I chewed my lip in frustration.

"What do you think?" Marie asked.

"I haven't found the perfect one yet."

Mac smacked her forehead with the palm of her hand. "Thank God. I'm trying to keep my mouth shut over here, but nope. None of those dresses say Gemma Thompson. I know my girl, and although they're pretty, they're not her. They don't scream Gem-ma. You know what I mean? Probably not, huh." Mac sipped her champagne, her forehead creasing in thought.

Marie's eyebrows shot up, and I offered her an apologetic smile. Mac was right, but Marie wasn't used to her directness.

"What if … wait, I think I have an idea." Mac stood, then darted toward the front of the store. "Hey, Marie, can you help me for a minute? Gemma, stay there so I can figure this out."

"I'll be right back." Marie's heels clicked against the tile floor as she disappeared.

I sank onto the couch and waited, wondering what Mac was up to. I reminded myself it couldn't be any worse than the ones that I'd already tried on. A few minutes later, the ladies came back in, their arms overflowing with dresses.

"Here, bestie." Mac hung up her first choice and waved me into the changing room. "You're going to keep your eyes closed, and I'm going to put this baby on you. No peeking. Not even a little."

"Seriously?" I joined her in the cozy space.

"Yup. Get those yoga pants and shirt off, girl. I haven't got all day." Mac snapped her fingers and grinned.

"Remember when we went to Nordstrom and you helped me pick out a dress for my first date with Hendrix?"

"Ohmigosh. That was so fun." Mac snickered. "When Hendrix saw you, he dropped his phone and stared at you. Poor dude's mouth just hung open."

I laughed softly and removed my clothes, placing the palm of my hand against the wall for balance.

"Eyes closed and arms up." Mac hopped up onto the seat, the material of the dress rustling as she moved. "I'm so glad you didn't change after your transformation. You're still Gemma. Just more badass."

I barked out a laugh. "I'm not a badass."

"Gem-ma. You single-handedly took down Carl, not to mention saving my ass from Bra—" She shut her mouth. "You're a badass girl. Not once did you ever give up."

"That's because you and Hendrix wouldn't let me. Plus, I love you guys so much I refused to lose either of you."

Mac slid the material over my head. "You'll need a strapless bra if this one works, or just let the girls be free." She hopped down, then the sound of the zipper filled the small space. "No peeking yet."

The door creaked open, and Mac turned me in the right direction. "Take about ten steps forward."

I lifted the front of the dress and proceeded cautiously.

"Oh my. You're stunning," Marie whispered. "Let me help, Mac."

I continued to not look as they twisted and tugged at the material, lining it up. Mac's petite hands landed on my bare shoulders and turned me gently. "Okay. You can look now."

My eyes fluttered open, adjusting to the bright overhead lights. My attention settled on the image in the mirror, and I gasped. I strolled closer, the long train flowing behind me as I walked.

"Your boobs look phenomenal!" Mac clapped her hands together, and an elated grin spread across her beautiful face.

The room remained silent as I took in the beaded, fitted bodice and the full satin skirt and train. A wide sash rested beneath my breasts, a sapphire stone in the center of it. I pressed my hand over my heart, and my eyes grew misty. I glanced over my shoulder, gaping at my reflection. "Oh wow. There are sapphires all the way down the middle of the train." I turned in a slow circle, taking in all the magnificent details. "Mac, it's perfect," I said softly.

"Yes!" She did a small victory dance and smiled at Marie. "This one caught my eye when we were walking back here. I stripped the mannequin just for you."

"Do you want to try anything else on?" Marie asked, approaching me.

"No, this is it." I winked at Mac and blew her a kiss.

"Well, let's make the necessary adjustments, then you can pick up the dress in a few days."

I stared at myself one more time in the mirror, a waterfall of emotions cascading over me as I realized I would soon be Mrs. Gemma Harrington. I couldn't wait. Out of all the hell I'd lived through, Hendrix was the one thing I was sure of. I loved him with all my heart.

After several minutes of Marie noting measurements for the alterations, I was ready to change.

"I'll be right back while you slip out of the dress." Marie disappeared to the front of the store.

"Are you all right?" Mac took my hand and gave it a gentle squeeze.

I nodded, unable to find my voice. "I just—I love him so much, Mac. Sometimes it just overwhelms me." I offered her a reassuring smile.

"Girl, he loves you too. We all do." She gave me a brief hug, then moved the train so she wouldn't trip, and unzipped me.

I held the front of the dress and proceeded to the changing area, the soft material rustling behind me. Within a few minutes, I was back in my yoga pants and T-shirt.

"Gemma, I have fantastic news." Marie sauntered into the room, all smiles. "The gown you selected is by a new designer who is trying to make a name for herself. She wondered if you would be interested in mentioning her as the designer, and if so, she would give you the dress."

I stared at her. "How much is it? I don't mind doing both for her. I know when I started my singing career, getting paid was huge." I hurried to the gown and glanced at the price tag. "She's only charging twenty-five hundred? No way. The quality is worth at least eleven grand. I've done my research. I'll pay for the dress and mention her, but only after the wedding is over. We're not announcing where or when due to the media stalking our every move. Do I need to pay for it today or when I pick it up?"

"Today would be great. I think Lydia will be beside herself. She's from Oregon and is an amazing designer with a bright future in front of her." Marie gathered the dress, nearly giddy.

Lydia's story sparked my curiosity, and I had another idea. "Do you think she would mind if you gave me her contact information?"

"Oh, of course not! But we can call her to double-check if it would make you feel better." Marie picked up her phone and smiled.

Mac cocked an eyebrow at me, and I smiled at her.

"Hey, Lydia, Gemma Thompson would like to speak to you." Marie handed me her cell.

"Hi, this is Gemma."

"Oh. My. God. *The* Gemma Thompson." Lydia's voice climbed in pitch as she spoke.

"I love the gown. It's more than I could have ever dreamed of. How fast can you make three bridesmaid's dresses for me?"

"I can work up some sketches in a few days, then it will take a few weeks to make them. Will that work for you?"

I split my attention between Mac and Marie. "Marie, if Lydia overnights the items here, is a week for final alterations enough time?"

"Gemma, we'll make it happen. Lydia is phenomenal, though. I doubt we'll need to do much if anything, but yes. Have her send them here. She and I can work out those details, so don't you worry."

I grinned. "Lydia, did you hear Marie?"

"Yes. We can do it. I need to have an idea of what you want, and I'll provide some sketches by tomorrow. We can facetime and dial in all of the details. What do you think?"

"That sounds fantastic. What's your cell number?"

Marie handed me a pen and paper, and I jotted the information down. I also provided Lydia with my number. "Call me later."

"Thank you! Thank you so much. This could be a career changer for me," Lydia said.

"I hope so. You deserve it, and if I can help, then I'm happy to. I'll talk to you soon." I disconnected the call and handed the phone back to Marie.

"Here." Mac shoved my phone at me. "I didn't want you to forget it."

"Thanks. I probably would have." I tucked the paper in the back of my case and wrapped up the details with Marie. After paying for the gown, Mac and I slipped out of the shop and into my Beemer.

"Whoa, girl. That was amazing and emotional and ohmigosh. You're going to blow my poor brother's mind when he sees you in that dress."

I laughed. "I hope so. You always amaze me with your sense of style. Maybe I should start paying you to choose my clothes for me while we're on tour. You're really talented, Mac."

"Really?" A light pink dusted her cheeks.

"Yeah. I don't know why I didn't think of it before, but if you want the job as my stylist, you've got it. We can discuss salary and benefits, then we can sign a contract. I'll need you on the road with me again." I peeked at her from the corner of my eye, waiting for her to catch what I'd said.

"What? Oh shit. Oh, hell yeah!" She did a fist pump in the air. "I don't have to say goodbye to you, Cade, or Hendrix anymore. It's a sweet deal, Gemma. Are you sure?" Her expression grew serious as she stared at me.

"Yeah, today confirmed it. We'll sign a six-month contract, so if you're not happy or if you decide it's not for you, then no big deal. At least we'll all be together again while on tour. If you love it, then I'll mention who my stylist is, and you can build a business from there if you want to. Or you can just stick with me forever."

Mac leaned over and hugged me tightly. "I've always loved doing it. Now I have a chance to pursue my passion."

"You're super talented, Mac. I wouldn't have asked if you weren't."

"Thanks, bestie." She straightened in her seat and beamed at me.

"I'm starving. Do you want to grab some dinner? It's my treat. Maybe Clinkerdagger won't be too busy." I pushed the button and started the car.

"You know I'm always hungry, plus I love their food. I'll follow you." Mac hopped out of my Beemer and waved as she hurried to her electric blue Mini Cooper.

I drove quickly, wanting to beat the dinner rush, but it was Saturday, so I didn't have my hopes up. Pulling out of Marie's parking lot, I glanced at the clock. It was nearly six. My pulse spiked with the realization that Pierce would most likely be contacting me that day or the next. I hoped like hell it was sooner rather than later. There was nothing in the world I wanted more than to hear Pierce tell me it was a lie and that Brandon was screwing with me.

Ten minutes later, I eased into a parking space at the restaurant, and my phone began to ring. My heart hammered against my ribs, and I gasped for air. It was Pierce.

2

I picked up my phone, fumbling it in my shaking hands. It dropped to the floor, and I swore under my breath while I retrieved it.

"Hey," I said, trying to disguise the fear in my voice.

"Where are you?" Pierce asked.

Mac waved at me to hurry up.

"Hang on a second." I tapped the mute icon and rolled my window down. "I have to take this call. Why don't you go in and grab us a table? I'll be in shortly."

Her gaze narrowed at me. "Something has been a little off with you today. What's going on?"

"It's about the wedding. I just need to focus."

Mac placed her hand on her hip, her toe tapping impatiently against the pavement. "Are you sure?"

"I swear." I attempted a smile. "Get a booth in the back corner if you can."

"Okay. I'll see you in a few." She headed in the direction of the entrance and glanced over her shoulder at me, her forehead creasing.

I rolled up the window and unmuted the phone. "Sorry. Mac was with me. She had questions, and I needed to pacify her so we can talk.

She knows something is off with me. I'm having a difficult time hiding it."

Pierce chuckled. "Give her a hug for me."

"I will." An uncomfortable silence filled the line while I waited for him to continue.

"Gemma, it's not good."

I gulped over a sudden lump in my throat as I lifted my head, glancing out the window at the Spokane River. "Just say it. Please."

"Brandon will be released three days before your wedding." Pierce's voice was low. Haunted.

"Dammit." I white-knuckled the steering wheel and drew in a deep breath in order to contain the turbulent emotions that had erupted inside me. Fear, my forgotten friend, settled in next to me and wrapped her frigid fingers around my heart.

"You need to tell Hendrix tonight. I'll assign bodyguards to everyone. You guys are my family and top priority."

My head throbbed as I tried to absorb the news that the son of a bitch would be free again. "I have to wrap my head around this before I tell Hendrix."

I imagined Pierce rubbing his face, determination settling into his handsome features. "Would it help if we met with Franklin tomorrow morning? Let's see what legal rights you have and put a restraining order into place. Then we can talk to Hendrix."

I hesitated. "*I* need to tell Hendrix. He's not going to be happy that I hid the letter for a few days, but I had to know the truth first," I said, my voice cracking. I nervously played with an imaginary string on my shirt. "Text me what time to meet with you and Franklin. Right now, I have to pretend nothing is wrong and have dinner with Mac."

"I will. And Gemma?"

"Yeah?"

"We have almost four weeks to prepare for his release. Try to breathe."

"Thank you. I need the reminder." I rubbed my temples, teetering on a full-blown headache.

"I'm going to speak to Franklin and fill him in. I'll text you in a little while."

"Dammit, he'll call Hendrix. Before you say a word to him, make him promise he'll wait to talk to Hendrix until after we meet tomorrow. Please, Pierce. Franklin is going to flip his shit." My chin trembled with my words.

"I know he will, but I won't explain anything to Franklin until he's given me his word that he won't tell his son. Gemma, I realize you're scared, but Franklin is on your side. He'll want to dig into things before he talks to Hendrix. Go eat. Talk to your fiancé and let me take care of Franklin."

My stomach growled in agreement. "Okay. Thank you. I'll talk to you later." My head swam, and my breathing came in short bursts as I battled with my anxiety. Gritting my teeth, I willed myself to calm down. Regardless of how I felt inside, I had to be strong.

I WAS RELIEVED when I didn't see Hendrix's car in the driveway. I hurried up the sidewalk. When I reached the door, I punched the numbers on the keypad, then placed my finger on the scanner. Hendrix had hired a company to install a new entry system at the front and back. We each needed to use our own code, then it scanned our fingerprint. I loved it because I never had to worry about locking myself out of the house, but it also helped me feel more secure, which apparently would be needed soon.

I entered our home and immediately set the alarm, then strolled through the living room toward the kitchen. I set my phone on the counter, removed my car keys from my pocket, and placed them in the basket that Hendrix and I kept on top of the stainless-steel fridge. After living here for a few years, this was still one of my favorite rooms. Not only was Hendrix sexy as hell while he cooked, but the marble countertops and cherry cabinets created a gorgeous contrast to the light hardwood floors.

After grabbing a glass of wine, I sauntered into the living room. I plunked down on the leather couch, slipped my tennis shoes off, and propped my feet up on the coffee table. I looked up the weather on the television. It might be cool enough to use the fireplace, which meant we could curl up on the sofa and relax. All I needed was a good rain to make it a perfect evening. We deserved to have a peaceful night together before all hell broke loose.

For some reason, I thought I would be able to catch my breath, but my brain was running at high speed, wondering how I was going to break the news to Hendrix. My phone chirped, and I groaned as I realized I'd left it in the kitchen. I stood up and made my way back to my cell to see who was calling. It was Lydia on FaceTime.

"Hey!" She gave me a beautiful smile as we filled each other's screens. "Is this a good time?"

"Yes, it's perfect actually."

Lydia's dark wavy hair fell around her shoulders, and her hazel eyes flashed with excitement. "I still can't believe we're working together."

I sat back down in the living room, tucking my feet beneath me and taking a sip of my drink. "The dress is stunning. I'm really eager to see your ideas for the bridesmaid's dresses."

She flipped her hair behind her shoulder and reached for her sketch pad. "I've been playing with a few new designs. If you like them, we can use one. If not, that's completely fine. This is your wedding, and I want it to be perfect for you."

"Let's dig in. I'm excited."

Over the next half hour, I explained what I was looking for, and Lydia shared her designs and ideas. She sketched mock drafts within a few minutes, and I chose the two I wanted her to flesh out more. By the time we were done, my excitement about the wedding had taken front and center stage in my thoughts. Brandon could fuck himself.

Lydia and I scheduled our next FaceTime appointment, and I hung up, a huge grin settling into place. The sound of the door opening warmed my heart.

"There she is. The most beautiful thing I've seen all day, my future wife with a smile on her face."

I shifted in my chair. "Hi, babe. How was your afternoon?"

Hendrix strolled over, kissed me tenderly, and sank into the couch next to me. "Wedding planning takes a lot out of you." He chuckled and winked at me.

"Here." I placed my wine on the coffee table and hopped up to grab him a beer. I removed the cap and set it next to my glass and joined him again.

"Did you choose a dress?" He took a long pull from his beer, then rested his hand on my leg.

"I did. It's incredible and—" I pursed my lips into a thin line. "I can't tell you."

His blue-eyed gaze softened as he stared at me and tucked some loose strands of hair behind my ear. "I want to give you the wedding you deserve, but I won't lie. I would marry you tomorrow."

"I thought about it tonight, and I'm torn. Does it make me selfish that I want the dress and our family and friends on the coast of Maine?"

Hendrix pulled me into his lap. "It's okay, Gemma. I'm just impatient." He gave me a gentle kiss.

"Me too, but as long as we can keep the wedding secret, I want our day. We deserve it. In my heart, I'm already married to you. The only thing that hasn't happened yet are the papers."

Hendrix's hand slipped behind my neck, his thumb stroking my cheek. "I love you," he whispered before his lips pressed against mine.

I sighed softly. He tasted like home. I placed my hands on his broad shoulders and straddled him. "Show me how much."

Hendrix lifted the bottom of my shirt, his fingertips tracing up my spine. I was on fire. Every part of me hummed with expectation and desire. His eyes darkened as he released the front clasp of my bra and cupped my breast.

I drew my top over my head and tossed it on the floor. Hendrix gently tugged on my nipple with his teeth and slid the bra straps off my shoulders. Threading my fingers through his shoulder-length hair, I whimpered as his erection pressed against me. I rocked my hips against him, growing needier.

With one quick move, he flipped me over on the sofa and trailed kisses down my stomach. He worked my yoga pants and thong down my legs and over my ankles. I sank my teeth into my bottom lip, waiting for him to look up.

"Holy shit." His eyes widened as he stared at my core, then glanced up at me. "You shaved."

"Do you like it?" I asked, growing more nervous by the second. It had taken me a long time to be comfortable with the thought of shaving my bikini area. Trimmed was one thing, but completely bare was another.

"Hell yeah." He fumbled with the button and zipper on his jeans and freed his thick cock.

Raw desire ignited my body. The mere thought of his touch stoked the fire that raged through me.

He ran a finger up my folds and released a low guttural growl. "I'm going to come just looking at you." His thumb circled my clit slowly, and his tongue darted out across his lower lip. Hendrix slipped a finger inside me, and a soft moan escaped me. I dug my nails into the leather material of the couch cushion as he continued.

He pinned me with a heavy-lidded gaze while he lifted his hand from between my legs, brought it to his lips, and licked my juices from his fingers. "I want to taste you." His deep voice was hypnotic and elicited a whimper from me when his hot mouth brushed against my sensitive skin.

A moan escaped his throat as he ran his tongue up my slit. I fisted his hair in my hands and arched my back, my chest heaving as my walls throbbed with longing. Pleasure swirled low in my belly while he sucked my bundle of nerves, and I gripped his shoulders. "Hendrix. Please. I need you inside me."

He kissed the tender flesh of my thigh, then rubbed his dick up and down my folds and pushed deep into me. Hendrix grunted and thrust in and out, his body rocking with mine. My hands roamed the muscled planes of his back, and I scraped my nails along his sweat-slickened skin.

"Jesus, you feel so good." He nipped at my ear and sucked on my lobe.

I wrapped my legs around his waist, pulling him against me. He braced an arm on the back of the couch as he increased his rhythm. I closed my eyes as waves of ecstasy spread through me.

"That's my girl." Hendrix tensed and released a possessive growl.

I tilted my hips up and ground against him. Just as I came down from my pleasure, his climax hit, and he shuddered.

Hendrix stilled, his labored breath tickling my skin. He placed a kiss on my mouth, then a lopsided grin that turned my insides to mush spread across his face. "I get to do that for the rest of our lives." He chuckled, then eased out of me and stood.

I propped myself up on my elbows as he sauntered out of the living room. His ass was magnificent, and I would never tire of seeing him walk around our house naked. He returned with a damp, warm washcloth and gently cleaned me up.

"Thank you." My cheeks flushed. I wasn't sure if it was his consideration that made me blush or the fact that, for some reason, I felt exposed after we made love. Regardless, I loved him for the little ways that he took care of me.

My phone chirped, breaking the mood. I glanced at it, my heart hammering wildly against my ribs. Pierce and Franklin wanted to meet at ten the next day. After quickly giving the message a thumbs-up, I returned my attention to Hendrix. "How about a nice hot shower before bed?"

He extended his hand to me and, in one smooth motion, pulled me off the furniture and flush against his muscular body. "I thought you would never ask." He leaned his forehead against mine. "It's nights like this that I miss while we're on tour, so I plan on taking advantage of every minute we have alone."

I pushed up on my tiptoes and kissed him. "I'm all yours."

I spun around and darted out of the room, giggling as I ran up the stairs to our bedroom. His laughter filled the house as he caught up to me and playfully smacked me on the ass. Then my heart ached as I realized that after that night, there wouldn't be much to laugh about.

3

———————

The late-summer sky was a brilliant blue without a cloud in sight. I drove up the long, winding drive and parked in front of Franklin's garage. My stomach twisted into knots, and I sucked in a slow breath. I had no idea how Franklin would react to Brandon's release, and I hoped like hell he wasn't mad at me for keeping it from Hendrix. Deep inside, I'd decided that I wouldn't tell Hendrix until I learned more, and I stood by my decision.

I held my hand over the car handle and the *beep-beep* of my alarm broke the silence, sending my nerves skittering into overdrive. The front door swung open before I even reached it, and large-framed Zayne Wilson stepped outside. His green eyes flashed with protectiveness, and he brushed a dark curl off his forehead. He wore a white Westbrook Security polo shirt tucked into his black pants.

Every bodyguard who worked for Pierce was mouth-dropping gorgeous. Unlike Mac, I'd never verbalized my thoughts, though. The first time we'd met Vaughn Reddington and Zayne, Mac had gushed full on.

"Hey, Gemma."

"Hey, Zayne." My brows furrowed. "What are you doing here?"

"Pierce and Franklin will talk to you, but I'm assigned to you and Hendrix."

I approached him and removed my sunglasses, then tucked them into my handbag, which was slung over my shoulder. Self-consciously, I tugged on the hem of my green shirt, then rubbed my sweaty palm along my jeaned thigh. "On a personal note, it helps to be surrounded by friends even though it's business." I gave him a brief hug. "I figured I should get one in before it all became official."

A corner of Zayne's lip curled upward. "I'm sorry about the circumstances, but I'll do everything in my power to keep you and Hendrix safe."

"I know." A lump formed in my throat. I squared my shoulders, preparing for the meeting with my future father-in-law. I loved Franklin more than my biological father, but I'd seen his aggressive-attorney side, and I wasn't interested in being in that line of fire. As much as he cared for me, he was protective of Hendrix. I didn't blame him. I was too.

"Are you ready?" Zayne's eyebrow arched.

"No, but time has never done me a favor and stood still when I needed it to." I cracked a small grin. "Full speed ahead."

I entered Franklin's home and followed Zayne through the marble entrance past the formal dining area with the white pillars, through the casual living room, and down the hall to Franklin's office. Zayne cleared his throat as we approached. Franklin stood near his desk, his blue button-down shirt almost matching his eyes. To my surprise, he wore designer jeans. I rarely saw him in anything other than dress slacks.

"I'll let you all talk business," Janice said, hopping up from her chair and kissing Franklin.

She exuded class even in casual clothes. Her skinny jeans hugged her trim figure, and her plum-colored blouse was tucked into the front of her waistband while the back of the top hung free. Janice whispered in Zayne's ear, patted his cheek, then turned to me.

"Hi, hon." She embraced me warmly, and I fought back tears.

I loved Janice. Although she was Mac's biological mom, she was a mother figure to Hendrix, and me as well. I wasn't sure if it came naturally, but she was amazing. Kind. Genuine. Funny. She had the ability to love and accept someone until their heart healed. Those types of people were rare, and I was so grateful she'd given Franklin a second chance.

"Hey. How are you?" I pulled back.

Her large brown eyes flickered with worry, and she tucked her shoulder-length, sandy-blonde hair behind her ear. "It's going to be okay. Take a breath. We're all in this together."

Franklin had told her. I'd assumed he would, but I wasn't prepared for her comment, and I burst into tears.

"Franklin, Gemma and I will be back in a few minutes." Janice took my hand and led me out of the office and into the kitchen. "Sit." She pointed me toward the barstool at the counter.

I hiccupped and grabbed a few tissues from the box in the corner. "I'm sorry. I've been holding this in, terrified I would fall apart in front of Hendrix. Keeping this from him while I figured out if it was real or not is tearing me into pieces. I—I just can't believe Brandon will be a free man." My shoulders shook with my sobs.

Janice wrapped her arms around me, and I rested my head against her. "It's okay. You're allowed to cry, hon." She rubbed soothing circles on my back as all of my bottled-up feelings suddenly rushed out.

"I've already been a little emotional, missing Ada Lynn and Mom as we prepare for the wedding. I can't wait to marry Hendrix, but my heart aches when I remember they won't be at the ceremony with me."

Janice sat next to me and remained silent until I began to pull myself together, then she handed me a tissue. "When I married Franklin the first time, my parents were against it. He was already drinking heavily when we met, but I was too young to see the signs of alcoholism. Daddy refused to walk me down the aisle." Sadness filled her expression. "Mom was loyal to Daddy even when she disagreed with him. I had no family at the wedding. I understand my parents were alive at the time, but it hurt like hell not to have them with me on that special day. If you need someone to listen, I'm here." She squeezed my hand. "As for the Brandon situation, Franklin is going to help manage it. Hendrix might be angry with you for withholding the information about the release, but it's because he'll be scared to let you out of his sight." She glanced at the floor, then looked at me again. "We're all worried, Gemma. Claire went through hell and back to put Dillon Montgomery away, and the second the jail door clanked shut, Brandon signed his early-release form."

Confusion descended over me. "What?"

"Franklin has the details, but apparently Brandon helped the FBI capture Dillon in exchange for his freedom."

"Dammit. This crap sucks. All we did was trade one devil for another." Sucking in a deep breath, I dabbed the moisture from my eyes and cheeks and blew my nose. "I better go talk to Franklin." I hopped off the barstool. "Thanks for being there for me. I love you."

"I love you too, hon."

I headed to Franklin's office, promising myself I wouldn't fall apart again. Poking my head into his room, I spotted Pierce, Zayne, and Franklin. "Sorry about that. I'm still trying to digest all of the news."

Franklin stood from behind his desk and approached me. He placed a hand on my shoulders, his features clouding with worry. "Before we start, I'm not mad at you, Gemma."

"You're not?" My voice cracked uncontrollably. "I thought you would be."

"I was upset for five seconds, but it had nothing to do with you not talking to Hendrix yet. Honestly, I respected your decision to wait until we had more information. You did the right thing in contacting Pierce."

I glanced at Pierce, who stood next to me, and he nodded. "I wasn't sure what to do," I said. Some of the tension eased from my shoulders with Franklin's words.

"I'm going to shut the door so that we can talk freely. Have a seat." He offered me a sad smile.

As soon as Pierce had confirmed that Brandon would be released soon, I knew it would profoundly affect all of us, not just Hendrix and me. Brandon had kidnapped Mac and held her at gunpoint. I'd given him what he'd really wanted in exchange for Mac: me. Thanks to Pierce, I'd made the swap with a plan in place. It worked, but it hadn't ended there. Both Mac and I had been plagued with nightmares, and she'd even started mixing pills and alcohol in order to numb the pain. Thank God Cade had been there and loved her unconditionally while she healed.

I sank into the leather wingback seat and clutched my purse in my lap. It might come in handy if I needed to dig my nails into something.

"I'm not sure what Pierce updated you on, so I'll just start." Franklin sat down in his plush office chair and folded his hands on his desk. "The short version: Brandon worked with the FBI and provided inside information on his father. It was enough that the FBI was able to pinpoint his whereabouts and where he entered the country. Brandon also gave up Dillon's right-hand man. The FBI is looking for him now."

My brows shot up. "Then why is he still alive? My dad—I mean, Kyle—gave up names, and he was murdered in front of his house within a few weeks." Disgust tightened my chest. The very thought that I was related to a monster made me sick to my stomach.

"I don't know. I suspect Brandon will have a target on his back when he rejoins the rest of the world."

"I can only hope." I glanced at Pierce, but his stoic expression was firmly in place as he stood still, his hands at his sides. Zayne remained near the door and stared straight ahead at the wall, standing in the same position as his boss. They were on high alert, their bodies ready to strike at any sign of danger. I leaned back in my chair and reminded myself I was safe. *For now.*

"Moving forward, I'll be contacted with any updates up to the day that Brandon is a free man. If anything changes—if he pisses anyone off, gets in a fight, or causes problems while he's still on the inside— his early release could be revoked."

"Really?" A rush of optimism surged through me.

Franklin held up his hand. "I wouldn't count on it, though. His deal is pretty solid. The FBI got what they wanted. To them, Brandon is the least of their concerns."

My shoulders sagged forward, hope slipping away from me as Franklin continued to talk.

"For now, let's focus on the wedding, and I'll help you file a protective order. Brandon won't be allowed within three hundred feet of you or any of us."

I snorted. "You and I both know that's too close. He's smart."

"He is smart, but his emotions tend to overrule his judgment. We'll be counting on that as we formulate the next steps after the wedding."

My breath hitched. "What do you mean?"

"Pierce and I will do some more digging, and we'll try to determine how much of a danger he is at that point. He'll need money after he's released, and I have plenty."

I briefly closed my eyes, then opened them again. "You're going to pay him to disappear in exchange for our freedom." My gaze connected with his. "Do you think it will work?"

Franklin rubbed his chin and leaned back in his seat. "I'll do my research, and if I think it's feasible, he'll get a nice fat check to set him up for the rest of his life. Far away from all of us. That's for me to work through, though. Not you. It might not be an option at all, but I'm contemplating every possibility at this point, including setting him up so his parole is revoked."

"What if it's not?" I massaged my temples, attempting to alleviate the pounding in my head.

A heavy silence blanketed the room. "Then we leave. All of us."

Internally, I groaned with frustration. Nothing about this conversation was encouraging. "And go where? Franklin, I know we need a plan, but Hendrix and I are in the middle of our careers. We have tours …" I trailed off when I met the steely eyes of my future father-in-law.

"I will keep my family safe at all costs." His tone was clipped and left no room for argument.

Franklin didn't pull rank on us very often, but when he did, it was because he was protecting us. I nodded, unable to articulate what I wanted to say. All I knew was that Brandon needed to be silenced once and for all.

"I need to talk to Hendrix." I glanced at the clock on Franklin's shelf. It was already eleven thirty. Hendrix would be home by the time I returned. He'd planned to work on song selections and writing in the studio that afternoon. I got up and sighed. "I'm sure he'll want to speak to you after we talk."

Franklin stood and shoved his hand into the front pocket of his jeans. "I support your decision, Gemma. I know it's difficult not sharing information with Hendrix, but you made the right call. Let me know if I can help. Neither of you say anything to Mac, though. I'm going to have you, Hendrix, Mac, and Cade over for dinner tomorrow night. Let's try to relax and enjoy each other before—" Franklin's lips pursed together. "Before I have to tell my other daughter that her kidnapper is about to be released from prison."

A small cry escaped from my lips, and my hand covered my mouth. "Oh God, Franklin." I rushed over to him and threw my arms around his neck. "My heart is breaking. Mac and Cade are finally doing well. Mac's nightmares have calmed down too." Guilt whispered in my ear that once again I'd brought danger to the people I love. "This is all my fault."

Franklin wrapped me in a fatherly embrace. "You can't blame yourself for someone else's actions, and you can't reason with insanity, Gemma. You're not responsible for Brandon's choices. Just remember that we're family, and we will get through this situation together."

I stepped away and nodded, a heavy weight crushing my chest. "Please be honest with me. Claire and Vaughn just took down Dillon Montgomery. Now Brandon is coming back. There are always other people waiting in the wings to take over if something goes wrong. Even if Brandon is removed, we've pissed off the entire Dark Circle Society, which makes me wonder." I looked at the floor, then back to Franklin. "Will we ever be rid of the society?" A high pitch rang in my ears, and I reached for the corner of Franklin's desk to steady myself.

"Gemma?" Franklin's hands gently grabbed my arms. "Gemma? Are you all right?"

Playing it cool, I shrugged, refusing to meet his protective gaze. "Yeah. When I get stressed, my ears ring. It was just worse this time."

"Sit." Pierce slid a chair up to my legs, and I sank into it gratefully.

"I haven't eaten anything today either." I leaned back in the seat and tried to relax.

"Zayne, can you have Ruby get some food for Gemma, please?"

"Yes, sir." Zayne quietly left the room.

"How long has this been happening?" Franklin asked.

"I don't know. Not all the time, but more often in the last few days since I received the letter from Brandon."

"If it occurs again, I need you to call your doctor and schedule an appointment. I can't have anything happen to you. You're too important to Hendrix, Mac, and our family." Franklin squeezed my hand and made himself comfortable in his office chair, his perceptive attention never leaving me.

A few minutes later, Zayne arrived with a plate that included an omelet and fresh fruit. "Thank you." I popped a grape in my mouth, the sweet juice exploding on my tongue as I chewed it. "You didn't answer my question." I took a bite of my eggs, and my eyes rolled into the back of my head. "Man, I miss Ruby's cooking."

"She's great." Franklin glanced out the window and sighed. "I'm a fantastic bullshitter, Gemma. I built my life on it, in and out of court and in business dealings. I've always been honest, but I understand how to spin information in order to get what I want or to soothe someone."

"You're an attorney, and I wouldn't expect anything different." I set my fork down and rolled a grape in between my fingers.

"Keep eating." Franklin pointed at my breakfast. I took another bite, and he continued. "I don't know, Gemma. Most people don't find themselves in the middle of a dark corner of hell. The society is vast. Even if Dillon and Brandon are removed, we're still in a difficult situation." He rubbed his chin, worry evident in his features. "I'm not sure, and honestly, I don't want to say it out loud." He shifted in his chair, his expression solemn. "I think we might be looking over our shoulders for the rest of our lives." His voice was sad, lost. Franklin swallowed, stress pouring off of him in waves.

A cold, sinking feeling overwhelmed me. Even though I'd suspected it might be the case, hearing Franklin verbalize my fear made it real. Now it felt ingrained. There was a possibility that we would never truly be free. I gripped the collar of my shirt, struggling to breathe. *Focus. Take a breath.*

I quickly finished my eggs and stood. "Thank you for feeding me. I'll take my plate to the kitchen on my way out."

"Gemma, you need to take care of yourself." Franklin's features were filled with fatherly love and concern.

"I will. I'll talk to Hendrix when I get home. I can't wait until tomorrow at dinner. Plus, we both know he'll need to process all of this before he's ready to help Mac." I turned to Pierce, but remained silent. The protectiveness in his eyes spoke volumes. Not only was I crushed that we were dealing with a maniac, but I was also well aware of how dangerous the situation was.

Zayne fell into step behind me, and I paused, turning back to Franklin. "Brandon's not out yet. Do we need Zayne right now?"

Pierce stepped forward. "We're not taking any chances. Brandon is well connected."

I bit my bottom lip. "Can Zayne wait to appear until I've talked to Hendrix? The second he sees him, he'll know something is wrong."

"He'll be out of sight but surveying the perimeter. Once Brandon is released, a bodyguard will be inside the home with you, and one on the outside."

Dammit. There went our privacy around the house. "Just like on tour." The moment I said it, I realized there might not be any more concerts. I balled my hands into tight fists. I refused to let this motherfucker steal our lives. I didn't care what I had to do, but I would win, and this time, it would be for good.

4

Storm clouds had drifted in, darkening the afternoon and my mood even more. I punched in my front-door code and placed my finger over the sensor. It unlocked, and I opened it, glancing over my shoulder at Zayne's car up the road. I wasn't sure if he planned to stay there or look for a more concealed spot, but at the moment, I didn't care.

"I'm in the kitchen!" Hendrix called out.

Rummaging around in my purse for the letter, I gave my fear a kick in the ass and moved my feet forward as I offered a silent prayer that Hendrix wouldn't come unglued.

"Hey." My pulse kicked up as I drank in the sight of Hendrix's sculpted body as he unloaded the dishes from the dishwasher and put them away. His black sweatpants hung low on his hips, and he'd ditched the August Clover concert T-shirt he'd been wearing earlier that day. He was sexy as hell when he cleaned the house, and I loved him for never treating me like a maid. We were equals. Partners.

"I figured I would get some things done before I disappeared into the studio." He smiled as he placed the glasses in the cabinet. Finally, he looked at me, his expression falling as his beautiful blue eyes connected with mine. "What's wrong, Gem?" In a few quick strides, he was in front of me, his gentle lips on mine. "Talk to me, babe." He pressed his forehead against mine, and my heart melted. I couldn't bear the thought of what I was about to do to him.

"I'm so sorry," I croaked. "I'm so sorry."

Hendrix rubbed my arms, attempting to soothe me, his expression confused. "For what? Whatever it is, we can work it out."

I stepped away, our gazes connecting. "Do you promise?" I knew the moment the words had rolled off my tongue that I wasn't being fair. He might never forgive me for keeping this from him or trust me again. At least, that was my greatest fear.

"Yes."

I buried my head in my hands, gathered all the courage I had, and looked at Hendrix. "Zayne is outside. Pierce assigned him to protect us."

"What? Why?" Hendrix took my hand and guided me to the dining table. "Sit."

If the situation hadn't been so damned serious, I would have laughed. He sounded just like Franklin. I sat down, my spine ramrod straight. He settled into the chair next to me and waited patiently for me to speak.

"Zayne ..." I shook my head, trying to form the words that I needed to say. "Baby ..." Tears blurred my vision, and anger stirred deep inside me. I tilted my chin up. "You're going to be mad at me, and I'm sorry. I had to protect you until I knew the truth."

"What truth?" Hendrix's forehead creased in confusion.

"Brandon mailed me a letter, and I received it three days ago. He's being released early." I slid the envelope across the table to him, then remained silent as he read it.

Hendrix bolted out of the chair and sent it skittering backward into the kitchen. He shook his head. "Are you sure?"

"Positive. It's why I waited to tell you. I needed to be a hundred percent positive that he wasn't fucking with us. He'll be released three days before our wedding."

Rage rippled through him, and his eyes glowed with fury. "God dammit!" His fists clenched, then it snapped out in front of him, connecting with the wall. The sheetrock groaned as it tore apart, and a gaping hole was left behind.

"Hendrix!" I jumped up and ran toward him. "I'm sorry." I grabbed his hand, but he jerked it away. A storm of emotions—anger, disbelief, and fear—clouded his features.

Then his mouth dropped, and he wrapped his arms around me and hugged me tightly. "Jesus, Gem. I'm sorry. This can't be happening." His fingers dug into my back as he clung to me.

I embraced him, feeling his racing heartbeat against my ear. Somehow, I managed to choke out my next words. "He's coming for me."

Hendrix's knees buckled, and we sank to the floor, clinging to each other, struggling to find a thread of hope to hold onto.

"You're mine. He can't have you. I won't let him," Hendrix whispered against my hair.

We sat in silence. The weight of the situation nearly suffocated me. After a few minutes, Hendrix shifted, and he leaned against the wall and pulled me into his lap. I laid my head on his shoulder and snuggled into him.

"Are you mad at me?" I peeked up at him.

He tilted my chin up and kissed me gently. "Yes and no. I'm trying to wrap my brain around how Brandon will be walking free. Gem, I wish you'd told me the minute you opened the letter. At the same time, I would have gone straight to Dad to find out if it was true before I gave you the news."

His fingertips traced my cheek, and my pulse began to slow down. "I did. I made an appointment with Pierce, slid an envelope full of cash across the desk for payment, then said I wouldn't talk until a confidentiality agreement was in place."

To my surprise, a low chuckle rumbled through Hendrix. "Smart move, babe. He would have told me if you hadn't done just that."

"I know, and I wouldn't have blamed him, but I needed time to find out if it was true. Pierce made some calls and confirmed it for me, then I met him and your dad this morning. I've felt sick keeping this from you. Please don't be upset with me."

Hendrix kissed the tip of my nose. "I'm not. It just hurts that you carried the burden around on your own, but you made the right call."

"It was hell, and seeing your reaction was worse," I said. Tenderness filled his expression, and it took my breath away. "I love you so much." I cupped the side of his face and stroked his cheek with my thumb.

"I love you too." He closed his eyes briefly and leaned into my touch. "So what's next?"

"Your dad said for now that we keep planning the wedding, and he'll find out more. At this point, we know that Brandon worked with the FBI and helped them capture his father." I frowned, an idea dawning on me. "For some reason, I could have sworn that the FBI had told Pierce and Claire that Dillon was in California, though."

I sat up, and a glimmer of hope coursed through me. "After he was arrested, she filled me in. It's why Pierce and Sutton assumed she was safe, then she and Vaughn were at the park when Dillon arrived." A sharp pain of anxiety hit me, and I pressed my hand to my chest and attempted to rub it away. I stared at the floor, puzzling through my racing thoughts. "Babe, what if Brandon fed the FBI the wrong information?"

Hendrix's expression lit up. "If we can prove it, then his release might be revoked."

"Call Franklin, just in case this is what we need to keep him behind bars." I crawled off his lap, and we both stood. "I'll let Zayne know he no longer has to park up the street."

"He's up the street?"

"Yeah, I wanted to talk to you before you saw his car. It would have tipped you off that something was wrong."

Hendrix scrubbed his face with his hands. "Let's hope we're about to turn the tide and we can send Zayne on his way soon."

Hendrix picked up his phone off the counter and called his dad. I hoped like hell this was enough to stop Brandon, and Franklin wouldn't have to tell Mac that her worst nightmare was coming back.

5

"Are you ready?" Hendrix asked me as he parked his Lexus next to Cade's convertible BMW 8 at the side of Franklin's house Monday evening.

"No, but if I were, you would need to have my head checked. I can't imagine Franklin is looking forward to delivering the news to Mac and Cade. It's going to tear me up seeing her reaction."

Hendrix leaned over and kissed me tenderly. "I know but remember that I love you."

"I love you too. I'm just sorry that I brought all of this crap into your life." I stared out the passenger window, refusing to look at him. I couldn't lose my shit right before we went inside Franklin's house. "I realize you and Brandon had your issues before I arrived in Spokane, and his brother, Matthew, drove the car that ..." I couldn't say it out loud. "If I hadn't moved and attended college here, maybe you and your family would be free from him. For whatever reason, he's obsessed with me and hell-bent on hurting everyone I love."

"Bullshit. I have my own issues with the son of a bitch. He should have turned his brother in for what he did to Kendra, not to mention he raped Mac's best friend from high school, Eva, at a frat party." His voice held a sharp edge to it. "Brandon is fucked-up, Gem. This isn't your fault. If you weren't here, I would still have a gaping hole in my life. Mac and Dad would too."

I dared a peek at him.

"Babe, I'm a better man with you next to me. You taught me to love —to live again."

My heart fluttered. "Really?"

"Yeah, really."

I pressed my mouth against his, tasting heaven.

"Let's go. Zayne is probably tired of watching us in our car." Hendrix winked at me, then hopped out.

I glanced over my shoulder. Zayne was patiently waiting a few feet away from Hendrix's Lexus, but his body language was unreadable. He could have glared at me behind his Ray-Ban sunglasses and I would never have known it.

A cool summer breeze blew across the property and rustled the tree leaves as we approached the front of the house. I looked down the hill to the guesthouse. Suddenly, the memory of knocking on Pierce's door and asking him to train me in self-defense came rushing back. A small smile tugged at the corners of my mouth. At the time, he'd terrified me, even though I knew we were connected on a deeper level after Carl had attacked me. I never would have imagined that he would walk me down the aisle in less than a month.

"We're here!" Hendrix called as he entered the foyer.

"Hi, hon." Janice appeared from the casual living room, looking stunning. Her long hair framed her face, and she smoothed her designer jeans and turquoise top. "How are you?" She hugged Hendrix, then me. Her expressive dark eyes surveyed us. "You didn't sleep much last night, huh?"

I glanced at Hendrix.

"How did you know?" he asked.

"I know my son." She patted him on the cheek. "Don't forget that we have brilliant minds involved in the situation with Brandon, not to mention exceptional bodyguards. We're all personally invested in how his release plays out. It's going to be all right." She reached for my hand. "Plus, we're weeks away from a fabulous wedding." A sparkle flickered in her eyes.

"I'm ready." I smiled up at my fiancé.

"Let's go into the dining room. Mac, Cade, and Franklin are already there. I was waiting for you two. Your father wants to eat first and spend time together before he drops the news."

"That sounds nice. I'm in no rush to turn Mac's world upside down." I nervously tucked my hair behind my ear.

"Me either." Hendrix threaded his fingers through mine.

We followed Janice into the dining area, and my attention immediately landed on the empty chair where Ada Lynn used to sit. Although I missed her more than I admitted to anyone, I was grateful she wasn't here to live through this shit show. She'd endured enough, but at least she'd experienced Washington and a few months of living in luxury before she passed on. I inhaled deeply, attempting to clear the ache in my chest.

"Bestie!" Mac hopped out of her seat and hugged me.

I laughed. Her excitement was contagious. "Did you tell Cade and Franklin about your new job offer?"

She bounced on her tiptoes. "Not yet. I thought we could share the news with them over dinner."

"What are you two up to?" Hendrix asked while he embraced his sister.

I feigned shock. "Us?"

"Mac and Gemma are always up to something, and usually, it's pretty entertaining." Cade snickered, then stood and gathered me in an awesome hug. He released me and squeezed my shoulder. "It's been a few weeks since I've seen you. How are you doing with all the wedding planning?"

I gave Franklin a knowing look while we all settled in at the table. "I'm good. Excited about the big day and changing my last name." I beamed at Hendrix as he wrapped his arm around my shoulders and pulled me into him.

"You decided to take Harrington?" Franklin asked, appearing pleased.

"I did. I don't think it will affect the band at all. I'll hyphenate my name on the music if I need to. If I were a solo singer, it might have mattered. Regardless, I no longer want Thompson as my last name. It's tied to a lot of bad memories and people. My mom is the only one that matters, and if she were here, I think she would support my decision."

Hendrix kissed the side of my head. "Gemma Harrington. I love the sound of that," he whispered.

Butterflies scattered in my tummy, and I placed my hand on his knee. "Me too."

"Although I would have understood if you'd chosen not to change from Thompson, I'm happy that you'll officially be a Harrington." Franklin reached for Janice's hand as they exchanged an affectionate glance. At one time, they'd been married and divorced. A few years after Franklin admitted he was an alcoholic and rebuilt his life, he and Janice had decided to begin a new chapter together.

Janice hopped up from her seat, a broad smile on her face, and strolled to the hutch. She began removing wineglasses and set them on the table. Although she already knew about Brandon, she was doing an exceptional job of staying positive and keeping our time together light and fun.

"Cade, there's a nice chardonnay in the fridge. Why don't you open a few bottles, and let's make a toast."

"You bet." Cade placed a sweet kiss on Mac's forehead, then excused himself and went to the kitchen.

When he returned, he and Janice poured the wine, and we each took a glass. Except for Franklin. He stuck to his water.

Janice raised hers. "To family."

"Cheers." We all clinked our glasses together, and I happily took a sip.

"So, what's this talk about a job offer, Mac?" Franklin asked, his blue eyes twinkling with pride as he looked at her.

My heart warmed. In addition to Franklin becoming a father figure to me, his relationship with Mac had strengthened over the last few years.

"Well ..." Mac peeked at me. "Gemma offered me a position as her stylist." Her attention bounced to Cade.

"Wait. Does this mean she would tour with us?" Cade asked me, lighting up like a Christmas tree.

"It does." I laughed as Cade pulled Mac into his lap, then kissed her on the cheek and hugged her tightly.

"I love the idea, babe." Cade's expression had filled with adoration for my best friend.

Mac slid out of his lap, eyeing Franklin, but he just smiled.

"Damn, why didn't I think of that?" Hendrix asked. "Mac, you've always done a fantastic job dressing Gemma for special occasions."

"Right? I mean, your response to her transformation the night you took her out on her first-ever date was priceless." Mac giggled.

A low chuckle rumbled through Hendrix's chest. "I'll never forget that evening. Ever." He cleared his throat, desire flashing in his gaze as he stared at me. "Dad, that was the same evening you met Gemma at the event in Spokane."

"Oh, that was your first date?" Franklin said. "I didn't realize that."

"Yeah. Mac took her shopping and picked out her dress and accessories. She's a natural."

"She is," Janice added. "Even when she was younger, Mac would select or put together my outfits." Janice laughed. "Her changes were always better than what I'd originally chosen."

"We just need a contract drawn up with a salary. After that, it's official. She'll tour with us, shop for me, and pick out my clothes for concerts and photo shoots." I grinned at her.

"Speaking of which, I found Gemma's wedding gown!" Mac said, bouncing in her seat.

"You found one already?" Cade asked me.

"I didn't. Mac found me *the* one." I grinned at my bestie. "It's perfect. Stunning." A dreamy sigh slipped from my lips.

"The wedding will be here before we know it." Janice smiled and took a sip of her wine.

"Well, I think hiring Mac is a fantastic idea. It'll keep my man focused while we're on tour too. He tends to get a bit mopey and cranky without you, Mac." Hendrix flashed her a lopsided grin.

"Aww, babe." Mac leaned over and gave Cade a smooch on his cheek.

"It sucks when we're apart for that long," he muttered.

"I think it's good that you'll all be together on the next tour. It seemed to go well last time." Franklin's poker face was intact, but I didn't miss the small hint of worry in his expression.

The timer on the oven buzzed, breaking the comfortable conversation and reminding me why we were really here tonight.

"Oh, the roast is ready. Girls, I gave Ruby the night off, so why don't you help me in the kitchen?" Janice excused herself, and Mac and I followed.

The guys continued to chat as we talked about the upcoming nuptials and gathered plates and silverware. This was how life was supposed to be—spending time with the people you loved. Brandon's letter bombarded my thoughts, and I shoved the fear away, refusing to let him steal my happiness. Not yet anyway. He would have enough attention from us in a little while.

Half an hour later, we all relaxed in our chairs with full bellies. Franklin picked up his napkin and wadded it, then tossed it on his empty plate. "Mac ..."

Hendrix's body tensed next to mine, and I moved my hand beneath the table and placed it on his leg. Dread bundled inside me, and my dinner churned in my stomach. I wondered if I would make it through the announcement without needing to run to the bathroom. Willing the nausea to settle down, I released a quiet breath. Hendrix's arm eased around me, his fingers slipping beneath my hair and lightly rubbing my neck.

"Yeah?" She flashed him a big smile, then it slipped away as she registered his seriousness.

Janice shifted in her chair and took Mac's hand. Bewilderment shadowed Mac's face. Cade shot Hendrix a *What the hell?* look, and Hendrix tilted his chin up slightly in response. Then his focus landed on his sister.

"You're scaring me. What's happening?" Mac's leg began to bounce beneath the table, shaking the silverware.

Janice rubbed Mac's back in an attempt to calm my bestie, but Mac wasn't stupid, and she only grew more agitated. My heart thundered in my ears, and I mentally urged Franklin to hurry up and tell her.

"I want you to know that I'm already working on a solution with Pierce and Sutton, but you and Cade will have bodyguards when you leave here." Franklin's fingers tapped against his water glass.

"What? Why?" Mac looked at me, a million questions in her big brown eyes.

"Brandon Montgomery will be released from prison three days before Hendrix and Gemma's wedding."

Mac didn't say a word, and her focus bounced from Cade to her parents, then to Hendrix and me. "I know you wouldn't mess with me about something so important, right? I mean, he broke federal law and transported a fourteen-year-old across state lines. That bastard raped her!" Mac placed her hand on her forehead, her expression changing from disbelief to fury.

"I'm sorry, Mac." Franklin kept a calm demeanor, but he gripped the chair arm so tightly that his knuckles had turned white.

Mac jumped out of her seat and began pacing behind Cade and Janice, then she spun around and glared at Franklin. "You can fix anything. You have connections. Stop this from happening." Her hands clenched into fists.

"I can't, Mac. I don't have any pull with the FBI."

Her petite body visibly trembled as a whimper escaped her. "No." She shook her head vigorously. "No."

Without a word, Cade pulled her into his lap and held her. A heartbreaking silence filled the room as I watched my best friend fall to pieces. Janice reached for Mac's hand, her eyes brimming with tears.

Franklin leaned his elbows on the table, and a deep frown etched into his forehead. "Gemma received a letter from him a few days ago."

"Bestie?" Mac asked, peering at me, then her mouth formed an O. "The dress shopping ..."

I nodded, confirming her suspicion that something had been wrong that day. "I wasn't sure if it was true yet, so I didn't want to say anything."

Cade massaged Mac's shoulder as he continued to hold her.

"That day, I hired Pierce to look into it. He called me right before you and I went to dinner. Pierce was the call I told you I needed to take. He'd confirmed that Brandon wasn't trying to scare me. He really is being released from prison. I'm so sorry, Mac." I bit my lip, attempting to control the tidal wave of despair and rage that threatened to crash down on me. I couldn't allow it to take me over. I couldn't lose sight of what was important.

Franklin rubbed his chin and leaned back in his chair. "From what we've been able to learn, Brandon worked with the FBI to catch his father. He offered details about Dillon and a few other men in the society."

"What about the misleading information?" Hendrix asked. "If Brandon told the FBI Dillon was in California when he was actually here in Spokane, then can't the deal be revoked?"

"I talked to my friend in the FBI, and since they apprehended Dillon, they're still honoring Brandon's release. Not only did he help track Dillon down, but he provided key evidence against him as well. The situation was kept quiet in order to protect Brandon's life."

I snorted and rubbed my face with both hands, willing myself to wake up from this fucked-up nightmare. "Because *Brandon* deserves to be protected."

"No shit," Mac added.

"It doesn't make sense, though," Cade said, speaking up for the first time. "Wouldn't they want to keep both of the Montgomerys behind bars?" He sounded afraid.

"My contact couldn't share any additional details, but they're after something bigger or someone further up the chain." Franklin said.

His words weighed heavily on my mind. Although I understood how an organization this large worked, in some ways, I didn't have a clue about the inner workings. Since Dillon was behind bars, who had taken his place? In order to shut the entire operation down, the FBI would have to dismantle it from the inside and arrest anyone who had helped run the Dark Circle Society.

"They're using Brandon as bait?" Hendrix asked hopefully.

"I think so, son." Franklin sighed. "Pierce's team is in place as we speak. Right now, Vaughn, Zayne, Tad, and Greyson will keep an eye on us. Once Brandon is released, then there will be security in our homes and on the property at all times."

"What about the wedding?" Mac asked, sliding out of Cade's lap, her eyes wide.

"We're continuing as planned. No one knows the date or location. It will be fine," I promised, though a tiny voice in the back of my mind said otherwise.

"We have three and a half weeks to plan for his release," Janice added. "However, he can't be trusted, so Franklin and I wanted Pierce's men now."

I took a sip, allowing the smooth white wine to travel across my taste buds and down my throat. "I've already paid Pierce, so part of the fee is covered."

"Pierce refunded your money, Gemma. I took care of the bill. It's my responsibility to protect my family." Franklin's tone carried a note of finality that I knew not to argue with.

"You didn't need to do that but thank you." I tapped my fingers against the stem of my glass as images of Brandon dying a slow and painful death flickered through my imagination.

Hendrix gently stroked my hair. "What's next?"

"Stay alert and try to live your life as normally as possible. Pierce and I are working together to see what can be done. If Brandon is open to a negotiation, then I'm open to resolving this matter once and for all."

"Dad! You can't do that. He's a liar and a rapist. What in God's name makes you think he won't take your money and still come after us?" Mac asked, her pitch climbing with each word.

"Mac, sweetie. You need to let your dad figure that out. His goal is to keep everyone safe," Janice said.

Mac slumped in her chair, her shoulders slouching. "Will August

Clover still tour?" Sadness crept over her features as her attention bounced between Cade, Hendrix, and me.

"That's our goal, but no one knows right now," Franklin replied.

A blanket of quiet stretched over the table, then I stood. "Thank you, Franklin, for your help. I don't know what I would do without you." I strolled over to his seat and hugged him.

"Gemma," Mac whispered while she wrung her hands. "What did the letter say?"

"Just that he was getting released early." I'd just lied to my best friend, but there was no need for her to deal with his threat against me.

"I'll drop it for now, but I know Brandon. I also realize you just lied to protect me. We'll continue this conversation later." Mac pointed at me for emphasis as her eyebrows rose. If the situation hadn't been so grim, I would have laughed. She knew me well.

"Please know that I love you, Mac." I pursed my lips into a thin line, silencing myself from saying anything else.

"Love you, too, bestie." She heaved a sigh and glanced up at Cade.

"Go ahead, babe," he said softly, brushing loose strands of hair off her cheek.

She nodded and gulped. "I need to tell everyone something."

6

"I'm pregnant."

Holy. Fucking. Shit. A palpable tension hung in the air as we tried to process Mac's news.

"Cade and I found out today. We're keeping the baby. We were already planning on getting married after Hendrix and Gemma. I was going to tell everyone at dinner tonight, but the conversation took a shitty turn and messed up our news," she said, blurting each revelation in rapid succession.

Janice was the first one to respond. "Honey, this is wonderful. As long as you're happy, then I am too." Janice sniffled as she threw her arms around Mac. "Wow, I'm going to be a grandma. My baby is having a baby." Janice laughed and released her daughter. "That's why you only took a sip of wine. I knew something was off, but with the news about Brandon, I missed the sign."

"Finally! I have someone to spoil rotten, then send home." Hendrix laughed. "Congratulations, you two."

Hendrix and I hugged our best friends, then we returned to our seats. "I would love to help with the nursery. Oh, and a baby shower." I grinned at her. "I'll even make trips to the store when you get a craving if Cade is busy."

"I'm definitely going to take you up on that," Cade replied. "Her appetite seems to have already grown." He gave Mac a silly grin.

"Thanks, guys. I've always been back and forth about having kids, but this feels right. Cade and I are committed. We can easily provide a good home. Our finances are in great shape. I just got hired ..." The rest of Mac's response was muffled as she hugged Janice and buried her face in Janice's neck. "I'm terrified and excited at the same time." She backed away and wiped her runny nose. "Dad?" Mac asked, worry lines creasing her forehead.

"I'm going to be a grandfather?" Franklin's voice faltered, a look of bafflement registering in his expression.

"Yes, sir," Cade said. "I love Mac. This wasn't planned, but eventually, we wanted kids. The timetable just moved up. Honestly, I'm thrilled."

"I know you love her, Cade. I've never doubted your feelings for my daughter." Franklin cleared his throat, his eyes misting over. "So, we also have a reason to celebrate. This is great news. Hell, I'm about to be a grandfather!" He grinned and stood, waving Mac over. She darted out of her chair and threw her arms around him, finally breaking down in loud sobs.

Franklin held her tightly, allowing her to cry. "I swear to you that I'll do everything humanly possible to protect you and my future grandbaby."

"I know." Mac released him and wiped the tears from her cheeks. "I didn't want you to be disappointed in me." She glanced up at him, a look of concern on her face.

"You're my daughter, Mac. How could I ever be disappointed in you?" He wrapped her in a warm embrace and planted a kiss on the top of her head.

"Thanks, Dad." Mac sat down again and took a drink of her water.

"The pregnancy changes things." Franklin shoved his hands in the front pockets of his slacks.

Janice nodded, worry moving across her beautiful features. "When is your first appointment?"

"In four days. It's this Friday at three. From what I can tell, I'm about fourteen weeks along. The doctor will confirm it though." Mac looked up at Cade, and he kissed the tip of her nose. "We were wondering if you and Dad would want to come with us. We'll listen to the baby's heartbeat for the first time. You too." She sniffled, her attention landing on Hendrix and me.

"We'll be there." Hendrix glanced at me for confirmation, and I nodded.

Franklin pulled out his phone and tapped the screen a few times. "I cleared my schedule for the afternoon. I'll take everyone to dinner afterward. We need to remember that we also have plenty to be grateful for." The doorbell rang, and Franklin excused himself.

My attention drifted in the direction of my best friend. "How are you feeling now that we all know?"

"Better. Scared. Tired." She offered me an exhausted smile. "I think we're going to call it ..."

I followed Mac's gaze and muffled my laugh in my arm. Vaughn, Zayne, Pierce, Greyson, and Tad all stood in the formal living room with Franklin. No matter how hard I tried, I always stared at Vaughn's beautiful mismatched eyes. Even though I was about to get married, there was no way I could ignore the gorgeous men in Franklin's house. Testosterone rolled off them in waves. I glanced at Mac, whose cheeks were bright pink.

A petite and beautiful blonde poked her head into the dining room. "I feel the same, Mac. Trust me."

"Claire!" Mac yelled and hopped out of her chair, engulfing her in a warm embrace.

Claire laughed, then hugged me as well before she sat next to me. "I talked my brother-in-law into letting me come over and see you guys."

Claire Forrester, my friend and August Clover's choreographer, flipped her long blonde hair behind her shoulder, her expression growing grim. "Pierce updated us on Brandon." Her voice faltered and the spark dimmed in her green eyes.

"I'm glad you're here. We were just discussing the situation." Since we weren't touring, I hadn't seen Claire in a few weeks. She and Vaughn had been busy settling into their new home.

"How are you guys doing?" Claire's attention landed on each of us.

"I'm pregnant," Mac announced as she returned to her seat.

Then Claire said what I'd initially been thinking. "Holy shit!" Her hand flew over her mouth as she muttered an apology to Janice. "Are you happy about this? I mean, do I congratulate you?"

"Yeah. We're excited," Cade said, grinning.

"What he said." Mac pointed at him and attempted to stifle a yawn. "Baby Cade is making me tired."

Claire shot me a quick look. I suspected she was concerned about Mac with Brandon's upcoming release. She wasn't the only one, but no one had vocalized it yet.

"Pierce said Vaughn is on frontline duty again," I said, wondering how Claire felt about that.

After Dillon Montgomery had been sentenced, Pierce had reassigned Vaughn from security to work behind the scenes. Claire had been elated that her fiancé wasn't in the line of fire any longer. *Until now.*

Claire pursed her lips together. "Yeah. I think it's because it's you guys. You're family, and Pierce and Sutton will do whatever it takes to keep you all safe. I feel better with him taking care of you guys, but honestly, there's nothing about this situation that I'm comfortable with. I haven't had any experience with Brandon, but if he's anything like Dillon or his sister ..." Claire's cheeks paled.

"He's not as smart, which works to our advantage," Hendrix said, offering us all a little bit of hope that we might have the upper hand.

"I'm not sure we can count on that anymore, son," Franklin said from behind us. "He's spent two years in prison with criminals worse than him. There's an excellent chance that he'll come out a different man, and not in a good way."

Goosebumps pebbled my arms, and an eerie feeling crept up my spine. Franklin was right. We had no idea what to expect.

Over the next several minutes, Pierce assigned Greyson to Cade and Mac, then Tad to Franklin and Janice. Vaughn and Pierce would alternate days with the men, providing them a break before Brandon was set free, then everyone would be on full-time duty, including Pierce. The security systems in our homes would also be inspected and upgraded. My mind wandered to my best friend while plans were put in place to protect us. I suspected Hendrix would have a lot to say about Mac and Cade's pregnancy, but I wasn't ready to discuss it yet. My hand slipped down the top of his thigh to his knee. I gave it a firm squeeze and hoped like hell Hendrix would be happy as an uncle for the time being.

"I BET I can guess what you're thinking. The answer is no." Hendrix started the car and shifted into drive.

"I'm thinking a lot of things right now. It was a big night." I leaned my head against the headrest and stared out of the passenger window as Hendrix drove down the winding driveway.

"Gem, I'm not in any hurry to have kids. At this point, my main priority is keeping you safe and getting married."

My heart was heavy as I tried to sift through all of the feelings that were running rampant inside me. "Are you sure?" I shifted in my seat and looked at him. "I love you, Hendrix."

"I know, babe. Just because I'm going to be an uncle doesn't mean I'm going to want us to have a baby of our own right now. Hell, it might send me running in the other direction when we babysit for them."

I laughed. "You're going to be an amazing uncle." I paused, searching for my next words. "I just want to marry you. Our time alone is special and rare if we're touring a lot. Maybe I'm being selfish, but I don't want to share you. That's how I feel."

"I feel the same way. We're on the same page, Gem. I'm only bringing it up so you don't feel pressured by the fact that Mac and Cade are having a kid."

"Thank you." I relaxed a little bit. "I think Mac and Cade will make great parents."

Hendrix's laugh filled the car, and a smile graced his lips. No matter what was happening, his laughter made my heart happy. "They will. I suspect my sister will get pretty overwhelmed, but she has all of us to help. We'll probably be fighting Mom and Dad for extra time with the baby. Mac and Cade will have plenty of opportunities to rest and have date nights. Hell, they can easily afford a night nurse if they choose to. Financially, they're super solid since the band has taken off. Mac can work for you and have a flexible schedule during the pregnancy too. I'm guessing Cade will buy them their own bus so they can tour with the little one. Asa can continue to ride with us, but eventually, we'll have a bit more privacy."

My thoughts drifted to the evening August Clover had performed in Colorado—the night that Dillon Montgomery had hired a hit on Mac and me. Instead, his shooter killed John, leaving everyone devastated. John, Cade, and Hendrix had grown up together, but the loss affected us all deeply. Asa joined us not long after. He was a fantastic drummer and had fit into our tight-knit group quickly.

"It seems like you already have all of this figured out for them," I said. He might not be ready to have kids yet, but it was clear that he'd put a lot of thought into it.

"I can't help it, Gem. I've considered all of those things for my own life. When you meet the right person, at some point, you want kids, the house, the vacations." He raised my hand to his lips and placed a gentle kiss on my knuckles. "On the other hand, I love our life the way it is. It's perfect with just you and me."

"It's not that I don't think about it. I'm just not ready yet." I paused while I gathered my thoughts. "I'm worried, though. Hendrix, if I were Franklin, I would ... I think he's going to move Mac and Cade somewhere safe."

Silence filled the car as Hendrix focused on the winding country road. Deer and wild turkey often darted across it, which kept a driver on constant alert.

"I was thinking the same thing. Dad will go to any length to protect his family, especially his unborn grandkid. If he doesn't mention it soon, then I'm going to bring it up to him. As much as I want to see my best friend and sister, they have to stay safe."

My heart plummeted to my toes, leaving a hollow ache inside of me. Life wouldn't be the same without my bestie next to me every day.

"After the wedding, though." I'd just taken selfish to a whole new level. "I can't get married without my best friend. She's the reason we're together. Cade's your best man, and she's my maid of honor."

A heavy weight pressed against my chest at the thought of her and Cade being forced into hiding to protect the baby. A deep, slow-burning anger spread through me. *Fuck Brandon. Fuck the FBI.* They were playing with people's lives. No matter how they justified releasing Brandon, I couldn't. He was just as much of a monster as his father was. It ran in the family, apparently. Brandon's half-sister, who had stepped up and taken Brandon's place when he was tossed into prison, hadn't even been on the FBI's radar when she came after Claire.

"I think we need to move the wedding up, though. Let's sleep on it for a few days, and we'll talk about it after Mac and Cade's first baby appointment. I think everyone will have a better idea of what needs to happen." Hendrix pulled into our driveway, then checked the mirror for Zayne's headlights.

"Okay. I'll see if I can get the dresses finished sooner too." I made a mental note to call Lydia the next day.

Hendrix leaned over the console and cupped my cheek with his warm hand. "Tonight, while we still can, I want to put all of the good and bad news that we learned at dinner on the back shelf. I want to taste every inch of you and make love until we collapse. In a few weeks, Zayne will be sharing the house with us, so I want you screaming my name every chance we get before then."

I bit my bottom lip, understanding precisely what he was saying. A mental break was desperately needed. "What if I'm not in the mood to make love?" I peered up at him through my eyelashes, mentally undressing him already. I leaned over and whispered, "I want it hard and fast, baby. Make me forget all the shit we're dealing with. Just for a little while."

Hendrix gulped. "Anything you want, babe." He pressed his mouth against mine, then we exited the car, and I waved at Zayne as I entered the house. Hendrix stayed behind to chat with him.

The front door closed behind me, and I leaned against it, willing the feeling of impending doom away. Hendrix was right. It was only a matter of time before our privacy was no longer ours, and I planned to take advantage of our night alone.

With a burst of energy, I ran up the stairs to our bedroom. I dropped to my knees and searched underneath my side of the bed for a brown shoebox I'd been saving as a surprise. It had taken me a while to muster up the courage to experiment more in our sex life, but Hendrix was truly my safe space. After the Valentine's Day pictures, I'd been able to prepare for the next step. Not only had my heart healed since we'd first met, but tonight was a perfect time for what I had in mind. We needed a reprieve from all the pressures of the wedding and Brandon.

My fingers gripped the top of the container, and I slid it toward me. Hendrix's voice floated up the stairs, and I lifted the lid. I couldn't wait to see his expression.

7

"Gem?" Hendrix called.

"I'm in the bedroom!"

Hendrix's footsteps grew closer. My pulse thundered in my ears as I sat in the chair next to the floor-to-ceiling window and waited for him.

"Zayne said he—what the …?" Hendrix's eyes widened as they swept over the bed.

"I thought we would mix it up a little if that's okay." My voice sounded more confident than I felt. Even though Hendrix and I had made serious progress in our sex life, I was still terrified to try new things.

"Hell yeah." He approached the bed, his fingers trailing the edge of the comforter as his tongue darted across his lower lip. "Who gets the blindfold and handcuffs? I assume the vibrator is for you." A grin split his face.

"Yes about the vibrator, and I'm fine either way concerning the other items." I unbuttoned my blouse, exposing the swell of my breasts and stomach. "Or you can watch." I flipped open the front closure on my bra and allowed the material to slowly reveal my nipples. Arching my back, I trailed my fingers down my belly and to the top of my jeans. I flicked them open and slid my hand inside them.

"Jesus, Gemma. I'm going to come before you even get naked."

"What do you want tonight, Hendrix?"

"Keep going." His voice was husky as he sat on the bed, his attentive eyes never leaving me.

I stood long enough to remove my clothes and toss them into the corner, which left me in my red lace bra and G-string. I sat down and propped a leg on each chair arm. Slowly, I slipped a bra strap over one shoulder, then the next. I cupped my breast and moaned.

Hendrix flipped the button open on his Levi's, the sound of the zipper filling the room. "Gemma."

Our eyes locked, then I pinched my nipples and rolled them between my fingertips. His fingers disappeared into his jeans, and he freed himself. His hand wrapped around his thick shaft and he stroked himself.

"No touching. You can only watch," I ordered.

He removed his clothes and did as he was asked, longing burning in his heavy-lidded gaze. I let my fingertips graze the inside of my thigh, then I brushed them over the thin material and rubbed small circles around my clit. I quickly removed my G-string and returned my legs to the arms of the chair. I gave Hendrix a full view of my core. He growled as I spread myself apart for him. Jolts of pleasure passed over me while I massaged my sensitive nub. I tilted my head back, and a soft sigh of pleasure escaped me.

"Baby." I glanced at him. His desire rippled off him in waves. He was sexy as hell sitting on the bed, naked and hard.

"Can I?" He reached for the vibrator.

"Please," I panted, my center throbbing at the mere thought of him watching.

Hendrix knelt in front of me, then pulled me to the edge of the chair. His warm breath caressed my inner thigh, and I trembled with need.

"Have you ever used one before?" Hendrix turned the toy on low, then rubbed it up and down my wet slit.

"No." My fingernails dug into the chair cushion, waves of ecstasy moving through me.

"Relax, babe." He eased the tip inside me, then pushed it in a little deeper.

"Oh my God," I whispered, closing my eyes and allowing him to take control. "Hendrix."

"That's it, Gemma. Let me watch you."

I tilted my hips upward as he continued, but his strong hand held me in place. He withdrew the vibrator and stood. "Stand up."

I wasn't sure if my wobbly limbs would support me, but somehow, I managed. Hendrix turned me around, then picked up the blindfold. "If at any time you want me to remove it, let me know."

"I will." My chest heaved as he slipped the blindfold in place.

"Are you all right?" He asked in a concerned tone, squeezing my shoulder gently.

"Yeah."

His hand glided over my skin, sparking a fire low in my belly. He guided me to the bed and grabbed my ass cheek. His fingers dug into my flesh before he let me go. "Bend over."

I did as he said. No longer able to see what he was about to do. I released a little yelp as his hot mouth sucked my clit. "Be still." After a bit of movement, Hendrix's hand landed on my waist, then he eased the vibrator inside me again. "Do you like that?"

"Yes." And I did. For the first time, I was pretty sure that Jungle Gemma was about to make an appearance without any alcohol. "Harder," I begged, tilting my hips up off the mattress.

"Jesus, you're fucking hot."

"Fuck me, baby," I pleaded, spiraling into the depths of pleasure that were consuming me. On the edge of an intense orgasm, I whimpered.

And with that, he pulled it out of me. "You're not coming until I say you can."

A smile played at the corner of my mouth. I loved Hendrix like this, taking charge and not worrying if I was going to freak out on him.

"Lie down and put your hands over your head."

Attempting to gauge the middle of the bed, I crawled up the mattress and rolled over on my back. Seconds later, the cold metal of the handcuffs clicked around my wrists, then fastened to what I assumed was the headboard. "Say the word at any time, babe."

"I'm good."

"Do you want this?" He rubbed his cock along my lower lip, and I ran my tongue along the tip of him, licking off the precum before he slid it into my mouth. "Gemma," he said as he quickened his pace. He gently pinched my nipple, and I bucked my hips off the bed. His large hand cupped my breast as he continued to thrust into me. "Looking at you cuffed to the headboard and blindfolded is hot as hell." In one swift movement, he pulled back. "I don't want to come yet, babe."

I relaxed and tried to anticipate his next move. The cool material of the vibrator pushed against my entrance, and I parted my legs so he would have better access.

"That's my girl." He nipped the inside of my leg while he turned on the toy. His tongue swept across my clit, and my back arched off the mattress.

My senses were heightened without my sight or touch. Every part of me hummed with expectation and need. Hendrix sucked harder on my bundle of nerves as he continued to pump the vibrator into me, and I writhed almost uncontrollably.

"Baby! I'm going to ..." I panted.

Within seconds, Hendrix had removed the toy and shoved his long shaft into me. My head tilted back, my mouth parting as he filled me.

"You're so wet." His hot breath grazed my ear and neck.

I linked my legs around his waist, my desire reaching new peaks with every deep thrust. Hendrix tugged off the blindfold, and my gaze immediately found his.

"I want to see your face as your tight little pussy clenches around my cock."

I groaned and lifted my hips, greedily grinding against him. "Fuck me," I whispered against his ear.

A low guttural growl escaped him as his hands trailed down my sides and to my hips. He dug his fingers into my flesh. "I can't hold on." He tensed, and I bucked wildly against him as he released inside me, triggering my own earth-shattering climax.

Sweaty and satisfied, my body went limp beneath him. Hendrix relaxed his weight on top of me, and he reached up and undid the handcuffs. My arms dropped, then I ran my fingertips over the muscled dips and valleys of his back and broad shoulders.

"I had no idea you were planning any of that." Hendrix pressed a sweet kiss to my mouth.

"I've been working up to it for a while. Did you like it?" I looked at him, but by the silly smile on his face, I already had my answer.

"It was amazing. You're amazing." He smoothed my hair off my cheek. "I can't believe I'll have the rest of my life to have mind-blowing sex with you."

I giggled and rolled us over with him still inside me. "Promise me." My mood grew serious. "Promise me, Hendrix, that we have the rest of our lives together."

Hendrix sat up, and I adjusted my legs around his waist as he wrapped his arms around me. "I promise, Gemma. I'll move heaven and earth and break every law there is to keep you safe."

I rested my head against his shoulder and inhaled his musky scent, which immediately comforted me. "I promise you the same." There was no doubt in my mind that I would protect him no matter the cost.

8

Hendrix and I slept late the next morning, then took a leisurely shower together. After he dressed in jeans and a black T-shirt, he insisted on brushing and blow-drying my hair. I immersed myself in an oversized plush towel, then slid my butt onto the counter and let him pamper me.

I giggled as he planted kisses on the back of my neck and shoulders. Even though him drying my hair was a mundane task, I thought he loved it as much as I did. More than once, it had led to another sexcapade, but not that day. We had a lot to take care of.

"Asa will be here shortly." Hendrix put the hairdryer away, then brushed out my long red strands.

"Is he excited about his drum solo?"

"Yeah. He's so damned good too. I mean, I knew he was, but when he has the spotlight on him, he shines. That kind of talent can't remain in the background." He smoothed my hair with his hand, then put the brush in the drawer.

I hopped off the counter and dropped my towel on the floor. There were only so many more opportunities I would have to run around naked, and I planned on taking as many of them as I could.

"Dammit, Gem. I'm going to be hard all day while I'm in the studio."

I snickered. "At least I'll be on your mind." I gave him a wink, then sauntered over to the dresser, where I selected a pair of jeans and a V-neck white top. Next, I rifled through my bra and panty drawer and picked a beige matching set. I glanced at him as he leaned against the doorframe of the bathroom, his eyes darkening with longing.

I turned, allowing him a full view of my ass while I bent over and stepped into my G-string, then stood.

"You're killing me, babe."

"What?" I gave him the most innocent expression I could muster. "I would never want to do something like that to you."

Hendrix's attention swept up and down my body as he rubbed his cleanly shaven jaw. "It's all right." In a few swift steps, he closed the gap between us and pulled me against him, flattening my breasts against his broad chest. His fingers threaded through my hair, and he bent down, his soft lips grazing my ear. "Make sure your schedule is clear tonight. I plan to fill it up."

A delightful shiver rippled through me. Before I could utter a word, his mouth crashed down on mine. My lips melted into his, and I moaned as his hot tongue explored my mouth. Even his kisses swept me off my feet. He backed away and chuckled softly, then he pointed to my cheeks.

I peered in the mirror and groaned. "Asa is going to be here any minute, and my neck and face are all flushed from you playing with me." I fanned my heated skin, then continued to get dressed.

Hendrix quirked a brow at me and laughed. "Who started it?" His tone was playful, and it was nice to see that we could have fun regardless of the Brandon situation looming over us.

The doorbell rang, interrupting our teasing. I giggled as I ran down the stairs. My bare feet smacked against the hardwood floor of our living room, reminding me of when I was little and ran through Mom and Dad's house. A flicker of sadness welled up inside me, but I would have to miss Mom later.

I checked the peephole, then threw the door open. "Hey."

"Hey, Gemma," Asa said, his large brown eyes filled with excitement.

I waved him in, then peered around outside. Zayne sat on the hood of his Mercedes across the street, his Ray-Ban sunglasses in place. He gave me a discreet nod, then I entered the house again. None of our neighbors had said anything about him yet, and I wondered if all the women were secretly drooling over him from the windows of their houses.

"Do you want anything to drink? I have coffee, milk, water, or tea."

Asa flipped his long bangs off his forehead, a freshly inked drum tattoo peeking out from beneath his navy-blue tank top. He was the tallest member of the band and lanky. "Water is great. I like to stay hydrated while working." A boyish grin tugged at the corner of his mouth. "Then when we're drinking at night, it won't hit me as hard the next morning. I haven't had a hangover in a really long time."

I laughed and led us to the kitchen. "I'm not sure I've ever heard that as a reason to drink a lot of water."

Asa shrugged. "What can I say? I like to party."

"Hey, man," Hendrix said from the stairs. "You ready?"

I handed Asa his glass and selected a few snacks for them to take to the home studio. It was easy to lose track of time and forget to eat.

"Yeah, definitely ready." Asa pulled his drumsticks from his back pocket. "Not that it's my business, but why is Zayne outside? I haven't seen him since I first started with the band. I'm no genius, but I'm taking a wild guess something is wrong."

Hendrix glanced at me, and I nodded. Asa needed to know what was happening. He was a part of our band and a good friend. This would affect him too.

"I'll explain while we're getting set up to record. Your drums are ready for you too."

"Thanks, Gemma." Asa lifted his water glass, downed it, then refilled it from the refrigerator.

Without a word, I grabbed a reusable bag and tossed six bottled waters in it along with the Gatorades and protein bars.

"You guys have fun." I handed the items to Hendrix.

"What are you doing today?" He twirled strands of my hair around his fingers.

"I'm going to call Lydia and see what can be done. I'm not sure after that."

"Okay, text me if you leave," he said, then kissed my forehead.

"I will."

Hendrix and Asa chatted as they walked down the hall to the studio, leaving me alone in the kitchen. A tidal wave of fear crashed down on me, stealing the air from my lungs. I grabbed the corner of the granite countertop while I tried to calm my anxiety. "I'm safe. I'm safe." I wiggled my toes, the cool floor helping me remain in the present moment. I was home with Hendrix, and Zayne was right outside.

When my heart rate slowed to nearly normal, I made myself a quick breakfast of scrambled eggs and an organic white peach. I wanted to keep my strength and wits about me, which meant I needed to prioritize my health. I hoped Zayne enjoyed running, because I was about to incorporate it back into my schedule.

After I ate, I rinsed and loaded my dishes into the dishwasher. I ran up the stairs and located my cell phone on the nightstand. It was time to see what kind of magic Lydia could work with the dresses.

LYDIA and I spent a few hours on FaceTime while she showed me the final designs and sketches. She had a couple of variations for Claire and Sutton with different necklines and lengths. Since Mac was the maid of honor, Lydia had three other versions for me to choose from.

After I'd selected one, she promised to get back to me about the schedule. If she were able to pull it off, we could move up the date of the wedding. At this point, I would have married Hendrix in a potato sack, but once I'd allowed myself to dream again, I longed for a white dress, bridesmaids, and an outdoor ceremony. Although I reminded myself that we might not have to move the date up, a strong nudge in the pit of my stomach told me otherwise.

Since we owned the house in Maine, we wouldn't have to deal with a venue. Hendrix and I had agreed on a small number of family and close friends. They were the only ones that mattered to us, and I wasn't interested in having a bunch of drama surrounding our special day. I would ask Mac to contact Kami and see if she was available for wedding photos and video. She'd done an amazing job on the Valentine's Day photoshoot. If at all possible, I wanted to work with people we trusted. Since we'd planned on having a separate reception with more people, we still had time to pinpoint a date and plan the food and music.

My phone chimed, and I smiled at the screen before I answered. "Hey, bestie." I strolled into the living room, then sank into the leather couch.

"Gemma." Mac hiccupped through her tears.

I sat up ramrod straight. "Mac, are you okay? What's wrong?"

"Dad and Mom called. They want Cade and me to relocate and hide for a while."

Reality crashed down on me, and my shoulders tightened. *Fuck.* My bestie would no longer be up the road from me anymore. I struggled with conflicting relief, anger, and sadness that swirled around inside me like a cyclone. "When?"

"After my first doctor's appointment this week."

"Shit. That fast? Why? We have a few weeks before ..." I couldn't even manage to say the bastard's name.

"Gemma, the wedding." Mac sucked in a shuddering breath.

"Hey, we'll figure this out. I won't get married unless you're there. Hendrix needs Cade too. They're best friends."

"How? How is this happening again, Gemma?"

My heart cracked wide open as she sobbed uncontrollably. "I don't know." I rubbed my temples, searching for what to say to help her. She didn't have to explain what she was going through. I knew she was dealing with traumatic memories of what Brandon had done to her. I was dealing with mine, too, but there was no reason to talk about them.

"How does Cade feel about it?" I suspected that I already knew the answer.

"He agrees with my parents. He's already looking for a backup caretaker for his mom and sister. That way if anything goes wrong, or the current lady gets sick, he's not frantic trying to make sure they're taken care of. Hang on a minute." The sound of Mac blowing her nose reached my ears, and I wished she were next to me so I could comfort her better.

"Are you busy today?" I asked when she returned to the phone.

"No. Cade is at his mom's, which is good since I'm a blubbering mess."

"How about I come over so that we can talk? Maybe we can figure out what to do."

"Please. And would you mind picking up some crackers and sugar-free ginger ale?"

"Is baby Cade making you sick to your stomach?" I stood and gathered my purse and car keys.

"Omigosh, it's the worst. I've puked all morning."

I cringed, recalling my own pregnancy, before I shoved the pain back into the corner of my mind. "I'm happy to get anything you need. I'll be over in a little while."

"Thank you, Gemma."

"It's what besties do for each other." I ended the call, a smile pulling at my mouth as I recalled the first time Mac had said that to me. We'd shared a dorm room together at college, and she'd agreed not to question my floppy hat and tinted glasses. In exchange, I would be her best friend. It wasn't long before she really was my bestie. I released a heavy sigh. A part of me missed those days, but I would always have the memories.

I texted Hendrix that I would be at Mac's, and seconds later, he responded: *Take Zayne with you. Asa and I will be fine here.*

Since the studio was soundproof, Hendrix had insisted we keep a handgun and ammo in a locked cabinet in the room. Brandon and his father had left some deep scars, and we were constantly on alert.

I texted back: Okay. I love you.

Love you too.

9

In less than an hour, I'd run to the store and purchased Mac's requested groceries, then showed up at her and Cade's house.

"You're the best," she said as she peered outside. "I see you brought the hottie." She flashed me a toothy grin and motioned to Zayne, who had parked in her driveway.

I grinned. "Yeah, I've gotten used to having him around again." I closed and locked the door behind us.

Slipping off my shoes, I lined them up in the tile entryway so no one would trip over them, then followed her through the living room and into the kitchen. Mac and Cade's house had a fantastic open floor plan that was great for entertaining. It was warm and cozy but not cramped. With four bedrooms, they had plenty of space for the upcoming addition to their family as well.

"Where's Greyson? Is he with Cade?" I definitely didn't like the idea of Mac not having security around the clock.

"He parks up the street, then patrols the property. I don't think he sits still very well. I totally get that." She tugged on the sleeve of her pink-and-black-checkered flannel shirt. "I still fit in my skinny jeans today." She stuck her bottom lip out slightly. "I know it won't last for long, though."

"You'll probably fit into them for several more months. You're tiny, which means you'll end up all belly."

"I hope so." Mac flipped her dark hair behind her shoulder and leaned against the refrigerator. "I suspect it's pregnancy hormones, but I omigosh, I want to have sex twenty-four seven. Cade loves it, but I swear to God, my twat gets sore." She barked out a laugh, then covered her mouth with her hand.

I slid onto a barstool and placed my purse on the white marble counter. "Soon, you'll have a bowling ball coming out of you, and *that* will make you sore."

"Oh my God," she wailed, tears streaming down her cheeks. "My sweater will be all stretched out, and Cade won't want me anymore. It won't even look like a vagina! They're not pretty, but still … do they have surgery to stitch that shit back up?" She placed the bag with her ginger ale and crackers on the table, her shoulders shaking.

Shit. Apparently I'd said the wrong thing. I rushed over and hugged her. "Mac, that man loves you more than life itself. He waited for years to be with you. There's no way he's going to let you go because your body changes a little."

She nodded against my shoulder. "Logically, I know you're right, but between the crazy hormones and Brandon, I'm a fucking mess." She released me and grabbed a Kleenex from the box near the refrigerator. They weren't usually there, so I guessed she was having a lot of emotional days.

"Go sit down, and I'll bring you some crackers and soda. Let's get something into your stomach and see if it helps."

"Thanks, bestie." Mac's shoulders slumped as she made her way to a chair and plunked into it.

I grabbed a paper plate from the cabinets and loaded it with saltines. "Here." I placed the food in front of her. "Hopefully this helps with the nausea."

"If not, I'll talk to the doctor about it. I hear they have medication for that. Cade's worried I'll lose weight between the puking and stress from that fucker's release. Normally, I eat like crazy when I'm stressed, but the pregnancy is making me so sick, I can't."

She picked up a cracker and nibbled the edge of it. She definitely wasn't feeling herself. Normally, Mac could eat twice her weight and never gain a pound.

I sat across the table from her. "Don't you think you'll feel better if you and Cade are tucked away somewhere safe? You won't have the stress of Brandon in your face. You can just relax."

Mac's eyes widened, and she shook her head adamantly. "No! Gemma, you don't understand. Not only will we miss your wedding, but everyone thinks hiding will fix the problem. Please, I need you to think about this. I'm going to be hidden away from my family and support, wondering every minute of the fucking day if that sick bastard has hurt someone I love. What if he kills one of you?" Her hand flew over her mouth as a whimper escaped her. "I can't lose any of you. The constant worry will tear me up. It would be better to be here where I can see my family and my brain can't torment me with horrible scenarios."

"I hadn't thought about it that way. We're all so invested in keeping you and the baby safe."

"I know, and I would be the same way. I would ship you and Hendrix off in a heartbeat, but this isn't what I want. Dad said we would have two of Pierce's men with us, and a doctor would make house calls for my care, then I could go to a private clinic as needed. Gemma, I can't hide. I can't leave you guys. You're my bestie, and I just got Dad back. He and Mom are so happy. I need my people."

"Mac, we need you too. You're my bestie. I would feel completely lost without you. We all would." My stomach twisted in knots. With what she'd just shared, I no longer thought it would be best to move her and Cade. Unfortunately, this wasn't a matter that I had control over.

"Have you talked to your mom and dad about how you feel?"

Mac took a sip of her ginger ale and nodded. "Mom, Dad, Cade, and I were on the phone for an hour last night. I tried to explain it to Dad, but everyone is taking his side. He can't see past his decision. I thought for sure Mom would, but she's supporting Dad. So is Cade. You're the only person that's listened to me and taken a minute to see where I'm coming from." She took another bite of her cracker and chewed it slowly. "If I suddenly jump up and haul ass out of here, I'll be back after I'm done tossing my cookies—or in this case, crackers."

"Okay, but I hope that you talking some of this through with me will help you calm down a little bit."

"Me too."

A thick silence hung in the air, then I gave a shitty situation the best idea that I had. "Do you want me to talk to Franklin and Janice? I can try to explain where you're coming from."

Mac gave me a sad smile. "No offense, Gemma, but I think they might listen to Hendrix over you."

She was right. Hendrix would have more pull than me. "Okay. Do you want me to talk to him tonight, or do you want to?"

"Would you? I'm afraid I'll just burst into tears. Fucking hormones." She sniffled and wiped her runny nose with the back of her hand.

"Of course I will. He and Asa are in the studio today, but as soon as he's done, I'll talk to him, then I'll text you."

Mac nodded and finished her cracker. "One down. That's progress."

My chest ached at the thought of Mac and Cade moving. I wasn't even sure if we would be able to talk on the phone or FaceTime. Our phones were traceable, but I assumed Sutton would have a safe way for us to communicate. But Brandon and his goonies were smart, so I wasn't sure any type of contact would be safe. I didn't think Janice and Franklin would be okay not speaking to their daughter for any length of time either. There was no way I could be sure, though. Shit had taken a dark turn the moment Brandon's letter had landed in my hand, and I was scrambling to make sense of the impact. It had rippled into all of our lives.

"I talked to Lydia today about the dresses. Hendrix and I are thinking that we need to move the wedding up."

"Really?" Hope lit up Mac's tearstained face.

"Yeah. We'll make it happen even if I don't get them in time. We can have another ceremony later. It's more important for you and Cade to be with us."

"Gemma." Tears began to stream down Mac's cheeks again. "Thank you. I couldn't stand to not be at the wedding. It would gut me. I mean, who gets married without the person that made it all happen in the first place?" She giggled and sniffled.

"That's what I said to Hendrix too." I offered her a smile, then grabbed her some tissues from the kitchen counter. I handed them to her and knelt down in front of her. "You're my sister, Mac. I'll do everything I can to make it happen. Hendrix needs Cade as well. So no more worrying about the wedding, okay?"

"Shit!" She nearly bolted out of her seat, nearly knocking me over. "We need a bachelorette party, like, ASAP."

I laughed as I sat down again in my chair. "It's not important. Let's just have everyone over to my place. We can pump up the beats, drink, and dance around like we have no worries in the world."

Mac halted me with her hand. "No. No. No. And in case you didn't hear it the first time, no. You deserve to have the real thing, bestie." Her petite hand clenched into a fist. "Brandon will not take our lives and happiness away from us. Fuck him."

Although the customary celebration wasn't that important to me, the time with my friends was. "Are you okay planning something as soon as Hendrix has talked to Franklin? We'll have a better idea of what our schedule looks like." My heart stuttered against my rib cage at the thought of Mac and Cade not being with us.

Excitement flickered across Mac's expression, and I realized she needed to plan the details. It would occupy her overactive mind and give her something other than Brandon and the pregnancy to think about—something fun.

"Yeah. That works, I'll just have to cancel the stripper I hired."

I was pretty sure that I could feel the color drain from my cheeks. "Mac. No."

A playful smile spread across her beautiful features. "I'm kidding. I just had to see the look on your face when I said it."

"Ugh." I released a big sigh and placed my forehead on the table.

The thought of seeing a guy nearly naked and thrusting his hips in my personal space sent my flashbacks into overdrive. Although I could appreciate a gorgeous man, that was as far as it went. Hendrix was the only one I'd even fantasized about. He was the only male who didn't trigger the memories of my brutal, soul-staining rape and pregnancy.

I lifted my head.

"Oh shit. Gemma, you look really pale." Mac hopped out of her chair, selected a glass from the cabinet, and poured some ginger ale. "Here." She placed it in front of me, her hands on her hips as she assessed me.

"I'm fine." I wasn't, but I didn't want her to feel bad. I sipped the carbonated drink, focusing on the little bubbles bursting on my tongue and imagining my fear slipping away.

Mac sat down and pushed the crackers toward me. "Flashbacks?"

I nodded, unwilling to say anything else about them. I'd made up my mind that they wouldn't control me. There might be times that I lost the battle, but I refused to lose the war.

"I'm sorry. Sometimes I forget," she said.

"It's not your fault, Mac. There's no reason to apologize. Brandon is bringing up a lot of memories, and some days, they have a life of their own." There were moments, no matter how hard I tried to manage them, when I couldn't control the onslaught of reminders.

"You've made so much progress, though. I'm so proud of you. I mean, you went from wearing a frumpy hat and tinted eyeglasses to singing on stage with August Clover, taking sexy pictures for your man, and planning a wedding. Don't get stuck on the fact you still have flashbacks. Just focus on all the wonderful things you have now."

"Thanks, Mac. That does help."

We hung out the rest of the afternoon and brainstormed ideas for the nursery. I was grateful there was something to take our minds off Brandon. Mac's appetite came back, too, so we ordered some pizza and had it delivered. I remembered what kind Zayne and Vaughn had eaten when we visited Claire at Sutton and Pierce's house, so I bought one for Zayne and Greyson too. For the first time since he'd been on duty, he smiled when I brought his dinner to him.

♥

"Hey, babe," I said as I entered my home a little after ten that evening. Hendrix was stretched out on the sofa with a spy novel in his hand. He'd pulled his hair into a man bun, and my fingers itched to take it down and run my fingers through his soft brown strands. "How did it go with Asa?"

He placed a bookmark between the pages, flipped the book closed, and placed it on the coffee table. "It went great. I can't wait for you to hear it."

I strolled over to him and tossed my purse on the floor. I flopped down and sank into the plush sofa, allowing the buttery feel of the leather to caress me. "I'm excited to hear it too. Are you guys close to finishing?"

"Yeah. We'll lay down the vocals around his solo next." Hendrix leaned over, grabbed my ankles, and stretched my legs out between his. "You look stressed, babe." With a quick tug, he removed my shoes and socks and set them on the floor. "Talk to me." He began to massage my foot, his curious gaze penetrating mine. "How's my sister?"

"Hormonal." A soft moan escaped my lips as Hendrix's thumbs rubbed my arch. "That feels so good."

My eyes fluttered closed, and Hendrix chuckled.

"Mac is scared and pregnant. Her worst nightmare is reemerging and she's struggling. Everything inside of me wants to take her pain away and bury Brandon for what he did to her. To all of us." I bit my lower lip, willing the tears to not spill down my cheeks. I gently moved my legs away and sat up. "If you keep rubbing my feet, I'm going to fall asleep, and I need your help, babe. Plus, I'm not sure if you know."

Hendrix relaxed his hand on my leg. "Know what?"

"Franklin and Janice called Mac and Cade last night. We were right. They want to relocate Mac and Cade. Although a part of me agrees with the decision, I'm not sure it's what's best for her. Besides, they want them to leave after her doctor's appointment."

"Damn, that's faster than I thought." Hendrix's face fell. "What about the wedding?"

"I've thought a lot about that." I tucked my hair behind my ear. "You know I would marry you tomorrow if it meant that Mac and Cade would be there. I need my family with us more than a dress, so that's not the issue. We can have a second ceremony later."

"I feel the same way. A justice of the peace works for me. But hell, for that matter, Dad has so many connections that he could get someone to marry us in a few days. The media hasn't found out about our house in Maine, so I say we just fly over. We still have a hidden location."

"True. I know we can figure it out. Honestly, now that I've had time to think it through, a date isn't even my main concern."

"What is, then?" He looked worried.

"Mac explained why hiding isn't the best option for her."

Hendrix's forehead creased. "I don't get it. She's pregnant, not to mention Brandon used her to get to you."

"Which makes her a target again. But she said if she can't be with her family, she's going to be constantly worried that Brandon has hurt one of us. Her imagination would torture her more than if she stayed close. I would be more concerned about her mental health, Hendrix. She does need to stay safe, but anxiety and depression aren't good for her or the baby."

Hendrix rubbed my leg, appearing deep in thought. "If it were you, I would put you in a fortress, and there's only one place that makes sense."

"Franklin's," we said in unison.

"Why don't you think your dad suggested they move in with him and Janice? Janice would spoil her every day. Mac needs her mom too. Janice has been pregnant before, plus I hear a lot of women really want their moms as their bodies change." My words trailed off as grief roared through me, and my heart ached so hard it cowered inside my chest. I would never have those special times with Mom or Ada Lynn if Hendrix and I ever had kids. Though she'd taken me to doctor's appointments, Mom hadn't been happy about my pregnancy or anything related to it. To her, it had been an abomination.

Closing my eyes briefly, I attempted to rein in my sadness. Logically, I understood that another baby would be a celebration, but the darkness that surrounded my last one threatened to consume me.

"Hey." Hendrix moved my legs, then scooted next to me. He gathered me up in his arms, pulled me into his lap, and placed a gentle kiss on my forehead. "I know you love Mac, and she's going to be fine." His fingers ran up the length of my arm, and I snuggled against him. "I also realize this is a difficult situation for you concerning the pregnancy. Please don't shut me out, Gem."

I nodded. "It's just that Mom and Ada Lynn are gone. I don't want to sound like a broken record."

"You don't. Grief is hard, and I understand the varying levels. Kendra should be here with us as well. As for Dad, I suspect that if anything happened to Mac or Cade while they were staying with him, it would destroy him. He's already lost one daughter."

A heavy sigh escaped me. "That makes sense." I glanced up at Hendrix. "What can we do, then?"

"Why do I have a feeling that you and Mac already have a plan, and it involves me calling Dad?" A small smile tugged at the corner of his mouth.

I sat up and pressed my lips against his. "Because you're the smartest man I know."

Hendrix chuckled and continued to kiss me, then he relaxed in his seat again. "I don't mind talking to him. I just need to think about the best way to approach the conversation. Once Dad has made up his mind, it takes an act of God to change it. But ... we have access to Janice. I'll start with her."

Straddling Hendrix, I locked gazes with him. "I love you so much. Thank you. I hope like hell this works and Mac can stay, but I understand if Franklin and Janice say no. The bottom line is they have to do what's best for her and the baby. Mac and Cade could say no, too, but I don't think they would. Mac's too scared."

"I'll call Janice in the morning since it's late."

"Do you think we should wait until after Mac's doctor's appointment on Friday? If Franklin and Janice hear the heartbeat first, it might change his mind. I mean, after that they might not want Mac out of their sight." I giggled. "Mac will hate that, but it beats the alternative."

"And if they agree, we don't have to change the date. You can still have your dream wedding, Gem."

"As long as I have you and my friends, nothing else matters."

10

The next few days were busy with wedding details and finalizations. On Friday, Franklin, Janice, Cade, Mac, Hendrix, and I filed into the small doctor's office. The afternoon sunshine streamed through the third-floor window as Dr. Whitaker introduced himself to all of us.

His gray-blue eyes were framed with long dark lashes, and his smile was warm and inviting. I guessed he was in his late thirties.

"Mackenzie, why don't you hop up on the table, and let's listen to your little one's heart today."

Mac's lips formed a big O. "Um. You're a dude." She placed her hand protectively on her lower belly and tugged on the hem of her baby-blue top.

I covered my mouth with my arm, hiding my snicker at Mac's bluntness.

"I am. Are you all right with me, or would you like a female?"

"Neither, but I guess I'll never get used to someone touching my lady bits." Mac looked at Janice, then at Dr. Whitaker. "I was just under the impression, when I made the appointment, that I would see the doctor recommended to me. I didn't realize that anyone in the practice could see me unless I specified one in particular."

76

Janice stepped forward and took Mac's hand. "Honey, you decide who you'll be more comfortable with. I know you've been with Dr. Madison for a long time and you like her for your general health care and annual female visits. Maybe a woman OB-GYN would be a better fit. And you're right—I don't think any of us get used to all the pap smears and checkups. Why don't you think about it, then you can decide next week? I can tell you what to expect with the pregnancy as well. I think it will help. Today, though"—Janice looked at Dr. Whitaker—"he'll put some cold jelly on your tummy, then move a wand around until they locate the heartbeat. Right?" Janice glanced at Dr. Whitaker while she patted Mac's arm.

"That's it for today, Mac. No exam yet. Your mom's right. Take your time and think it over. I've delivered lots of babies, and if you choose for me to be your doctor, I promise I'll take the best care of you and your little one."

Suddenly, my pulse kicked into overdrive, and my hands started to shake. It hadn't occurred to me that Mac's appointment would trigger me. All I'd thought about was how much I wanted to be there for her. My pregnancy and child had been a product of rape. There was no happiness surrounding the situation, only mind-numbing depression and darkness. I'd been so devastated and hormonal I'd blocked out most of the memories of the exams and prenatal care. *Until now.*

I swallowed hard and snuggled up to Hendrix. Mentally, I kicked myself for not preparing. I trembled, and Hendrix guided me over to the chairs. We sat down, and he rubbed my back as we waited to hear baby Cade's heartbeat.

"Okay. I'm fine with you today." Mac appeared a bit relieved with her decision, and she hopped up on the table and laid down. Janice stepped back and joined Franklin while Cade stood near her head and smoothed her hair.

Hendrix's arm encircled my waist and I looked up at him. Compassion flashed in his expression, and he leaned down and asked softly, "Are you all right?"

Before I had time to reply, a fast *whoosh, whoosh, whoosh* filled the room.

"There it is." Dr. Whitaker smiled and turned up the volume.

"Is it supposed to be that fast?" Cade asked, his voice filled with awe.

"Yeah. The baby's heart sounds absolutely perfect."

"Ohmigosh," Mac whispered and glanced up at Cade. "Ohmigosh." Tears slid down her cheeks, and Cade took her hand and kissed her knuckles repeatedly. "We're having a baby."

"I love you so damned much, Mac. I can't wait to meet our little boy or girl."

Franklin slipped his arm around Janice's shoulders and cleared his throat. Tears brimmed in his eyes, and he attempted to discreetly dab the moisture away with his finger. Janice wiped her own away, then peeked over at me as a realization dawned on her.

"Are you okay?" she mouthed.

I offered her a reassuring nod. Hendrix kissed the side of my head and looked down at me. Wonder filled his beautiful face, and he gave me a sweet smile. "I'm going to be an uncle."

I placed my hand on his chest, feeling his heart beat beneath my palm. "I'm going to be an aunt."

For the first time since Mac and Cade had announced their news, I was able to feel a twinge of excitement deep inside. *Holy shit. I'm going to be an aunt.*

I sprang out of my chair and darted over to my bestie. "I love you, and I'm so proud of you. You're going to be an incredible mom." Even through all of my pain and memories, I embraced this new chapter in all of our lives, grateful for the healing.

"Love you, too, bestie." Mac grabbed my arm and pulled me down for a hug. "You're going to be a kickass aunt."

We giggled, then released each other. I glanced at Hendrix. He wore a cute, goofy grin that made my heart melt. He was elated about the baby. We all were.

After the appointment, Franklin took us to Cedar's Floating Restaurant in Idaho for dinner. Everyone's mood was light with constant chatter about possible names for a boy or girl. Mac soaked up the attention, and Cade refused to let go of her. He had a perma-grin on his face and waited on Mac hand and foot. It was beautiful to see. Mac deserved only the best.

Before Cade and Mac had gotten together, I would never have suspected that he would be a family man, but he was. He'd helped his mom care for his sister, Missy, so he had some experience already. Plus he'd been in love with Mac for years. He'd just been too scared to admit it to her.

My mood shifted as I realized there was still a big possibility that Mac and Cade would leave soon. I wasn't sure if my heart could take it. I knew hers couldn't. That day was proof. She needed us. We needed her.

After dinner and a few drinks, we wrapped up the evening. "I'm going to use the bathroom before we leave." I excused myself from the table, noting that Janice was right behind me.

"I thought the restroom sounded like an excellent idea," she said. We entered the small ladies' room, but before I could make it to a stall, Janice spun me around and engulfed me in a big hug. "I didn't want to embarrass you in front of everyone, but I love you, Gemma. You're so good for Mac, and I can't imagine how hard it was for you today, but thank you. Thank you for going to the appointment and being there for my daughter."

And just like that, my grief and rage concerning my own experi-ence ripped through me like a tornado, gutting me in seconds. I released a big sigh while she held me. "I've been so worried about Brandon seeking revenge and Mac's safety. It didn't hit me until this afternoon when we were at her appointment."

"It's okay, hon. It's all in the past, and I'm here anytime you need me." Janice smoothed my hair.

"Thank you." I gathered my courage, then took a chance that Hendrix might be mad at me. "I do need you, Janice. I'm going to apologize now for overstepping my place, but ..." I inhaled, my breath stuttering. "Please don't send Mac and Cade away. I'm scared that mentally, Mac can't handle Brandon's release and the pregnancy without her family. She begged me to help her stay. She said it would be more stressful not to see us every day and not knowing if we were safe. It's going to tear her up and affect the baby."

There, I'd said it. I just hoped it was enough to win Mac's case. Time stood still while I waited for Janice to respond.

11

J anice played with the gold bangles on her wrist and leaned a hip against the black bathroom counter. "I don't know how to tell Franklin that I can't send my baby away. I was concerned about Mac falling into a depression if she and Cade were hiding, but I wanted to wait until after her first appointment. I hoped that once my husband heard his grandbaby's heartbeat, it would change his mind. Franklin nearly melted into a puddle today, which is what I was counting on. I don't think he'll be able to handle not seeing her every day during the pregnancy, but if anything happened to her … Gemma, he lost Kendra. He's never forgiven himself, and …"

Relief rushed through me. She was on Mac's side. "I feel the same way." I took Janice's hand. "You don't have to explain. I get it, and so does Hendrix. He and I have an idea. He was going to talk to you later this evening, but now seemed like a good time. What if Mac and Cade move back in with you and Franklin? You guys could hire additional bodyguards, and she could limit her out-of-the-house activities. The property is large enough that she can walk. Plus she can swim in the pool, which will feel really good as she gets bigger. Hendrix and I will be over all the time too. She needs you most of all. You're her mom. She's *your* baby. You're the one that can help her decide if a male or female doctor is going to be best for her when they reach inside of her for the exams." My cheeks flamed red.

Janice laughed. "Right? And not just once, but the last few doctor's visits before the baby is born."

I rubbed my forehead with the palm of my hand. "Yeah. Even in the best of circumstances, it's awful."

"I'll talk to Franklin tonight. I'll let you and Hendrix know what we decide, but I'm going to do my best to keep Mac with us."

I hugged her. "Let me know if I can do anything to help."

"I will."

HENDRIX and I arrived at the house a little after eleven, and I dragged my exhausted body up the stairs and to our bedroom. On the way home, I'd given him an update concerning my conversation with Janice in the restroom. Fortunately, Hendrix wasn't upset that I'd taken advantage of the situation to talk to her. The day had depleted the last of my emotional reserves, and I wanted nothing more than to curl up next to my future husband and sink into a deep sleep.

"It was a big day," Hendrix said from the doorway.

"Yeah." I offered him a tired smile as I removed my earrings and placed them on top of my dresser. I flipped the button of my jeans open and unzipped them.

"Let me." Hendrix strolled across the room, then guided me to our bed. "Sit, babe." He opened the top drawer and pulled out my favorite sleep shirt, a black Billy Raffoul concert T-shirt. It was his, but I'd claimed ownership not long after we'd moved in together. "Raise your arms." Hendrix gently eased my top over my head, then took off my bra. His eyes flashed with desire, but he slipped the other shirt over my head and guided my arms through the sleeves as though I were a small child. I couldn't help but smile.

"I can change clothes. I'm not that tired."

He knelt in front of me, and I leaned back and shifted my hips off the mattress so he could remove my jeans. Hendrix tossed them in the corner and glanced up at me. "I'm the luckiest man in the world."

"Hendrix." I tilted his chin up, locking my gaze with his. "I love you so much. Thank you for being patient with me at Mac's appointment."

"It's the other way around. You put all of your personal feelings about your past aside to be there for my sister. I was such an ass. It hadn't occurred to me how hard it was for you until I saw the expression on your face. It fucking gutted me, Gem."

I shook my head adamantly. "Babe, don't say that. You're not an ass and never have been. Hell, with so much happening so quickly, it hadn't even crossed my mind that it would send me into a mental tailspin. Plus I'd blocked out so many of the memories during those years and giving Jordan up for adoption. It didn't hit me until Mac was in the room and the doctor came in." I blinked rapidly, refusing to cry any more that day.

Hendrix took my hand and led me to my side of the bed. He turned down the comforter and sheet. I crawled in, and he tucked the covers beneath my chin. He quickly changed into shorts, then joined me. "Come here." He patted his chest and raised his arm.

I snuggled against him, the warmth of his skin soothing my frayed nerves. I peeked up at him. "Hendrix, I can't promise you a baby, but I can promise you my heart."

His gorgeous facial features softened as he rubbed my back. "That's all I want. You're all I want."

Even though I was exhausted, I slid my leg over his and moved on top of him.

"You're tired, Gem." His thumb stroked my cheek, his body already responding.

"Make love to me." I kissed him softly. "Remind me how good my life is."

Hendrix's fingertips danced down my spine and beneath my shirt, and for a little while, I was able to lose myself in his touch. In our love. Hendrix was the spark that ignited my soul and wrapped me up in his light every time I felt as though I was teetering on the edge of darkness again.

No matter how hard I tried to sleep, my mind continued to reel. Brandon. Mac. Jordan. The numbers on the digital clock glowed red, indicating it was nearly two in the morning. Hendrix had fallen asleep after we made love, which allowed me to slip downstairs undetected. At least I could take advantage of the quiet time and work on my wedding vows. I honestly thought they would come easily since Hendrix and I wrote songs together, but I'd been mistaken. How could I possibly articulate how much I loved him?

I chose a soda from the fridge and made my way down the hallway to the office. I closed the door part of the way, flipped on the light, and settled into my office chair. The crack of the Fanta can opening broke through the silence, and I took a sip. I wasn't a huge soda fan, but it sounded good at the moment. My brain scrambled for a starting point, but it faltered. I drummed the top of the desk with my fingers, then I began to write down all of the words that reminded me of Hendrix. My heart warmed with a growing list, and I began threading together what I hoped would work.

"Babe?"

I startled awake. My eyes were bleary from sleep, and I blinked several times, attempting to clear them.

Hendrix's smile lit up my view. "You fell asleep on your desk. I can't imagine your back is going to thank you."

"Ugh." I sat up, my entire body screaming at me.

A chuckle filled the room. "You've got a little drool on your chin."

I frowned, then wiped it off. "That's some sexy for ya in the morning." My Southern drawl resurfaced when I was tired.

"You're always sexy, even with a little drool on your mouth." Hendrix sat on the corner of the desk and waited for me to stretch and pop my neck. "You're so adorable. I'm not sure I can take it anymore."

"Sarcasm isn't a good idea this early in the morning." I peeked at the clock on the wall to see what time it was. I groaned. It was after nine.

"I'm not being sarcastic, Gem." A sweet smile spread across his face. "My phone woke me up, then I realized you weren't in bed. Why were you sleeping in the office?"

I cracked my neck a few times and sighed. "I couldn't sleep, so I thought I'd work on my vows to you."

"I can't wait to hear them." His expression softened, and my heart melted. "Well, I have good news."

"Yeah?" Hope rose in my chest.

"Dad is going to move Mac and Cade into his place. Mac and Cade have already agreed. It's all settled. They're not leaving."

"Yes!" I hopped out of my seat and performed a happy dance in my sleep shirt. "Oh my God, I'm so relieved to hear this. Oh! I need to text Mac. I'll need to help her get some things together." I searched for my phone.

"I thought you might want this." Hendrix handed me my cell.

I stared at him briefly, then flew into his arms, nearly knocking him backward. "I love you so much. Thank you."

"I love you too, babe. I'm as happy as you are. Your talk helped, but apparently Janice has Dad wrapped around her little finger."

I released him and stood back, taking my phone. "I don't think she had to work too hard to bring him around. Did you see his face when the doctor found the baby's heartbeat?" I sank into the office chair. "It was beautiful. My heart was breaking and singing all at the same time. I just want to continue to heal from what happened with Jordan so that I can be there for my best friend and our niece or nephew."

Hendrix pinned me with his intense gaze. "I did see him. I saw two people I love break inside."

My throat tightened with his words. "I'm sorry," I whispered, wishing like hell he didn't have to go through this with us.

"Don't ever apologize, Gemma. Not ever. You and Dad aren't the same people you were then. Both of you. Hell, all of us have come so

85

far. Let's look ahead. Today, we have Mac and Cade here with us. Let's celebrate that win."

"Should we offer to help them pack some belongings to take over to Franklin's?"

"Yeah. Janice said that they want them over there by this evening. Dad will have one of Pierce's guys taking care of the house and keeping an eye on the property. It will look like someone's home, which I thought was a good idea."

I stood, gave Hendrix a long kiss, and batted my eyelashes. "I'm going to call Mac, then I need a shower. Care to join me?"

"Always."

12

An hour later, Hendrix and I arrived at Mac and Cade's house. I realized that there wouldn't be a lot of packing needed, but I wanted to be there to support Mac. It was easier to focus on her needs and fears than my own. A part of me gave a mental fuck you to Brandon because, while I had Mac's best interest in mind, thinking about her gave me less time to fixate on him. He didn't win if I refused to let him take over my life.

Hendrix and Cade's voices carried down the hall, and I smiled. Those two were just as inseparable as Mac and I were. I wondered how Cade felt about moving in with Franklin since they had lived in their place for more than a year, but he would do anything to keep Mac safe, so the question of whether he liked it or not was moot.

"I love our house," Mac said, interrupting my thoughts. She smoothed the black-and-teal bedspread before she sat down on the edge of the bed. She patted the mattress and grinned. "This is where we made baby Cade. I'm *very* fond of this mattress."

"What are you going to call the baby if it's a girl? Cadette?"

Mac giggled and slapped the palm of her hand against her forehead. "Gem-ma. That was the worst joke I've ever heard come out of your mouth. Really?"

What could I say? At least she'd laughed. I leaned against the wall and glanced around the large room. Although their California king took up a lot of space, they still had a full-sized dresser and sitting area near the window. Cade had installed a new ceiling fan for Mac after she'd complained about being hot all the time. At the time, he hadn't known she was pregnant.

"I'm going to miss you being so close. Not that Franklin's is a day's drive away, but it takes longer to lock the house up and get in the car than to actually drive here. At least you're not leaving the state."

"I know, right?" Mac stood and walked to the window that over-looked the Spokane River. "I'm going to miss this view too. It's peaceful."

I joined her, gazing out across the body of water. "It is. I find myself on the back porch, listening to the sound of it rushing by all the time."

"Do you know what I'm excited about?" Mac grinned. "Ruby, because that woman can cook some seriously delicious food, but you already know that. And let me tell you. If you thought I could eat before I was pregnant ..." She shook her head. "If I'm not sick to my stomach, then it's buffet time. The increase in appetite is what trig-gered me to take a pregnancy test. It happened when Asher got me knocked up too." Mac's smile faltered. "It's funny how I thought Asher was all there was for me. And now I can't even imagine my life without Cade."

"I'm glad you were able to move on. You deserved so much more than being someone's secret."

"Damn straight." Mac sighed and rubbed her lower belly. "Well, guess we'd better get going, or Dad will call me wondering where we're at. Mom said he's practically pacing the floors. I told her we had Greyson with us. Zayne is with you and Hendrix, so we have two bodyguards, plus Hendrix can fight, and Cade won't hesitate to shoot Brandon or his minions." Mac arched a brow. "Motherfuckers wouldn't have any clue what hit them."

"If we could be so lucky. I know that sounds horrible, but, Mac, I've thought about it. What if the only way to stop him is—"

"Don't say it out loud, Gemma." Mac placed her hand on my arm and rubbed it gently. "We can think about it, but don't talk about it. Pierce and his men will take care of us. We'll all be all right."

I swallowed down my fear. Mac was right. That was why I'd gone to Pierce in the first place. I trusted him and his men with my life.

Cade entered the bedroom and made a beeline straight to Mac. "You ready, babe?" He approached Mac and slipped his arm around her waist. "Hendrix and I packed my car."

Hendrix joined us and leaned against the doorframe, glancing around the room.

"I think the suitcase is all that's left." Mac pointed to the luggage in the corner.

Hendrix picked it up, and his mouth opened and closed before he spoke. "What in the hell is in this? Are you moving your entire house into Dad's?"

Mac rolled her eyes at him. "I'm the one that's pregnant. I get to be dramatic, not you."

Hendrix's chuckle filled the room. No matter what was going on in my world, his laugh always made me smile. After the last items were loaded, we all filed into our cars and headed to Franklin's.

"How's Cade doing with all of this?" I asked Hendrix before we turned into Franklin's winding driveway. My mouth had gaped the first time I saw the house and property. The large colonial home was stunning. The rolling hills and mountains visible from the back of the home added a picturesque and peaceful view.

"Worried about Mac and the baby, but he and Dad have always gotten along, so he's cool with living here for a while. He didn't say it, but I think he's relieved to have Janice help Mac. He mentioned that her hormones and moods have been intense, and he doesn't know how to help her. I think the issue with Brandon is making the pregnancy worse."

"I understand that. Hormones can be a wild stallion all on their own. Add a shit show on top of it, and it's just not good." My voice trailed off as I recalled my journey. Shards of the devastation still existed, wedged into the cracks and crevices of my soul. No matter how much I'd grown, I doubted I would ever completely heal. At least with the Ada Lynn Foundation in Louisiana, I was able to help other rape victims, and that offered me some peace on bad days.

Hendrix parked the car and took my hand. "You haven't talked much about your pregnancy with Jordan, and I won't push you to, but it's comments like those that allow me a glimpse of what you lived through."

I placed my palm on his cheek. "I'm sorry, babe. Every time a memory comes up, I remind myself of what an amazing life I have now."

"Does it help?"

"Always." I blew out a heavy sigh. "I just no longer know what that life looks like with Brandon being released. What if we can't tour? What if we have to hide? What if—"

Hendrix gently placed a finger on my lips. "You can't do that, Gem. We have to stay in the moment as much as possible. I'll admit I struggle with it myself, but I think it might keep us sane."

I rubbed his cheek with my thumb. "We're sane?"

Hendrix chuckled, then pressed his mouth against mine. "As long as we're together, I don't care if we're sane or not."

"I love you, Hendrix Harrington. You're my always. I'm ready to make it official."

The moment the words left my mouth, my phone chimed. I dug around in my handbag until I located it. "Oh, it's Lydia!"

"Hopefully it's good news." Hendrix opened the car door, then hurried to open mine.

I accepted the FaceTime call. "Hey, Lydia. How are you?"

"Good! I have great news!" Her eyes sparkled with excitement.

I walked with Hendrix to the entrance of the house as Zayne trailed behind us. "Fill me in."

"Are you ready to see the dresses?"

"You're finished? I figured you were calling to give me an ETA." I glanced at Hendrix.

"Once we got the design down, it was just a matter of sewing. I would have felt awful if I'd overpromised and underdelivered. As you probably know, once the creative juices start to flow, you don't sleep much anyway."

"Yeah. We've pulled a lot of all-nighters while we were writing songs. I'm super excited to see them."

The camera on Lydia's phone changed angles and landed on three bridesmaid dresses. I spotted Mac's first. It was forest green with a cowl neck. The bodice hugged the mannequin but fell into a flowing A-line that graced the floor.

The two others were mulberry with deep V-necks and long A-lines. The ruffles at the hems added a touch of elegance without over-doing it. Sutton and Claire would look beautiful in that color.

"Babe?" Hendrix asked.

I hadn't realized I'd stopped walking, and my hand was over my mouth. He must have thought something was wrong. I was over-whelmed with gratitude, tears welling in my eyes. "I'm good." I waved him over to join me in the foyer. "These are the dresses."

"Oh. My. God. It's Hendrix," Lydia gasped. The image blurred, then a loud clatter filled the line.

"Lydia? Are you okay?" I frowned while I waited for her to respond.

"Oh geez. I'm so sorry. I dropped the phone." She turned the camera to her face and offered an apologetic grin. "I just fangirled. I'm so sorry."

Bright red dusted her cheeks, and I couldn't help but laugh. "He's used to it, and so am I."

"It's nice to meet you, Lydia. Thank you for making the dresses. I would love to see them."

"Oh crap. Right, of course." The camera angle landed on the sewing dummies once again.

"They're stunning," Hendrix said while he slid an arm around my waist. "The ladies are going to look gorgeous. Thank you for all of your hard work so this could happen, Lydia."

"No, thank *you*. This is actually helping me! As I explained to Gemma, I'm trying to break out as a designer, and the competition is insane."

"The dresses are more than I could have hoped for." I beamed at her, thrilled with the products.

"I'm so happy you love them. Okay, so I went with the sizes you provided. Sutton's length is five foot eight, and Claire is five foot six. From what you said, it should be a close fit. I'm hoping we're damned close."

"When can we get them so Marie can finish any adjustments?"

"What's today? Friday?" Lydia grinned. "I tend to lose track of days when I work."

"Today is Saturday," I confirmed.

"I'll overnight them first thing in the morning, so they should be delivered to Marie by Monday afternoon. I'll call her and let her know to expect them so she can set up a time for you all to come in. I'll start a group text so you have the information."

"That sounds great. Thank you so much. Please send me the invoice." I provided Lydia with my email address, then we disconnected the call.

"I'll know more by Monday, then." I tucked my phone back into my purse, my attention landing on Hendrix, who had remained next to me the entire time.

"She designed your wedding gown?" Hendrix's voice was low and gentle.

"Yeah. She's amazing."

Hendrix leaned down and whispered, "I can't wait to see you walk down the aisle to me, but I'm not sure my heart will be able to handle it. Sometimes my feelings for you are so intense I don't know what to do with them. So if I'm a speechless fool, then just know you're holding my heart in your hands."

I slipped my arms around his neck and kissed him passionately, completely forgetting we were standing in Franklin's foyer. A loud gagging noise came from the entrance of the living room. Embarrassed, I broke away and glanced over my shoulder.

"Not in front of the baby." Mac snickered and rubbed her lower abdomen. "Dad wants a family meeting." She waved us over and we followed her.

"I'll collect on that kiss later." Hendrix winked at me and threaded his fingers through mine.

"Hey, kids." Franklin stood from his wing-backed chair and embraced me, then he patted Hendrix on the back. We settled in next to Cade and Mac on the couch as Janice came in. She smiled warmly at us and sat down in the recliner.

Franklin scratched his chin and cleared his throat. "Ruby is making her lasagna, so I hope Hendrix and Gemma will join us for dinner."

My phone chimed, interrupting Franklin. I rifled through my bag and silenced it, noting that Lydia had texted Marie and me. Hopefully I would get a schedule soon. With each day that grew nearer to Brandon's release, I became more anxious. Maybe it was that Hendrix and I just needed to make up our minds and move the wedding up, get off the fence.

"We have four bodyguards right now," Franklin said. "Greyson will continue to be with Mac and Cade. You two are here for the duration and will only leave for medical appointments. Your safety is the number-one priority. If you take a walk on the property, take two men with you."

"Who are the others?" Mac glanced at me out of the corner of her eye.

Franklin shifted in his seat. "Zayne is already assigned, and we have Tad. Vaughn will join us here as well, and if we need another one, Pierce will send Jaxon Sullivan over."

"Oh, I thought Vaughn wasn't on duty until Brandon was released?" Mac's brow arched with her question.

"I'm not taking any chances. Pierce agreed and offered to have Vaughn work for now. Plus I know you ladies are friends with Claire. She's welcome over any time."

"Umm, Dad?"

"Yeah?" Franklin's expression softened as it landed on his daughter.

"I'm throwing Gemma a bachelorette party, so I need to leave then."

Franklin looked at Janice, and I wondered what they were nonverbally communicating.

"Mac, let's get it planned and talk about where. I'm willing to rent a place out for the evening for you girls to have fun if Pierce will work the get-together as well," Janice suggested.

"Sutton will be there too. That girl can kick her husband's ass, so she's an extra bodyguard," Mac said.

Laughter filled the room, then everyone grew serious again. Not only did I not want Mac to go to a lot of trouble, but I also wanted something small. "Let's keep it simple, though. Sutton, Claire, Tensley, and maybe a few others. Just a handful of people. Those are my friends and the ones who are important to me."

"Oh, Tensley! How could I have forgotten? Dammit." Mac grabbed her phone out of the back pocket of her jeans and focused her attention on the screen. "Noted."

"Son, are you having a bachelor party?" Franklin asked Hendrix.

Hendrix ran his fingers through his hair and chuckled. "I'm not sure you'd call it that, but the guys are taking me out for drinks."

"Yeah, Asa, Ramsey, and I are taking him out." Cade flashed a boyish grin at us, then chuckled.

"Let's see what last-minute options are available so I can talk to Pierce about additional men if we need any." Franklin paused, his attention sweeping across the room. His cell phone rang, and he picked it up off the coffee table. "This is Franklin." Silence hung in the air, then Franklin's face paled. "Are you sure?"

My heartrate kicked into overdrive, and I reached for Hendrix's hand. Something wasn't right.

"Thank you for letting me know. Have a good evening." Franklin lowered the phone, his troubled gaze landing on me.

"What's wrong?" I asked, my voice so soft I wasn't sure he heard me.

13

"Gemma, I already know the answer, but I have to ask anyway. Have you visited Brandon in prison?" Hendrix's body tensed, and the room grew eerily quiet while everyone stared at me, speechless, as they waited for my response.

"What? No! Why would you even ask me that?" *What the hell was said in that call?*

Franklin cleared his throat and folded his arms across his chest. "Someone used your name when they signed in to visit Brandon."

"That doesn't make any sense." Hendrix frowned.

"It was a conjugal visit," Franklin said.

Bile swam up my throat, and I swallowed repeatedly in order to force it back down. The mere thought of even being near Brandon raised the tiny hairs on the back of my neck and gagged me.

Janice gasped. "What? That's ridiculous. Gemma would never do anything like that." I appreciated Janice's vote of confidence.

Disgust twisted Mac's features, and Cade tightened his hold on her shoulder.

"I know that piece of shit is up to something, and I understand it wasn't Gemma. Unfortunately, we have to prove it and be prepared. When was it?" Hendrix asked, a sharp edge to his tone. "She's been with Mac or me most days. She wouldn't have had time to visit and return without causing suspicion."

"That son of a bitch," I muttered. "I'm betting that he wants that information leaked to the media. He's up to something."

"It was a week ago. Friday, September 11." Franklin sank into his seat.

"We were dress shopping, then we ate dinner at Clinkerdagger," Mac explained. "The only time we weren't together was when Pierce called her. Gemma took the call in her car while I went inside, but that's obviously not long enough to visit that asshole."

"I think you're right, Gemma. He's toying with us, and I bet it will be all over the media within a few hours. I'll have a statement ready to refute the information if this is what he has planned." Franklin rubbed his chin, his forehead creasing.

"Can't we stop him?" I wrung my hands, imagining they were around Brandon's neck and choking the life out of him.

Franklin shifted in his seat. "We might be able to get him on defamation of character since it's public knowledge that you and Hendrix are getting married this year."

"Whatever his reason, I don't trust him." Janice rubbed her palm along the leg of her jeans, her eyes flickering with fear.

"I need to make some phone calls. I'll meet you all at dinner." Franklin rose, then kissed Janice on the cheek and disappeared down the hall in the direction of his office.

"Mac, let's chat about the get-together and see if we can make something happen. I'm a bit concerned that everything is about to change," Janice said.

Mac hopped up. "Mom, please. We can't let Brandon win. Don't make us cancel the party. Gemma needs some fun. We all do. We can go back to being afraid later."

"I understand, but everyone's safety comes first." Janice appeared deep in thought. "I might have an idea."

Mac gave Cade a quick kiss, then followed her mom to the kitchen.

I glanced at Hendrix as he clenched his jaw. "Babe, if this gets out
—if that bastard ..." I shook my head.

"I say we take the motherfucker out. I'm sick of him messing with
us," Cade spat.

"I wish it were that easy, man. His asshole brother, Matthew,
would send someone after us." Hendrix ran his hand through his hair,
which told me he was more stressed than he was allowing me to see.

"Or Dillon would," I added.

"I don't understand what his angle is. He knows it won't stop us
from getting married, so what's the point?"

I peeked down as my phone screen lit up with text messages. "It
looks like Marie and Lydia are messaging me, babe. I need to see
what's going on." I squeezed his knee, then made my way upstairs into
the game room. Hopefully, Cade and Hendrix would have a few
minutes to process while I was dealing with the wedding details.

Sinking into the leather couch, I scrolled through the messages.
Marie was offering to stay open late for fittings and alterations
Monday evening. That meant I needed to see if the girls were available
then. I texted Sutton and Claire to see if they could meet us at the
bridal shop at six. I knew Mac was available, so we could ride together.

Marie messaged that if the modifications weren't anything major,
she could have the dresses done by Thursday. I bit my lip lower lip,
pondering how fast we could pull together the rest of the details.
From what I could tell, we could move the wedding up by a week.
Hendrix and I had never announced what month we'd planned on
getting married or where, which meant the media wouldn't have the
information. I honestly didn't see any reason why it wouldn't work.

I ran out of the game room and down the stairs. "Hendrix."

His head popped up as soon as I entered the living room.

"What's wrong?" He knitted his brows while he waited for me to
talk.

"Let's get married next weekend."

"She can have the dresses ready?" He stood and crossed the room,
his expression hopeful.

"Yeah. They should be available by Thursday. Let's see if everyone is available and go to Maine, baby. I'm ready to become your wife."

Hendrix wrapped his arms around me and lifted me off the floor, twirling me in a circle as I giggled. "That's the best news I've heard in a while." He kissed me, then set me back down on my feet. "I'll go talk to Dad. Why don't you tell Mac and Janice, then call Sutton and Claire to see if they're all available to fly over Friday. We can get married Saturday."

I nodded. "Perfect." Butterflies erupted in my stomach. I was only days away from marrying Hendrix. Giddy, I turned to Cade. "Do you want to tell Mac and Janice in case they're discussing any details I'm not supposed to hear about?"

A wide grin eased across Cade's handsome face. "I was just about to offer." He approached me, then stopped. "I'm really happy for you, Gemma. I've never seen my man fall so hard for anyone before. In fact, he hasn't shut up about you since the first day he saw you."

"What?"

"Yeah, he came to band practice talking about a girl he'd seen at the library. When I asked him what your name was, he just shrugged, then said, 'I don't know, but she's special, and someday I'm going to marry her.'"

My hand flew over my mouth.

"He's always loved you, Gemma. Never doubt it." Cade gave me a quick hug before he left to locate Janice and Mac.

Closing my eyes, I allowed Cade's words to sink into my soul. Hendrix had known even back then and had been so patient with me —tender when he needed to be and fiercely protective at the same time. He was the beat of my heart. Suddenly, I realized I had to write my vows. I scrambled to find my purse along with a pen and something to write on, then I jotted the words down as fast as I could. For a few blissful moments, no one and nothing else existed except for the man I loved.

"Babe?"

I turned to see Hendrix leaning against the doorframe. "Yeah?"

He strolled toward me and shoved his hands into his pockets. "We forgot something important."

"What do you mean?" My stomach clenched, and a nervous silence stretched between us, my mind scrambling to fill in the blank.

"We failed to apply for the marriage license."

A giggle slipped from my lips. "Hendrix, how the hell did we forget that?" Within seconds, the realization smacked me full force. "We can't get married this weekend?" I shook my head. "No. Don't tell me that, Hendrix." Frustration and disappointment collided inside me.

"I'm sorry, babe. With all the chaos ..." He wrapped me in his arms and stroked my hair. "We just spaced it. Plus, we weren't sure of a date." Hendrix's chest heaved with a sigh. "I let you down."

"What?" I asked looking up at him beneath my eyelashes. "No, you didn't. I should have put it on our calendar a few times to apply. I didn't realize there was a waiting period. Hendrix—" I stared at him, overwhelmed with emotion. Love. Respect. Gratitude. "You never let me down. You're the best thing that's ever happened to me. We made a mistake, and we'll fix it."

"My head agrees with you, but my heart broke. All I wanted to do was marry you this weekend." He tucked a piece hair behind my ear.

"Me too."

"Kids, it's taken care of."

My head snapped up at Franklin's words as he entered the room, a gentle smile on his face.

"What do you mean?" Hendrix asked.

"Maine doesn't have a waiting period like Washington does. You'll need to fill out the application when you get to Maine. I would encourage you to fly over Thursday so you can apply. The rest of us will join you on Friday. Zayne will go with you of course."

Without a word, I ran to Franklin and threw my arms around him. "Thank you."

"You bet. Don't stress over it. It's going to be all right." He gave me a fatherly kiss on the forehead, and I wondered whether he was trying to comfort me or himself.

"I'll have Sutton bring the dresses on Friday." I grabbed my phone and texted her. She immediately replied with a yes and a heart emoji.

Hendrix pulled me in for a hug, and Franklin excused himself. Hendrix gave me a quick peck before he took off to locate Cade. Exhausted, I strolled into the living room and plopped down on the couch.

"Bestie!" Mac darted into the room, grinning. "We're going out tomorrow night! Get your dance moves on." Mac wiggled her butt, then broke into the running man. I fell over giggling as she exaggerated each movement and continued to entertain me. She galloped in place and smacked herself on the ass, then she doubled over howling too.

"What are you talking about?" I struggled to catch my breath, then stretched my legs out in front of me. Leave it to Mac to make me laugh until I cried while our world is once again being turned upside down.

She snickered and sat down next to me. "Mom and I rented out Mik's downtown. She wanted to rent a space at the Davenport, but they were all booked. However, Mik's is available. I've already confirmed with Tensley, Sutton, and Claire. Tensley was hanging out with Avery, so I invited her too. I hope that was okay. She's part of the group by proxy, right? Cade invited Layne and Benji to Hendrix's bachelor party. We're going to have both parties tomorrow. No one will consider Monday a prime time to go out, unless they're in college —then every night is—but anyway ..." She finally slowed down long enough to take a breath and waited for me to respond.

Excitement swirled inside me as I realized that just a few years before, I never would have thought this would happen. I lay awake night after night and stared at the bedroom ceiling, dreaming of an existence outside the walls of my house, wishing for something different, and desperate to regain my life. Yet I never imagined I would have friends who loved me enough to get together and spoil me for an evening. "I never thought I would have a bachelorette party, Mac. All those years I hid at home, terrified to leave the house, and now ... thank you so much. This means the world to me."

"And ..." Mac looked around the room, then leaned close to me. "No, there won't be a stripper, but who gives a rat's ass, Gem-ma? Vaughn will be there, Pierce will be there, Greyson, Zayne, and a few others. Eye candy galore." She fanned her cheeks and giggled.

"Does Claire know you have a crush on Vaughn?" I nudged her playfully with my elbow.

Mac's expression grew serious, and she tapped her index finger against her chin. "I wonder if they would be down with a foursome. I mean, Claire's hot. I could probably play around with her." She paused, then her nose scrunched up. "Forget it. I couldn't even handle eating crab. I sure as hell couldn't get into some chick's pussy."

I burst out laughing. "I wondered when you were really going to think that one all the way through. Your face was hilarious!" I grabbed my stomach, nearly doubling over with a fit of giggles again. Finally, I dabbed the tears of laughter from my eyes and sank back into my seat. "I love you, Mac. You're the best bestie a girl could ever have."

Mac threw her arms around me. "Love you, too, Gemma. Let's try to focus on the party and the wedding. We deserve to have some fun."

"Oh shit. I forgot! We're all meeting at Marie's to try on the dresses tomorrow at six. What time did you guys reserve Mik's?"

"Girl, I got this." She tilted her head and gave me the peace sign. "Sutton and Claire told me. We're not starting to cause trouble until nine."

Mac looked rather proud of herself for organizing the get-together. Hell, I was proud of her too. I knew how hard it was for her to stay on track under normal circumstances, but this was a spur-of-the-moment plan due to the storm that was brewing in the air. A chill traveled down my spine, and I steeled myself for what I feared was yet to come.

14

Monday evening, Mac and I had prepared for the bachelorette party together from Franklin's house before we left for the dress fitting. We applied each other's makeup and had both opted to leave our hair down. However, since we would be dancing later, I'd shoved a few hair ties into my jeans pocket for later. Mac had scrambled to purchase T-shirts for the wedding party. They were black with bright pink lettering. Mine said bride-to-be and the other's bridesmaids. I absolutely loved them and I couldn't wait to wear the shirt later.

Franklin had rented us a limo for the night and Zayne and Greyson piled into the back along with us.

"I could get used to this." Mac stretched her legs in front of her and propped them up on the seat.

"Poor Marie is going to freak out when we show up with them." My attention bounced between the two men. I hadn't known Greyson long, but he was just as gorgeous as the rest of Pierce's men with his dark hair that was streaked with natural red highlights. His chocolate brown eyes were sharp and attentive. "Do you ever become used to people talking about you while you're around?"

"Most of the time, we don't even pay attention. Not to you two, anyway." A small smile cracked Zayne's tough-guy exterior. His emerald green eyes sparked with mischievousness.

"Holy shit, was that a joke?" Mac leaned forward, then nudged me in the side. "He's a real boy, Geppetto."

"Mac," I chided and laughed.

A low chuckle filled the limo, and I looked at Greyson wide-eyed. None of us had ever heard him laugh or seen him smile, but I would take it as a compliment. "You guys must be more comfortable around us. I'm glad. There's no reason we can't chat every once in a while."

"Right?" Mac leaned back and crossed her legs. She was adorable in her skinny jeans and black booties. Her plum-colored shirt provided a deep V-neck accentuating her abundant cleavage. After she and Cade got together, she'd confided in me, telling me how self-conscious she was about her breast size. I wasn't sure why. Petite and stacked was what a lot of women wanted. I was content with my B cups, but Hendrix had a lot to do with me growing more confident with my body.

"So, Zayne, are you seeing anyone? Got a little side piece?" Mac wiggled her eyebrows at him.

"Mac," I groaned. "I know you're not drinking since you're pregnant, so you can try to filter what comes out of your mouth. Give him a break." I rolled my eyes.

"I don't date," Zayne replied, his deep voice sending chills through me.

What the hell? He was hot, but all the bodyguards were. Apparently, being confined in a small space with two gorgeous men was more than I could handle. At least Hendrix would reap the benefits. My cheeks warmed as I realized Zayne and Greyson were staring at me. "What?"

"You're the first celebrity he's guarded." Zayne grinned and nodded at Greyson.

"Oh, no. I'm not a celebrity."

Mac barked out a laugh. "She's just modest, Greyson. She won't even admit how big August Clover is right now."

"I'm just me. That's all. Zayne, Pierce, Sutton, and Vaughn are all my friends. I mean, I know they have a job, but they're more than bodyguards."

"We're all extremely fond of you and the Harringtons as well." Zayne glanced out the tinted window of the limo. "We're here. Greyson and I will exit first, then check out the store. When we've cleared it, we'll return for both of you. Keep the vehicle locked."

With that, the men hopped out of the limo. Zayne headed in the direction of the building while Greyson stood outside the vehicle, guarding us.

"Sorry," Mac muttered, flinging herself dramatically across the seat and slapping her hand over her face. "I don't know why I asked Zayne that. Can I blame it on the hormones?" She peeked at me through her fingers.

"I don't think he really thought much about it, honestly. I just figured it was an incredibly personal question to be asked in front of other people."

"Didn't you hear his response? He doesn't date. Gemma, you know what that means, right?"

"That he doesn't date?" I quirked an eyebrow at her.

Mac sat up and waved her hand in the air. "No. That means he has one-night stands, then moves on to the next one. He dips his wick then blows the Popsicle stand. A smash and dash. A—"

The door opened, interrupting Mac's explanation.

"Ladies." Greyson extended his hand out for Mac and assisted her out of the limo. Someone had taught this man some manners. He presented his palm to me next, and I carefully stepped out of the car with my heels on. Although I wouldn't wear them to the bachelorette party after the fitting, I needed to see how the height of the shoes worked with my gown.

"Thank you." Suddenly shy, I ducked my head and dashed toward the entrance. Most days, a celebrity status was hard for me to digest, then there were others like today that I was grateful for security.

Mac and I hurried into the store, then I removed my sunglasses and stuffed them into my bag.

"Welcome." Marie beamed at us, then her focus bounced between Zayne and Greyson.

Her cheeks flushed, and I felt sorry for her. These guys had that effect on women no matter where we were. I would have bet money that if we showed up at a convent, the nuns would stutter and blush too.

"I'm sorry. I should have told you I had security with me tonight."

"No apologies necessary. I'm so glad you're here. Sutton and Claire are in the back with Lydia." Marie began to lead us to the fitting area.

"Lydia is here?" I asked.

"Oh my. That poor girl has had quite a day. There was a hiccup with FedEx, and the dresses weren't going to make it in time. She hopped in her car and drove seven hours to have them here for you."

"What? Oh my gosh. She could have sent them tomorrow."

"She's very serious about her word, and she promised she would have them here today."

I spotted Sutton standing on the step stool while Lydia knelt on the floor, pinning the hem of the gown.

"Gemma!" Claire came bouncing out of the fitting room with her mulberry dress on. "I love it! The color is amazing. I've heard so many horror stories about the bridesmaid dresses from hell, but these are gorgeous." Claire ran over and hugged me.

"I'm glad you like it. Does it fit?"

She stepped back and kicked her leg out in a wide sweep to the side, the skirt following her graceful dance moves. Her bright blue eyes sparkled with excitement.

Claire's body was to die for. Not only was she toned and slender, but she had a great ass. Her boobs were bigger than the traditional ballet dancers, which was one reason she hadn't pursued it professionally. It had all worked out, though since Hendrix and I had hired her to be our choreographer for August Clover.

"Just a few minor tweaks to that one, but you gave really accurate measurements for her." Lydia peered up at me and grinned. "Hi, Gemma."

Mac ran to the rack and selected her dress. "I'm going to change, then I'll help you with your gown, Gemma. But these two have to step out. They can't see you until the wedding." She pointed to Zayne and Greyson.

"Oh, I'll shut the curtain." Marie hurried and pulled it closed, separating us as much as possible while still keeping them close.

"Thank you for delivering them personally, Lydia, but you didn't have to."

She rose from the floor and shoved a pencil in the top of her bun. She flashed a beautiful smile filled with excitement at me. "I told you Monday. My word is very important to me. Besides, now I can help Marie, and we can make the adjustments quicker."

"She's a doll." Marie patted her on the back as she adjusted Sutton's dress and pinned it around the waist.

"Claire's right—they're gorgeous." Sutton tucked a strand of her long blonde hair behind her ear. "Are you ready to have some fun tonight?"

"Yes! I can't wait. Since we have security, I'm not going to worry about getting drunk." I bounced up and down on my toes with excitement.

"You drink, dance, and have a great time. Hell, even I'm taking the night off. Pierce and Vaughn will meet us there, so I'm going to let the four guys handle security," Sutton said.

"Gemma," Mac said softly. Her lower lip trembled as she stood in front of me. "I can't zip it." Tears welled in her eyes, then it dawned on me that she'd probably gained a little bit of weight, and I hadn't given Lydia the right size. "I'm getting fat."

"Oh no. Don't worry, Mac. I can add an extension without any problem at all. These things happen all the time." Lydia hurried over to Mac and soothed my bestie's stress. Lydia wasn't just a fantastic designer—her customer-service skills were off the charts as well.

"I'm pregnant," Mac admitted.

"Congratulations! You're with the guitarist in August Clover, right?" Lydia kept Mac's focus on Cade rather than the alterations, and within minutes, she'd sent Mac back into the changing room.

"Quick fix, Gemma. We've got this," Lydia said, encouraging Mac and me.

"She's a miracle worker." Marie slipped one last pin into Sutton's dress. "Other than just a few minor adjustments, this one is almost done. Step down, dear."

Sutton held up the hem and stepped off the stool. "Well?" She twirled around for me.

"I can't get over how beautiful the dresses turned out. Thank you so much, Lydia." I embraced her. "You're making my dream wedding happen."

Lydia bit her lip, suddenly shy. "I'm happy to be a part of it."

"She should come with us tonight, Gemma!" Mac yelled from the dressing room.

"You should! It's a very small and private bachelorette party. We'll have fun. Besides, you deserve a night off after not only creating and sewing the ensemble in a matter of days but driving up here too."

"Really? I would love to. And am I allowed to take a picture with you?"

"Yeah, that's fine. In fact, why don't we do a mini shoot of the dress and the other ladies? We have a signed contract that says you can't share anything until after the wedding, but we're all here, so why not?"

In my mind, if Lydia leaked anything to the press, it would only be to reveal the gowns. At that point, I wouldn't be able to trust her for future projects, but for the moment, I wanted to give her the benefit of the doubt. So far, she'd gone above and beyond what I'd hoped for.

"I would love to!" She hurried over to a handbag in the corner and removed her phone. "I need to power it on. I didn't want you to think I was recording the session or anything. It's important to me that you trust me." She offered me a kind smile, and I couldn't help but like her even more.

An hour later, Lydia had taken photos of me in my wedding gown, then the group of us in the dresses. She suggested some fun pictures as well. Maybe her eye for design helped her with photography, because even the playful images were really good.

"Can you text them to me?" I asked, strolling toward the dressing room, careful not to trip in my heels. It fit perfectly with the alterations Marie had made. I couldn't wait to see Hendrix's face when I walked down the aisle this weekend.

"You bet. So, where should I meet you guys? I need to run to my hotel and grab a quick shower. It's been a long day."

"Meet us at Mik's. We're heading there now, so just text when you're on the way so we can let security know that you're with us." Mac gave her directions, then we all changed back into our jeans and wedding party T-shirts before we headed to the parking lot of Marie's. Unfortunately, we didn't have one for Lydia.

"Where are you going?" I asked Sutton and Claire as they started to walk to Sutton's Audi.

"We're going to follow you."

"Nope. Come on. We're all riding in the limo. We can have someone pickup your car tomorrow."

The ladies ran over to us, and we loaded up. Mac picked up the bottle of champagne and handed it to Zayne. "Please open it." She flashed him a big grin.

A loud pop filled the small space, then bubbly spewed out from the bottle. We shrieked and giggled like teenagers.

"Let's get started!" Mac tapped her phone, then "Parable" by Mako thumped through the limo's Bluetooth speakers.

"I love this song!" Claire said as we all filled our glasses.

"Cheers! To a love that survives anything." Sutton raised her glass, and we all joined in.

The champagne flute touched my lips, and my attention swept over everyone in the limo. I grinned, then tilted my drink up, draining it in seconds. By the time I looked at Sutton, Claire, and Mac, their mouths were hanging open. Then everyone burst out laughing.

"I'm going to have some fun tonight." I held out my glass for some more, and Mac refilled it. "But please keep the water coming so I'm not sick as a dog tomorrow."

"I'll keep you hydrated. I'm not drinking, so it will be easy to keep the water coming for everyone. And snacks." Mac flashed a toothy grin and giggled. "I do plan on dancing my ass off."

"What's the music like?" Claire asked, moving her feet to the beat of the song. The girl couldn't sit still if there were tunes on. Dancing was in her blood, and she was damned good at it.

"I have a playlist for us tonight, so we have full control over the booty shakin'."

"I haven't danced in a long time. Too long," Sutton chimed in, then took a sip of her drink.

Zayne cocked a brow at her.

"What was that for?" I asked, laughing. Sometimes, I forgot that Sutton had grown up with Pierce, Vaughn, and Zayne. I suspected they could communicate telepathically, and occasionally, I was extremely curious about what their conversations would be like.

"Pierce told me to come home drunk and happy." Sutton grinned. "Zayne is reminding me of that, but we're just starting. He needs to give me a minute."

Zayne chuckled, his deep laugh floating over the music.

"So, Lydia. Do you like her?" Claire asked me.

"I do. She's been so amazing with the dresses, and her work is gorgeous. The few times we've worked together on FaceTime, it's been really good. I'm happy to endorse her. Do you all like her?" I glanced at Sutton and Mac. "Your opinion is important to me. If there's any suspicion, or something feels off, please share."

"Her background check is clean," Zayne said.

"Shit. I didn't even think about asking you to look into her, Sutton." I smacked my forehead with the palm of my hand. "I can't be that stupid right now, or ever."

"As soon as I saw her, I messaged Pierce to work with Vaughn to run it. Since we didn't have a lot of personal information on Lydia other than the state and her career, I had Vaughn run her through some other systems. She's clean." Sutton pursed her lips together. "But I never trust that knowledge on its own. All it means is that she's never been caught in any illegal activity."

"Is there a concern?" My brain kicked into overdrive as all the possibilities flooded me.

15

"I mean, none of my alarms went off around her. The opposite actually." I bit my lower lip while I waited for someone to respond.

I didn't miss the tension in Sutton's shoulders. *Dammit.* My mood had taken a hard dip. Tonight was supposed to be fun, but Brandon's bullshit continued to snake its way into my life, dampening my attempts to forget about him this week. Maybe if I drank myself into oblivion, and Jungle Gemma appeared, it would keep me mentally occupied. Hendrix could reap those benefits too.

"I found it interesting that she missed the FedEx deadline for the dresses and drove seven hours to get them here. It was too convenient." Sutton drained her glass. "Gemma, I'm sorry. I didn't mean to upset you. Don't panic. This is *my* job. Not only are we close friends, but you're a client too. I analyze and evaluate potentially dangerous situations and dig into people's lives. You hired us to be suspicious. My gut feeling says nothing is going on, but her actions were a little bit of a red flag. But listen: four bodyguards will be there tonight, plus me. I can be drunk and still kick someone's ass. There's nothing to worry about."

My heart thundered in my ears, and I sipped my drink much

slower this time.

"Did I ever tell you what happened when Sutton found out Vaughn and I were together?" Claire shifted in her seat and flipped her long blonde hair behind her shoulder.

"No," Mac and I said in unison. I loved Claire for changing the subject.

A little smile pulled at the corner of Sutton's mouth. "I didn't take it well to say the least."

"That's an understatement." Zayne's laugh rumbled through his chest.

Claire rolled her eyes. "I'll never forget it. Sutton was out for blood."

"Oh no, what happened?" Mac leaned in and propped her elbows on her knees.

"We were in my bedroom at Sutton's place—well, it's not mine, but still. Anyway, I had this big heart-to-heart with her about how I'd met this guy, he was wonderful, and we'd fallen in love. Sutton asked when she could meet him, and I told her she already knew him. When I explained it was Vaughn, she dropped her half-full glass of red wine on the carpeted floor."

I grimaced.

"Then she flew out of the chair, down the stairs, and to the workout room. I was running after her, hoping Pierce wasn't going to get wind of the chaos. Anyway, Sutton darted in the gym and attacked Vaughn."

"What?" Mac snickered behind her hand.

"I was going to kick his fucking ass for messing with my sister." Guilt clouded Sutton's expression. "Vaughn is my best friend, but I'll protect Claire no matter what."

"I have to admit, I fell in love with him even more that night," Claire said softly. "He handled the situation so well. He refused to fight Sutton and only blocked her blows, but she still managed to get a few hits in."

"Poor Vaughn," Mac groaned.

"What happened? I mean you obviously came to terms with their relationship." I lightly tapped the stem of my glass with my fingernails while I waited to hear the rest of the story.

"He stood his ground and explained that he didn't need my permission to be in love with Claire."

"My man did well," Zayne said.

"You were there?" Mac quirked an eyebrow at him.

"I saw the entire thing go down. I didn't think Sutton would take it so hard, but I was wrong. Vaughn told it like it was, then they talked it out. But she did call him a motherfucker, and I've never heard her call Vaughn that before."

"Oh God. I did." Sutton shook her head. "I was so mad that I lost my head a little. After that, I apologized and bought him an expensive bottle of whiskey."

"I hope I'm not overstepping, but why were you so angry, Sutton? You and Vaughn are super close, so why didn't you trust him with Claire?" I asked.

Claire laughed softly. "Vaughn was a major player."

"That." Sutton nodded at her sister. "Different girl every night, threesomes, foursomes, clubs, you name it. Nothing was off-limits for him."

Mac glanced at the bodyguards. "Why do I have a feeling it's part of the job? I mean, Zayne doesn't *date* either."

"We don't have time," Greyson finally piped up. "The job is demanding and often dangerous. Our biggest challenge is finding some type of work-life balance without pulling another person into a bad situation."

"I think Greyson summed it up well," Sutton said. "It's why Pierce struggled with Vaughn and Claire at first too. And honestly, I needed to trust that I knew who Vaughn really was. We grew up together, and I know his heart. After Claire was kidnapped, I felt as though I'd let her down, and the guilt ate me alive. Vaughn was there for me, along with Zayne and Pierce. Once the FBI had recovered her, I vowed that no one would hurt her again."

"Ahh, thanks, sis." Claire leaned her head against her shoulder. "I love you, too."

My heart melted as I watched the beautiful sisterly bond between them.

Mac nudged me. "We've got that."

"We do." I squeezed my bestie's hand.

"We're here. Greyson and I will check the perimeter, then we will come back to get you. Once we're inside the building, the entrances and exits will be locked and secured. The only people you should see are the owner, two bartenders, and the manager. No other employees will be there tonight. Pierce and Vaughn are already inside." With that, Zayne and Greyson hopped out of the vehicle, then Greyson disappeared while Zayne guarded the limo.

"He's so bossy," Mac said, laughing.

"Zayne's a really great guy. At first, we butted heads, but he's become one of my closest friends. I'll be glad when he finds someone too." Claire finished her drink, then placed it on the little table between the seats.

"If Vaughn can fall in love and settle down, I have faith that Zayne can as well." Sutton slid across the seat, waiting for Greyson or Zayne to give the thumbs-up.

"Ladies," Greyson said, opening the door and extending his palm to help each of us out of the limo.

"Oh, shit. I almost forgot." I slipped my shoes off and traded them for my comfy black flats. I had no idea how Claire or any other female danced in high heels.

Giggling, I ran after the group and followed them into the building. The champagne had already made me a little tipsy since I hadn't eaten much. The transition from daylight to darkness temporarily startled me until my eyes adjusted to the dim light. I followed everyone down the hallway, then into the small club. Three rectangular tables were set up to the left, and the dance floor expanded across the room. A bar was at the front and another on the right side. I assumed that meant they had a lot of business. I liked the idea of two bars. While touring, we'd gone to some huge clubs with only one, which made it nearly impossible to get drinks.

A large pink-and-silver banner hung near the back wall, congratulating me on my upcoming marriage. The deep thumping bass of a song reverberated through the speakers, and Mac grabbed my hand, pulling me toward a table that was full of gifts. A collage of pictures hung on the wall near our seats. My heart fluttered as I inspected the images of Hendrix and me kissing under the mistletoe, working in the studio, performing on stage, and drinking and playing games on the tour bus. Mac had been hard at work and had caught some beautiful memories. My breath hitched. I was suddenly overwhelmed with love and awe of my life.

"Do you like it?" Mac asked, leaning her head on my shoulder. "You two have something so special, Gemma. I couldn't be happier for you both. After all, you're my favorite people in the world other than Cade."

I draped my arm around her shoulders and pulled her to me. "I don't like it. I love it, Mac. You caught the moods so well, Mac. You have an eye for those hard-to-capture moments." I paused, my pulse picking up its pace. "Is that John?" I drew closer, identifying our drummer who had been murdered while we were on tour.

"Yeah. I wish I'd taken more, but at least there are a few with him."

"It's a great gift. Thank you." I rested my head against hers, and we stood silently, soaking in the feelings still alive in us from the pictures.

"Let's get you drunk and dancing." Mac smacked me on the butt and laughed, then she signaled for the bartender. Within minutes, we all had shots of tequila in our hands.

"To Gemma!" Mac raised her diet soda to us, and everyone toasted.

I slammed my shot down, allowing the liquid to seep into every nook and cranny of my being. I welcomed the hazy feeling and the renewed sense of determination to have a good time.

Pierce and Vaughn caught the corner of my eye, and I waved at them, a calm washing over me. I was safe. I could relax with my friends.

"Gemma," Zayne said from the left of me. "Lydia is here."

"Hey!" I said, yelling at her over the music. "Do you want anything to drink?"

"Only if you promise me that if I have a drink, you won't hold it against me professionally," she said, her expression serious.

I could respect that. "I promise." I offered her a reassuring smile. A tug on my elbow pulled my attention away from Lydia.

"Do you need another drink before we dance our asses off?" Claire asked, grinning at me. "Mm, never mind."

Before I could reply to her, she took off toward the bar and returned with two shots. "Bottoms up!"

I tipped it back and drained it, my head swimming. I shook the dizziness off, set my glass on the table, and followed Claire to the floor. Sutton and Mac were already dancing. I signaled to Lydia to join us. In minutes, we were swaying to the beat of "Ride It" by Regard. All of my stress and worry began to slip away as the alcohol numbed me and the pulse of the song pumped through my veins. Music always brought me to life. Even though I'd stopped singing, it had saved me after the rape.

"Hey, gorgeous! Wanna dance?" Tensley bounced up to the group and threw her arms around me.

Tensley was one of the acts that toured with August Clover. She was an incredibly talented drummer, and her shows were off the charts. Franklin had seen her perform one evening and sent Hendrix and me a video of her. Her energy was infectious as she bounced drumsticks off the drums, used props including metal garbage cans, and worked in dance moves as the music drove her. Ten also used paint, which added an extra layer of entertainment. She often walked off stage with purple, pink, blue, and green splatters in her blonde hair and lightly freckled cheeks and nose.

"I'm so glad you're here." I hugged her, then turned my attention to a dark-haired beauty, who I assumed was Avery, Tensley's best friend. Not only was Avery gorgeous, but there was a commanding air about her as well. As Tensley had mentioned, Avery's dad had recently died and she needed to get out more often and have some fun. Apparently Avery had taken over her father's multimillion-dollar financial business. The moment Ten mentioned the company, I immediately recognized the name. I had a lot of respect for her for filling her dad's shoes at only twenty-two.

"I'm Avery. It's so nice to meet you. Thank you for inviting me." Her face lit up with a kind smile, and I instantly liked her. Avery's black designer jeans hugged her thin frame, and her heels matched her teal top.

"Any friend of Ten's is a friend of mine. And yes, that sounded super cliché, but I've already had two glasses of champagne and two shots of tequila, so there's no telling what else I might say."

We laughed, then I introduced Avery to the group. I hadn't realized that Sutton and Avery already knew each other. I was aware that Tensely had met Sutton and Pierce. Although the wealthy ran in their own circles, I wondered if there was another reason Avery knew them.

"How's Layne?" I asked Tensley over the music.

A dreamy expression filled her blue eyes, and she smiled. "He's amazing. I'm glad Hendrix invited him to hang out with the guys tonight. He's still meeting people. Moving is difficult, and it takes some time to start over."

"I know. If it weren't for Mac, I would still be hiding in the back of the college campus library."

"Enough talking, girls." Mac danced around us and bumped my hip with hers.

After another hour of dancing, I was ready for a break. Beads of sweat trickled down my spine, and I wiped the perspiration off my forehead with my hand.

"Major humidititties over here." Mac pointed at her chest.

I nodded in agreement while we all crowded around the table and took our seats, and Mac signaled for the music to be turned down. Another round of drinks was brought to us, as well as a few appetizers.

"Everyone, this is Lydia. She designed my wedding gown and bridesmaid dresses," I announced.

"I can't wait to see your dress," Tensley said. "You're going to look beautiful."

Everyone chatted about the upcoming nuptials, and Lydia was

plied with questions concerning her work. I had no doubt this fantastic group of women would welcome her with open arms.

Mac scooted her chair away from the table and clinked her fork on a collins glass. "Since this was short notice, I didn't have time to plan any games, but we do have gifts. I say we get started and see how red Gemma's face and neck turn."

Laughter filled the room, and once again, I glanced around the area and eyed the bodyguards. Unfortunately, their presence was going to make me uncomfortable while I opened the gifts that contained God knew what.

"Ignore them, Gemma. They've seen it all. Not much fazes them," Sutton assured me.

The next hour consisted of barely there lingerie, sex toys, lotions, and a gift card to Adam & Eve. Everyone shared hilarious stories, and we laughed until my sides hurt. Mac kept the booze and water coming as well as the food. Thank goodness she was on top of it. Even Sutton had relaxed and was buzzed. The side effect of being drunk was also settling in, and my body was begging for Hendrix's touch.

A single envelope with my name on it was the only gift left unopened. "It's from me." Avery waved from the other end of the table. "I'll explain it to you."

"It needs explaining? Oh boy." I giggled, then carefully opened it. A white gift card with a purple lily on the front fluttered and landed near my drink. "The Lily?" I asked, a bit perplexed. "I haven't heard of it before."

"Wait, isn't that the women's clothing boutique downtown?" Mac asked.

Claire snickered. "Something like that." She flashed a huge grin at Avery, who returned her smile. "Oh, Gemma, Gemma, Gemma. That is probably the best gift you could have gotten."

Avery barked out a laugh at Claire's comment.

"I'm confused." I flipped the card over to see if there was any additional information, but there wasn't.

"Mac, would you trade seats with me for a minute so I can talk to

Gemma?" Avery slipped into the chair next to me, then leaned in close. "I got permission to give you this gift. It's not common knowledge, and it has to be kept a secret, but I assured the owner I would vouch for you."

I frowned as I raised my glass and took a healthy swallow of my Mai Tai.

"It's a sex club for women."

Startled, I spewed my cocktail all over the table. Gasping, I wiped my mouth with the back of my hand. "What?" I squeaked.

"Oh no. I'm sorry. I didn't mean to make you spit out your drink." Avery chuckled, grabbed a napkin, and helped me mop up the mess, then continued to explain. "It's also for the ladies who are in a relationship and want some spice. Whatever your and Hendrix's fantasies might be, you have a safe place to act it out. Toys, bondage, threesomes, role play—the world is yours. Every client is confidential, so no one would ever know. Also, there's no pressure to use it. It's meant to support women being comfortable with their sexuality."

"Oh. I like that idea. I mean, at least for me, it's not something I've been at ease with." *Dammit.* I was definitely drunk. I didn't share that information with just anyone.

"I think most women struggle with it. If you and Hendrix talk, and it's not for you, then regift it to your friend Claire. She apparently knows what the Lily is." Avery struggled to contain her smile.

I glanced over at Claire, my cheeks flaming red at the idea that I'd just learned more about her intimate life than I wanted to. Claire hadn't lived in Spokane long, which meant she and Vaughn had utilized the club.

Suddenly, I recalled the evening that Hendrix had shared his fantasy of having sex with me in a crowded restaurant. The thought of his hand sliding between my legs and his fingers grazing my clit sent a delicious tremble through my body. Maybe we could do something like that. I wasn't sure how it really worked, though.

"Thank you." I gave her a quick hug.

"Have fun," Avery said, then returned to her seat.

Mac signaled for the music to begin, and my core throbbed as Hendrix's words tickled my memory. "I want to taste you. Since the table has plenty of space, I drop beneath it, pull your dress above your waist, and spread your legs." I bit my bottom lip in order not to moan. Every fiber of my being tingled with desire. All I could think about was easing Hendrix's big cock into my mouth and sucking him until he begged me to stop.

"Let's go, babe." Claire grabbed my hand and led me to the dance floor. "Let's show 'em whatcha got." She winked at me, and we laughed.

"Secrets" by Regard began playing, and I gave Mac a huge smile for dipping into my Spotify playlists for the party.

Avery and Ten started dancing, and my eyes widened. My attention darted to Claire, and she giggled. "Honey, every guy here is going to go home ready to fuck. That is called foreplay."

Avery seductively slithered down Ten's body. I looked at the guys. I realized they were on duty, but there wasn't a male in the room who wasn't watching.

"Relax. Let your body move with the music." Claire's hands glided down my sides and rested on my waist, guiding my moves. "That's it. You know what we've worked on. Don't pay any attention to the bodyguards."

How did I let her talk me into this?

"Loosen up. Move the hips. You've got this."

I swept my hands beneath my long red hair and let go and relaxed into the music.

"There you go! Let's do it."

I yelped as Claire pulled me forward. Then she hopped on top of the bar. She held her hand out and tugged me up next to her.

She started with the steps she'd taught me, then I fell in beside her. I'd secretly hired Claire to teach me to dance for my reception, though she'd refused to let me pay her. Not only had she taught me some of the traditional dances, but we'd had a lot of fun trying other moves as well. Now that we were moving up the wedding, I wasn't sure we would have a large reception, but Claire was right. *Why wait when we can shake our asses right now?*

Claire was fluid motion when she moved. My style was clumsier, but I was learning. We faced the front again, our hips rotating in a seductive circle.

"Woo-hooo! You go, Gemma!" Mac yelled from the floor.

I continued to follow Claire's lead, and we danced across the bar. My hands slid up and down my body, and I dropped to my knees. I thrust my hips forward. Claire had a whole new take on sexy. My goal had been to save it for Hendrix while on the honeymoon, but apparently Jungle Gemma was out to play, and it felt damned good to finally let go and enjoy myself without any judgment.

Claire and I rolled to our stomachs, then crawled across the bar top, practically humping the counter. We hopped to our feet and continued while the ladies shouted and whistled. I turned to the west wall, and Claire cuddled up to the back of me. Her hand trailed down my torso and to my hip as we moved our bodies together. Until Claire, I'd never danced with a girl, but she assured me it was well worth the benefits. Apparently, mind-blowing sex was involved afterward.

A pair of guy's hands slipped over Claire's, and I glanced over my shoulder. Vaughn. I laughed and hopped off the bar. Stepping back, I allowed Claire and Vaughn to take over.

Jesus, they are on fire. The chemistry that rippled off them in waves was hot as hell, and all I could think about was how needy I was for Hendrix. Desperate raw desire coursed through me.

Vaughn moved his leg between Claire's, and she gyrated against it as though they were naked and alone. Claire leaned her head backward, hair cascading down her back. Her lips parted slightly as Vaughn guided her hips.

"Holy shit. They should make porn movies," Avery said.

"Claire's very comfortable with who she is," I added. A spark of jealousy flickered to life, and I squelched it. I wanted the confidence Claire and Avery had.

"You can get there," Avery said.

We dropped the conversation, and Avery danced with me, but not as close as she and Ten had earlier. Tensley and Mac joined in as well.

"Oh!" Mac clapped and darted across the room.

Before I could turn around, strong hands slipped around my waist, and a hard body rubbed against my back. Hips pushed against me, and an erection pressed into my ass. Immediately recognizing his touch and musky cologne, I sighed and leaned into him.

"You're sexy as hell tonight," Hendrix said, his breath grazing my neck.

I faced him and planted a big kiss on his lips. "Hi! What are you doing here?"

I slipped my arms around him. His hair was in a messy man bun. My fingernails traced the angle of his jawline, down his neck, and below the collar of his silver button-down shirt. His blue eyes sparkled as his hands slid over my ass and pulled me against him, our bodies moving in sync.

"We're all here. We got drunk and wanted to dance, but we all wanted to be with our girls. So here we are. I hope it's okay that we crashed your party."

"I'm so glad you're here." I kissed him passionately and slipped my fingers into the back pockets of his jeans.

I glanced around. Cade and Mac were dancing in the corner and making out like teenagers. Ramsey and Avery were inseparable as well. Even Sutton had dragged Pierce onto the floor while two body-guards kept an eye on the area so the others could have a little fun for a few minutes. Pierce and Sutton dancing like they were gearing up for the bedroom was something I never thought I would see. Layne and Tensley were laughing and swaying to the music in the middle of the dance floor and making out.

"Looks like Asa met Lydia," Hendrix said, nodding at the couple.

"Ohhh. Asa is a player. I hope Lydia is okay with that." I giggled. "I think we're all really drunk."

"Us too."

I pushed up on my tiptoes and nipped his earlobe with my teeth. "Meet me in the ladies' room."

Hendrix's mouth gaped, then a mischievous smile played on his lips. I discreetly massaged his dick through his jeans, then walked away.

16

Sneaking into the ladies' room, I performed a quick search to make sure no one else was there.

"Is it clear?" Hendrix poked his head in.

A flutter of nerves and excitement filled my stomach. "Hurry." I giggled and waved him in. "Does the door lock?"

"Yeah." Hendrix secured it, then approached me. "Are we really going to do this?"

"Oh hell yes. You know that Jungle Gemma comes out to play after several drinks."

His tongue darted across his lower lip, and he backed me up. "What do you want, baby?" He growled while his palm moved to the wall over my shoulder, and his eyes scanned my face with a fierce intensity. He frantically fiddled with the button on my jeans until they popped open.

"I need you inside me, Hendrix." My gaze connected with his, and I helped him tug my pants down.

Hendrix released a low growl "You should drink more often." He kissed my neck and slid his hand between my thighs. My legs turned to jelly, and I was afraid I couldn't stand. "You're soaking wet, Gem."

"It's Claire's fault. We were dancing all sexy and shit on the bar, then she snuggled up to me, and all I could think about was fucking you."

"Dammit. I missed you on the bar dancing with another girl?"

I giggled. Apparently Claire was right.

"And ..." I ran my hands beneath his shirt and up his muscular back. "I remembered how you wanted to get under the table and lick my pussy at a restaurant."

In one swift motion, Hendrix picked me up and set me on the edge of the bathroom sink. "Shit, babe. I love it when you talk like that." He knelt in front of me.

"Wait." I kicked off my jeans, then spread my legs for him.

He bent my knees, then pinned them to my chest. He dipped his head between my thighs, and I nearly orgasmed on the spot as he sucked and licked my sensitive core. I grabbed his hair, moaning loudly. My hips bucked against him as he continued. "Shit, Hendrix."

He worshipped my pussy, lapping up my juices until I screamed his name. He stood and hurriedly undid his jeans. I hopped down and bent over the counter, bracing my hands against the mirror for support.

Hendrix slipped into me and grabbed my hips. "Fuck." He withdrew slowly, then slammed into me, my body rocking from the impact. His thrusts were rough and needy.

"Yes, baby," I cried. "More."

A knock on the door startled us. "Just a minute!" I yelled.

Hendrix slowed his pace down but didn't stop. His hand slipped beneath my shirt, and he flipped the cup of my bra down, exposing my nipple to his eager fingers.

"Come with me, Gemma," he panted.

Seconds later, his body shuddered, and he released a low moan that triggered my orgasm. Stars exploded behind my closed eyelids as my inner walls clenched his shaft.

Collapsing against the counter, I gasped for air. "Oh God. We just had sex in a public bathroom."

Hendrix chuckled and collected my jeans and G-string off the floor for me. "I'm not sure who needs to come in, but there's no hiding what we just did." He laughed and pulled his jeans up, then fastened them. "Make no mistake, babe. I'm down for a quickie in public any time."

I stood and dressed as quickly as I could, attempting not to break into massive giggles. Hendrix washed his hands and mouth and dried them with paper towels. "Huh. I haven't been in the girls' bathroom before. It's definitely nicer than the guys." He chuckled.

I grinned and kissed him on the cheek. "I'm going to go pee and freshen up. I'll be out in a few minutes."

"Sounds good. I love you." He adjusted my top and smoothed my hair. "We should do this again." A mischievous twinkle flickered in his eyes. He pressed his lips to the corner of my mouth, then snuck out of the bathroom.

Glancing at myself in the mirror, I laughed. My neck and cheeks were bright red.

"It smells like sex in here."

Shit.

A cute brunette with multiple eyebrow rings sauntered into the room. I recognized her as one of the bartenders on duty and gave her a weak smile. The stench of cigarettes reached me before she did, and I struggled not to wrinkle my nose in disgust. Her black leather halter top and pants matched her eyeliner and short spikey hair. A studded collar circled her neck, and I wondered if she shopped at Spencer's in the mall.

"By the look on your face, I would say Hendrix Harrington is one hell of a fuck."

My mouth opened and closed as I struggled to find something to say. Regardless of whether or not we'd had sex, her comment was inappropriate. "That's not any of your business." My shoulders tensed.

"Chill out, Gemma. What did you think would happen? Did you honestly think no one would notice that you two had slipped away or that Hendrix just casually strolled out of the women's restroom? You're celebrities. Every move you make is watched."

Her phone chimed, and she removed it from her back pocket. She tapped the screen. "I'm ready," she said immediately. She held the cell to her chest and stared at me. "You need to listen very carefully. Don't make a scene. Don't hang up the phone. Don't scream. If you do, this entire bar is rigged to blow the fuck out of everyone. Pieces of your friends and fiancé will land all over the parking lot."

I struggled to register what she'd just said. *Who the fuck does she think she is?* "You're lying. My men searched the building before I got here." My nostrils flared. *How dare she waltz in here and threaten me.*

She sneered at me. "Honey, what do you think I've been doing tonight? Taking inventory in the back?"

My heart skidded to a stop. *Who is she?*

"Take the phone." She held it out to me.

With a trembling hand, I reached for it.

"Leave it on the counter when you're finished." She winked at me, then hurried out of the door.

"I have a great view of your tits," a male voice said.

Blistering rage licked through me, and I clenched my hand into a tight fist. "Brandon. How dare you send someone to scare me." Apparently, alcohol not only made me horny as hell—it gave me balls too.

"Oh, my girl has a feisty side these days. I like it." Brandon's chestnut-colored eyes narrowed. His light-brown hair was shorter than the last time I'd seen him. "From the flush and glow of your skin, I would guess that you just got royally fucked."

I chose to ignore his vulgar comment. "How did you get a phone?"

"I'm well-loved here. I have friends everywhere. Behind these walls and out in the big bad world too." He ran a hand over his short, light-brown hair and smirked.

"What do you want?" My voice came out confident despite the way I trembled inside.

"Gemma, don't be like that." He feigned hurt feelings. "I'm a reformed man. That's all I wanted to tell you, and to ask you to give me a chance." He set the phone down on a table and paced the small room.

"If you'd changed, you wouldn't have had a bartender rig the bar to blow with my friends and family here. How did you even know where we would be?"

"Whoever made the reservation mentioned it was for your bachelorette party and rented out the entire club. The cute brunette is an ex-girlfriend of mine from college. She knew I had a thing for you, and she made sure I was aware of the event. It all worked out perfectly, might I add. She does great work with explosives. When I offered her a price, she nearly creamed her panties." Brandon chuckled. "I had to make sure you would take my call, so I overpaid her." He gave a half shrug as though money weren't an issue even in prison.

"I'm not talking to you. You're a disgusting rat bastard." I seethed and raised my finger to end the call when he moved the phone to view his hand. My legs shook violently, and I sank to the floor. His thumb hovered over a red button of a handheld device. I assumed it would detonate the bomb that would kill Hendrix and everyone else that I loved. *Oh God. Mac's baby.*

"Never forget, Gemma. I. Am. Always. In. Control."

The clang of a door sounded, then a devious grin spread across his face. "Dessert." He turned the phone around to a young woman with brown hair who stared at the floor, hiding her facial features.

"Don't hang up, Gemma," he said in a matter-of-fact tone, a smirk tugging at the corner of his lips. Brandon indicated a boom with his mouth and free hand. His laughter filled the room while he flipped the phone down on the table.

A rustling sound reached my ears, then I saw Brandon's ugly mug again. He moaned loudly.

"Do you know how fucking turned on I am having you watch while she sucks my fat cock?" He shifted the camera and allowed me to see the entire scene. My stomach dropped like a lead ball to my toes, and I nearly retched. The girl no longer had brown hair. It was now long and red, and she was stark naked. Her head bobbed as she gave Brandon a blow job at the same time that she bounced up and down on the face of a guard who was lying on the floor.

"You disgust me." I squeezed my eyes closed, but it was too late. Brandon with this girl would be forever imprinted on my brain.

"You have five seconds to open your eyes, or you can say goodbye to your life as you know it. You'll love to hear that you're the farthest from the blast. I think you might actually live. There's a good possibility you would be disfigured, but the important thing to understand is that no one else could survive it. You would be the lone survivor. Alone without Hendrix or Mac."

Terror spiked within me, sending my heart racing into overdrive. I struggled to pull air into my lungs as I opened my eyes. I would focus on gathering information to keep him behind bars.

"Do you know what she likes?" A malicious grin slipped over his face. "She likes it in the pussy and ass at the same time. She loves to be dominated and chained to a wall like a prisoner. She spreads her legs like the little whore she is, and I bring anyone I want to the party. Hell, I'm paid to line it up. Everyone wants in on the action. *Everyone* in this hellhole owes me favors, including the guards."

I cringed. This was how he got a cell phone to facetime me. "Stop, Brandon. Why are you doing this?"

My stomach flip-flopped over and over as images of my rape assaulted my mind. My hand clenched into a tight fist, and I dug my fingernails into my palm as I attempted to rein in my fear. I refused to give Brandon the satisfaction of me falling apart.

He grunted and shoved his dick between her lips, grabbing her hair.

"Because I can."

The chick popped him out of her mouth and looked up at the camera. A loud gasp slipped from me.

"She has an uncanny resemblance to you, don't you think?" His laughter filled the room.

The girl moaned as she orgasmed loudly. When she was finished, she smiled up at Brandon. "You ready to be fucked?" She purred, running her long, manicured nails along the inside of his leg. Then she crawled into Brandon's lap, and he wrapped his fingers around her throat as she settled onto his crotch.

"The press will never believe this isn't you. By the time they see the video, it will be doctored even more. You'll be ruined." He panted as the girl rode him and he choked her, her face turning crimson.

Seconds later, she clawed at his hand, leaving thick red welts on his wrist and arm.

"Why are you doing this?"

He released his hold on her, and she collapsed forward as he continued to fuck her. "I can't tell you that now, Gemma. But get ready. I'll be *seeing* you soon." And with a tap to the screen the call was ended.

My heart raced, and my breathing was erratic and labored. *Oh shit.* I had to get to Hendrix. We had to get the hell out of there before Brandon killed us all.

17

I bolted out the door and onto the dance floor where my friends were laughing and having fun. Little did they know it might be the last time we all saw each other. Panic jolted through me, and I located Hendrix near the table with a drink in his hand.

"Hey, babe. Are you okay? Maybe we shouldn't have had sex in the—"

I cozied up to him as calmly as I possibly could. "Hendrix, there's a bomb in the club. We have to go right now. I don't know ... I ..." I had no idea if the bartender had a detonator as well, but I was guessing that she did. Hell, I wasn't even sure she was still on the premises. Fear was clouding my thought process, and I was torn between scaring everyone with the truth or leaving as swiftly as possible without an explanation.

The color drained from Hendrix's face as his attention swept across the room. He signaled to Pierce, and within seconds, he and Vaughn flocked to us.

"We're all in danger," Hendrix said. "Get us out."

Vaughn slid his arm around my shoulders, his mismatched eyes scanning the perimeter for threats. I suspected he wanted to grab

Claire as well, but his job was to protect Hendrix and me at the moment. Pierce fell in next to Hendrix.

A whimper escaped me as they ushered us out of the bar. Sutton had picked up the movement and rounded up everyone else. A hush fell over the group as we exited the building.

"We can't get into the limo, Pierce. I don't know that it hasn't been tampered with. Everything here might be rigged." I hiccupped, trying not to break down before we were safe. "Bombs. I have no idea how many."

Pierce's furious gaze narrowed, and he waved us closer to him. "Do exactly as I say. You all need to act as though you're having a great time and are on a pub crawl. Laugh and act drunker than you are. Got it?"

A soft murmur broke out between people as their unanswered questions heightened everyone's concerns.

"Move. Now." He jogged a few feet in front of us as we all followed.

Hendrix held my hand so tightly I was afraid it would lose the circulation. The sound of our feet smacking against the cracked, uneven cement sidewalk echoed in my ears. A few blocks down the road, we stopped, and Pierce ushered us into a small café that was still open. He excused himself while he made a phone call, and the rest of the group huddled in a corner near the entrance.

"Gemma," Mac said, approaching Hendrix and me. "What's going on?" Cade held her hand, a look of fear creeping into his expression.

"We'll tell you in a little bit." Hendrix draped his arm around his sister's shoulders and kissed the side of her head. "It's okay. Don't panic. I promise you're safe."

I resisted blurting out the horrid details, and although Hendrix had promised we were all right, we weren't, and we both knew it. Vaughn blocked the entrance, and Zayne and Greyson stuck close to the group. Pierce returned a few minutes later and chatted quietly with Vaughn and Sutton. Pierce was on full alert. His shoulders were squared, and waves of anger rippled off him. It wasn't long before four cars turned into the parking lot.

"That's us." Pierce waved Hendrix and me forward. I grabbed

Mac's hand and kept her close, ensuring that she and Cade would stay with us. Hendrix and I might be the celebrities, but I was taking our best friends in the same ride with us.

"There's not enough room for all four of you in the same car. Not since I'm riding in the front passenger seat," Pierce stated.

I pulled Mac next to me. "Then she will sit in my lap. Mac and Cade go with us." I jutted my chin in the air. Pierce knew me well enough to realize I wouldn't leave without her.

"Fine. She sits in someone's lap."

Hendrix wrapped his arm around my waist, then we left the café and made a beeline into the closest vehicle. Pierce opened the back door and we hopped in. I sat on Hendrix's lap so Cade and Mac could get in quickly.

The minute Pierce settled into the front passenger seat, my body betrayed me, and I began to shake uncontrollably.

"Baby," Hendrix whispered against my hair. "I've got you. You're safe."

I shook my head. He didn't know. No one knew what had happened. Hot tears burned my cheeks as we remained silent. I had no idea where we were going, but Maine sounded good to me. At least we could hide there for now.

I snuggled into Hendrix as he continued to speak softly in my ear, attempting to calm me. Images of Brandon and the girl who looked like me flooded my mind. A shiver shot down my spine, then my tummy turned inside out.

"I'm going to be sick. Pull over," I barked. The car whipped over to the side of the road, and before we completely stopped, I flung the door open. The cool air caressed my clammy skin, and I scrambled out of Hendrix's lap and to the cold, hard asphalt. Sharp pebbles dug into my palms while my stomach revolted, and I puked up the appetizers and alcohol I'd had at the club. I was sitting still, waiting to see if I was finished, when I felt gentle hands gather my hair and pull it back.

"I swear on my life, I will take the bastard down," Hendrix said, his words laced with steel.

I peeked up at him, trembling. "How did you know it was Brandon?"

He knelt beside me. "The look on your face when you came out of the bathroom was of sheer terror. You were laughing when I left you. I just don't understand how he got to you. Pierce and his men made sure the bar was clear, and there weren't any threats before you ladies arrived."

I shook my head. "It was all put into place while we were there. The short-haired female bartender is Brandon's ex-girlfriend. She ..."

"Son of a bitch." Hendrix's shoulders slumped forward in defeat.

I wiped my mouth off with the back of my hand and willed my weak legs to support me again. Hendrix helped me up, then we climbed into the car.

"Are you okay, Gemma?" Pierce asked from the front seat.

"I could lie and tell you that I am if you need to hear that." I settled into Hendrix's lap, then the vehicle began to move again.

"Never lie to me. Anything you want to say, you always have my ear."

"I know. I'm just—I'm trying to collect my thoughts first." I leaned my head on Hendrix's shoulder and gently kicked my best friend with my foot. "I love you guys."

"You're scaring me," Mac whispered, tears moistening her eyes.

"We're okay for now. I promise. Don't be scared anymore." I tried to assure my bestie, but I couldn't guarantee anything at the moment.

Mac grabbed my hand as her other one gripped Cade's.

"I have a feeling I know who," Cade said, anger sparking to life in his amber gaze.

"You guys, all four cars are going to Franklin's. He's aware that something happened. Gemma, you can fill us in once we're there."

"Lydia. Oh shit. Pierce, she can't know. I don't want to terrify her. Dammit. I should have never invited her. All I did was put her in danger." I covered my face with my hands.

"We have to include all of them, babe. Layne, Tensley, Benji, Ramsey, Avery, Asa, and Lydia are all involved, whether they like it or not." Hendrix tightened his hold on me.

"Hendrix is right," Pierce said. "Asa is part of the band, so he's automatically caught up in this. Lydia … well, I'm afraid her life just changed for the worse."

I bit my lip, holding the swell of feelings inside until I could hit something and scream. I was teetering on the edge of the abyss, but I would fight like hell before I allowed it to suck me in. A heavy silence blanketed everyone in the car. I attempted to slow my thoughts, but they continued bouncing around in my brain like an out-of-control rubber ball.

FORTY MINUTES later the group had settled into the living room at Franklin's. Janice made sure everyone had water, then sat in her chair next to her husband. Pierce hadn't given them any details yet. I suspected he was waiting to hear them from me, then he could address the issue to all of us together.

Claire stood next to Vaughn, and he discreetly took her hand. He looked down at her, and my breath stuttered. They had almost lost each other that night because of me. Because of Brandon's sick obsession with *me*. Guilt took root inside me and whispered what a piece of shit I was for endangering lives.

Sutton remained near the front entrance, but within hearing range. Greyson was outside, and Zayne was fully alert behind me. Hendrix, Cade, Mac, and I had taken the couch, and our friends sat in the additional chairs.

"I'm so sorry, Lydia." I gathered my courage and looked at her.

"I have no idea what happened, Gemma, so don't apologize." She tucked a strand of her dark hair behind her ear and offered me a weak smile.

I fidgeted, then hopped out of my seat. My mind went blank while I struggled with what to say next. How could I explain to everyone in the room that they'd almost died?

"What happened tonight, kids?" Franklin asked, his blue eyes sharp.

A phone rang, and Pierce fished his cell out of his back pocket. "Pierce Westbrook."

Sutton edged a little closer, her posture tense and on the defensive. Pierce placed his hand on his hip, his biceps flexing. I could tell by the rigid set of his jaw and the tightness of his shoulders that he was trying to contain the beast within. Pierce was a complex man. Although he was patient, I realized there was an excellent chance he was at his limit.

"Thank you." He disconnected the call and white knuckled the phone. Whoever had been on the other end hadn't delivered good news.

"The bomb squad found two C-4 explosives. It was enough to level the entire block."

A horrified snort burst out of Mac, and she slapped her hands over her face. She swore under her breath while she shook her head.

"Wait ... what?" The color drained from Lydia's cheeks.

Asa's mouth hung open, and for the first time since I'd met him, he was speechless. Everyone in the room was in shock.

"God dammit!" Franklin spun on his heel and stared at Pierce. "You and your team are supposed to protect my family," he snapped, his voice growing louder as he pointed at his friend and colleague.

Holy shit. This isn't happening.

"He did!" I jumped up and inserted myself between the men. Hendrix joined me and touched Franklin's arm. "Franklin, you don't even know what happened. If you want to blame someone, blame me." My heart pounded wildly. There had only been one other time I'd stood up to Franklin, and that was when he didn't tell me Hendrix had woken up from a coma. "It's my fault anyway."

Franklin stepped back, his attention landing on me. "You're not responsible for this mess, Gemma. This entire situation reeks of Brandon." He ran his hand through his hair just like Hendrix did when he was stressed.

"Please. We're all on edge, but we can't do anything if you don't know the full story. I'm going to sit down, and I trust there won't be any more accusations." Holding Franklin's gaze, I refused to back down. I loved him, but he was out of line.

Hendrix gave me a tiny nod and remained standing while I joined Mac and Cade on the couch again. Pierce didn't even seem fazed by Franklin's outburst, and he stood his ground.

"I'd gone to the bathroom ..." My attention landed on Hendrix. I realized that we were seen sneaking off together, but I wasn't going to share that with Franklin. "Before I left, the female bartender joined me at the sink. I didn't think much of it at first, then her phone rang. She handed it to me and said if I didn't take the call, the entire bar would blow up. All I could think about was—all of you dying." I shook my head while a sharp pang stabbed me in my chest, stealing my breath. "I told her that I thought she was lying, but she admitted to putting the bombs in place after we were already there." I wiped my damp face. "Franklin, it wasn't Pierce's fault. The building was clean before we arrived."

My comment was followed by silence, so I continued. "Somehow, Brandon had access to a phone and FaceTimed me. He had a girl ..." Panic crept up my throat, and my heart pumped wildly. I wrung my hands, and Hendrix moved away from Franklin and sat next to me. He pulled me into his lap and slid his strong arms around me as I continued to speak. "Brandon was receiving oral sex from a girl. A guard was also in the room. They were all engaged in the act." My cheeks flamed red as I tried to provide everyone with the details. "It was being recorded. I didn't realize what was happening at first until the girl looked at the phone. When she first entered the room, she had brown hair, but before they got started, she put on a red wig." My stomach churned as I recalled her looking at the phone. "She looks a lot like me."

"That's why he had a visitor that signed in with your name," Franklin said, knitting all the pieces together. "Brandon is setting a plan in motion so people will think you're cheating on Hendrix and sleeping with him. I'll contact your PR and we'll get ahead of this."

"When I asked him what he wanted, he said I would have to wait and see." My chin quivered, and I sank my teeth into my lower lip, allowing the pain to ground me in the present moment.

"Blackmail, for starters," Pierce added quietly.

"This is all terrible, but can someone please tell me who this Brandon guy is?" Lydia nibbled on the pencil that had been in her hair bun earlier that day.

"Brandon Montgomery," Hendrix gritted out. "He harassed and stalked Gemma her first year of college. A few years ago, he kidnapped Mac, and Gemma traded herself to let Mac be free. With Pierce's help, Gemma took Brandon down, then the police arrested him. He got off on probation at the time. We suspect his father, Dillon, had some powerful people on his bankroll. After that, Brandon kidnapped and raped an underage girl and went to prison. We just found out a few days ago that he assisted the FBI with capturing Dillon, so he's gaining early release."

"Oh my God." Lydia's pitch climbed with each word. She wrapped her arms around her waist and hung her head.

"I'm sorry you were caught up in this, Lydia. We had no idea that someone was working for Brandon inside the bar." Pierce's brown eyes filled with regret.

"Gemma," Mac whispered, her voice cracking. "He's really back, isn't he?"

I nodded and glanced at her for the first time since I'd shared what happened. "I'm so sorry, Mac. Not only is he back, but I'm pretty sure that he's worse than ever. I tried to hang up on him, but he was holding the detonator, and all I could think of was you and the baby. If anything had happened to you tonight ..." My chin trembled.

Mac sprang forward and hugged me. Our tears flowed freely as we clung to each other.

"Vaughn, you and Zayne stay in the house." Pierce ground his teeth together, and I secretly cheered him on, wanting him to snap and end Brandon once and for all. "Call Tad and tell him to assist Greyson outside. Even though we know that Brandon is still in prison, he's obviously not fucking around."

"Kids, I apologize for my outburst," Franklin said. "I allowed my emotions to get the better of me. It's late, and due to the situation, I'm not comfortable with anyone leaving quite yet. Janice will help everyone get settled into the guest rooms. The family room upstairs can hold several of you as well. I need some time with Pierce, so I'll see you all in the morning." Franklin turned to Pierce, his expression apologetic.

Pierce patted him on the back. "Your office?"

Franklin nodded and kissed his wife before he and Pierce disappeared down the hall.

"Girls," Janice said, holding out the tissue box to us. "Mac, do you and Cade want your bedroom tonight, or would you prefer everyone sleep in the game room?"

Mac looked at me through red swollen eyes. "If everyone is okay with it, we can all bunk in there. It has couches and a TV, plus plenty of floor space."

"We've shared quarters before, so I'm good with it. I think the only person that might feel strange is Lydia." Asa stood, then held his hand out to her.

"I'm fine with it. I don't really want to be by myself right now anyway."

"Lydia, I'll cover the cost of your hotel room. Please don't worry about that. I would rather you be here with us right now," I said. "Again, I'm so sorry you've been pulled into our hell."

"Thank you." Her shoulders slumped forward. "Gemma ..." Lydia approached me, her emotions on her sleeve. Regret, fear, and uncertainty flickered across her face. "I had no idea you all had gone through this. I never heard anything about it on the news."

"It was all sealed, including what Dillon Montgomery did to me, but we'll save that for another time."

"Holy shit, there's more?" Lydia's eyes widened, and she shook her head. I reached out and squeezed her hand.

Claire and Vaughn strolled over to us. "This wasn't how your special evening was supposed to go, Gemma."

Hendrix slipped a protective arm around my waist.

"Everyone is alive. I'll take it. We still have each other for the rest of the night. That's worth something." I reached for Mac's hand. "I'm going to help Janice get food, drinks, air mattresses, and anything else we need. I'll meet everyone upstairs."

"I'll help," Mac said.

"Me too," Hendrix added.

I shook my head. "I think we need a few minutes to talk, babe."

"Okay. Cade and I will locate the mattresses and pillows, then." He pressed a kiss to my cheek, then he and Cade headed up the stairs.

"The sleepovers at Sutton's were more fun." I attempted a lame smile at Claire.

"Girl, those kept me sane. Having you and Mac around helped so much. Now it's my turn to return the favor." She squeezed my arm, then her attention turned to Vaughn. "I'm going to help the guys grab pillows and blankets. I know you're on duty, so I'll see you in a bit."

Vaughn smoothed her hair. "Love you."

"I love you too, babe. Keep us safe."

I thought I saw Vaughn flinch. From what Claire had shared with me, he'd struggled after he hadn't been able to keep her safe from Dillon Montgomery's daughter. It hadn't been his fault at all, but sometimes it was easy to carry the guilt for something out of our control. I hoped he would be able to leave it in the past soon.

While everyone else headed upstairs, Mac and I joined Janice in the kitchen. Janice had her head in the fridge and her arms full of mayonnaise, lettuce, tomatoes, and mustard. "I'm gathering ingredients to make sandwiches if you two want to help." She unloaded the contents onto the counter, then hurried to locate more.

"Mom," Mac said.

Janice continued to dig in the crisper, ignoring her daughter.

"Mom. Mom. Stop."

Janice bolted upright, tears streaming down her face. "I can't, Mac. I can't. Oh my God. I almost lost you all. I almost lost my entire world." Sobs shook her shoulders as the loaf of bread dropped from her grasp to the tile floor. I hurried to grab it before it got stepped on as Janice walked toward us. "My girls." She wrapped an arm around each of us and held us tightly while she cried.

"We're all right, Mom. Gemma got us out really fast."

Unable to stop my outburst of anger, I broke down. "I hate him," I said between gritted teeth. "I hate that fucker. I've never wished death on anyone but Brandon."

"Me too, bestie," Mac hiccupped.

We stood in silence, holding each other until the pain and shock of the night ran dry. Janice released us and wiped her damp cheeks. "We should get these snacks finished and take them upstairs."

"Yeah." Mac grabbed a tissue and blew her nose loudly. "I'm starving."

I giggled through my tears, thankful for the distraction. "You danced your ass off tonight. I bet you're hungry."

Janice pulled out a fresh ham and began to slice off pieces.

"Well, I wasn't the one dancing on top of the bar!" Mac laughed.

Janice's head popped up, and a silly grin eased across her face. "Gemma danced on the bar?"

I barked out a laugh. "It was Claire's fault, and maybe the alcohol had something to do with it." Mac and I began to assemble sandwiches, laughing at the fun parts of the night. "It felt so good to just forget all the bad shit for a little while. It didn't end the way we'd hoped, but at least we're still together." I flipped my hair behind my shoulder and released a sigh.

"That's what's important," Janice said.

"Babe?" Hendrix said, entering the kitchen. "Dad wants to talk to us."

18

"Do you know what he wants?" I asked Hendrix as we walked down the hallway to Franklin's office.

"No, but I can take a guess." Hendrix knocked on the door, then opened it.

Pierce was seated in a chair in front of Franklin's desk. They seemed to have worked out their disagreement. Or rather, Pierce had accepted Franklin's apology, which provided me momentary relief. I wasn't sure I could handle any tension between them.

Franklin leaned back in his chair, and we sat down. "Let's get both of you to Maine tomorrow. Pierce and Zayne will go with you. The rest of us will join you in a few days. We need to get through the wedding, then we can decide where you'll be safe."

My mouth dropped open, and I attempted to find the right words.

"Why can't we stay here? Mac and Cade are," Hendrix said.

"Son, they're going to have to live elsewhere. None of us will remain in Spokane."

"What? Why?" Hendrix slid forward to the edge of his seat, his knee bouncing up and down. He was about to lose it. So was I.

"We won't be together?" My voice hovered above a whisper as

panic settled over me. "I can't be away from my family. Franklin, you can't ask us to do that!" I shot out of my chair. "You think by scattering us all across the world it will protect us?" I smacked my forehead. "I can't even do this right now. I don't understand what the hell you two are thinking. Mac is pregnant, for God's sake. She needs her mom. And I need all of you. I have nothing left. If that son of a bitch separates us, he's won. He'll find some way to pick us off one by one."

"Gemma," Pierce said, standing. "Calm down. We have a plan. We're going to scatter, then all meet up in a remote location. It's all right." He pulled me into a hug, then released me.

"You too?" I asked. A mixture of relief and aggravation flowed through me. None of us should have to give our lives up.

"Yeah. I can't risk Claire and Sutton. I know Vaughn will want to stay with Claire. What Zayne and the other men choose to do is up to them. I'll turn the reins over to someone I trust, and they can be the front man for Westbrook Security."

My knees wobbled. Pierce was walking away from his world to protect his family as well. *How did this happen?*

"Gemma." Hendrix lifted me into his lap.

"I can't lose you," I whispered, my mind reeling from Brandon's threat that night. "If anything ever happened to you ..."

"Nothing bad is going to happen, babe. This plan will work. We can start over anywhere."

"Except for the band. It's over."

Hendrix kissed the side of my head. "As long as I'm with you, Gemma, nothing else matters."

"I'm sorry, Gemma," Franklin said. "I'm rattled. I'm terrified for my family. Tonight fucked me up, and I should have led with that. I didn't mean to make matters worse by not communicating clearly."

"I know." I clutched Hendrix's shirt, allowing my pain to slip away enough for me to get my bearings. In my heart, I knew that Franklin was just as human as the rest of us, but with his legal expertise and ability to make things happen, sometimes I forgot that he wasn't really Superman. Because in my mind, he was.

"Hey." Hendrix tilted my chin up gently. "We're going to Maine tomorrow, then we're getting married Saturday. That's what I'm going to think about when I get worried."

"Yeah." I smiled at him and kissed him fiercely. Then I scrambled to my feet, embarrassed that I'd had a full-on meltdown in front of Franklin and Pierce.

Once Hendrix and I were in our seats again, Franklin continued. "The plane is being fueled up as we speak. Since Lydia hasn't been disclosed as the designer of your wedding gown, she should be safe to return home tomorrow. One of Pierce's men will follow her home and inspect her house before she enters. I'll pay for her and Asa's bodyguards. With tonight's events, I don't want to leave them unprotected. Also, I've spoken to Michael and Marilyn, Benji and Tensley's folks. Security is in place for everyone now. Avery and Ramsey as well." Franklin glanced at his watch. "It's nearly two in the morning. You'll need to be at the airport by ten. Try to get some sleep, kids."

"I'll speak with my wife and team and provide an update. I'm going to make a bit of a change. Sutton, Zayne, Greyson, and Tad will take care of everyone here, then fly over on Friday. Vaughn will go with you instead."

"Why isn't Zayne going with us?" I asked, suddenly curious about why Vaughn was going instead.

"Vaughn has some expertise that Zayne doesn't. I'll leave it at that."

I nodded, too exhausted to ask any more questions.

Hendrix and I stood. "Was anyone hurt tonight?" I asked. "Did they remove the bombs safely?"

"They did," Pierce said. "Unfortunately, the media showed up. There was no way we could stop the reporters once it was safe. The owner of the bar gushed details faster than a broken fire hydrant. Everyone will know you had your bachelorette party, Gemma."

I massaged my temples to alleviate the pounding in my head. "He had a confidentiality agreement."

"He did, but once his bar and livelihood were in danger ..." Franklin sighed. "It just added to our decision to get you out of town."

"Thank you. Both of you. Try and get some rest yourselves." Hendrix nodded at them, then took my hand and led me into the hall.

The soft click of the door closing behind us gained my attention, and I stole one last glance over my shoulder. A sinking feeling descended over me, and I wondered if I would ever see Franklin's office again.

19

The next few days were a whirlwind as we finished the final details of the wedding from our house in Maine. The rest of the family and crew arrived early Friday morning. It was a relief to have everyone under one roof again.

Hendrix and I hadn't had any time to remodel the eight bedrooms upstairs in the Victorian home. Each had a different theme, and I wanted a more cohesive design throughout the house. One of the things I loved the most, though, was that they all had fireplaces and en suite bathrooms, which provided privacy and made for an intimate ambience. It was perfect for our guests.

Sutton had suggested the ladies take over one of the rooms upstairs, so we had a place to hide and get ready for the wedding the next day. It was our designated space away from the men. Hendrix had taken over the kitchen and downstairs, which worked out perfectly. I couldn't wait to see him in his tux but, more than that, to slide a ring onto his finger. Originally, we'd selected our bands together, but I wanted something special for him. Without his knowledge I'd purchased a yellow-gold one with a row of diamonds and sapphires in the middle of it. My jitters were in overdrive with the surprise. I just hoped he liked it.

We were all attempting to be as lighthearted as possible under the circumstances. After the wedding, we would all fly to separate places across the world. We would remain there for six weeks and only contact each other through burner phones. Hell, we didn't even know where we would all end up together. As happy as I was about becoming Mrs. Hendrix Harrington, my heart was in shambles over leaving our homes and the band.

Franklin had given us a choice of where to relocate for the next six weeks. He said to consider it a honeymoon. Hendrix and I chose France. We originally wanted Italy, but we all agreed that since Pierce's wedding was public knowledge, we might be a target there. Hendrix explained to Asa that we were being forced into taking some time off, but as soon as we were able, we would tour again. He recommended that Asa get a new gig if he found someone to play with. I'd had a similar conversation with Tensley. She'd lived through her own hell, so she understood.

After another full day of planning, both for our relocation and last-minute wedding details, I needed a few minutes to myself. I found Hendrix gazing out of the master bedroom window over the ocean. His shoulders were squared, his T-shirt stretching across the muscles in his back. His designer jeans hugged every curve and muscle in his ass and thighs, and I longed to dig my nails into his skin while he buried himself inside me. He'd shoved his hands in his front pockets, which told me he was deep in thought.

"I never get tired of looking at the water." I slipped my arm around his waist and placed my cheek against the back of his shoulder, watching the waves crash against the rocks below us. "I'm going to take a walk and get some fresh air, babe."

He turned and encompassed me in his arms. "How are you holding up?" He kissed my forehead, the warmth of his lips sending ripples of desire through me; but with a full house, we would have to wait to make love until everyone was in their rooms.

"I was just thinking about how easy it would be for you to join me outside later. Maybe you could slide my dress up over my hips, and we could have a moment of privacy." I nipped at his bottom lip, then peeked up at him through my eyelashes. I sucked in a breath as his body responded to mine.

"That sounds so damned good, but you know we're not going anywhere without the bodyguards. I'm happy we've come a long way in our sex life, but I'm not cool with someone watching. I don't want anyone else seeing what's mine." His tongue flicked out against the sensitive place on my neck, and I bit my lip in order not to groan. "But trust me, as soon as we're back in this room, I'll give you a night you'll never forget."

I gasped as his hand ran up my thigh and to my core. He massaged my bundle of nerves through the soft fabric of my G-string, then whispered in my ear, "More later." He grinned, then stepped away.

I blinked several times, trying to clear my hormone-addled brain. A walk didn't even sound good anymore. I wanted to take him to the bathroom and ride him slow, basking in every touch, every lick, every thrust.

"Dammit." I laughed. "You've got me all flustered." I smoothed my hair and chewed on my thumbnail to shift my thoughts away from undressing him, but the moment his chuckle filled the room, desire swept through me again. I cleared my throat. "To answer your earlier question, I feel bipolar. I'm happy one second, because I'm about to marry the man I love, and grief-stricken the next. The thought of us leaving our lives behind ..."

"Hey." His eyes bore into mine, and silence descended over us. "It's only for six weeks. We'll talk to them once a week at least, probably more. Then, once a safe location is secured, we'll all be back together. As far as the band goes, I think we should write and record no matter where we are. It's not goodbye forever."

"I hope not." I pushed up on my tiptoes and pressed my lips to his. "Pierce is waiting for me, and I would prefer to take a walk before it gets dark."

"Take a minute to relax, babe. I'll see you in a little bit."

I descended the stairs, and my attention landed on Pierce, Zayne, and Vaughn deep in conversation near the front door. "Pierce, we don't have to go. I don't want to interrupt your meeting. I know you guys are working hard to keep us safe."

"Don't be silly." Pierce slid his arm around my shoulder, then pulled me against him in a brotherly hug. "It's the evening before your wedding. If you want to take a walk, then that's what we'll do."

I slipped my arm around him. "I don't say it often enough, but I really appreciate and love you guys. Vaughn, Zayne, Pierce. You're all out here risking your lives for us so we can get married." A lump formed in my throat. "And afterward—just thank you. Hopefully I'll be helping you and Claire with her wedding soon." I smiled at Vaughn, and his face lit up at the mention of his fiancée's name.

"He's whipped," Zayne said, laughing and smacking Vaughn on the back.

I laughed. "Some girls are worth it, right, Vaughn?"

"Don't answer that. I don't want to hear any details about my little sister," Pierce barked.

Laughter filled the air, and my heart soared. I loved these guys.

"You ready?" Pierce asked.

"Yeah." I followed him down the porch steps and into the late-afternoon breeze.

"You and Hendrix did well. This place is gorgeous. I love that it's tucked away and offers some privacy too." He paused and glanced around the property.

"Thank you. It was a Valentine's Day surprise." The sound of the waves and the smell of the saltwater massaged my overloaded senses. "It's peaceful. For just a minute, I can forget all the chaos in my life and just breathe." I took a deep breath and savored the exquisiteness that surrounded me.

Silence descended over us as we walked toward the ocean. A grove of maple and oak trees lined the path, and my heart briefly yearned for the comfort of Louisiana. A heavy weight pressed down on my shoulders. Tomorrow would be the happiest day of my life, but a part of me still felt empty without my mom and Ada Lynn. *But fuck Kyle.* There was no love lost with him.

"Oh! I had no idea that was there!" Excited, I continued down the small slope to the open area with a bench. "I can't wait to show Hendrix."

Pierce followed me, then we both came to an abrupt halt. The sun was suspended over the ocean, casting coral, rose, and indigo hues across the sky. My breath stuttered in my chest as the beauty of the moment captivated me. We stood quietly as the embers of the sunset kissed our skin, promising hope of another new day.

"I should get married at this time of day."

"Under normal circumstances I would agree, but not this time. The darkness can hide to many dangers."

Pierce's words snapped me out of my daydream, and I secretly despised him for a second. "Thanks for the reality check," I muttered, then continued down the path.

"Gemma, I didn't mean—"

I held my hand up to stop him. "I know. I'm not mad at you, but sometimes I get so fucking angry at the situation. I realize you're in this fucked-up mess with us, and Hendrix and I aren't the only ones with lives at stake. But it still ..." I spun around to look at him. "How do I handle this, Pierce? You've seen unspeakable things, done unspeakable things, yet you're a wealthy and well-adjusted man living a happy life. How?"

His expression softened. "It's one day at a time, Gemma. It took me years to come to terms with my military days. Let's sit down, and I'll share what I can." He motioned to the wooden bench nestled beneath a tree.

I plopped down and waited for him to provide the insight I desperately needed. Pierce remained standing, his eyes narrowing as he scanned the perimeter for any potential threat.

"It gets better, I swear, but you have to have those outlets in place. If not, then the hatred for yourself and others will drown you. As you get older, it manifests in physical ways as well. Your talent is singing and writing music, but you need to beat the fuck out of something too. Otherwise, all the destructive feelings will eat at you slowly until one day you lose your shit and blow."

"Is that what you do? Fight?"

"Sometimes." He rubbed his chin, his brown-eyed gaze holding mine. "The other night, when I learned the bombs were planted and we'd missed it ..." He swallowed hard and looked away, his features filling with regret. "If it hadn't been for Sutton, I would have fucking lost it and gone after Brandon myself. The moment that sick little fucker steps out of prison, I would be more than happy to end him. Hell, I wouldn't even feel guilty about taking out a pedophile. He and his family disgust me, but more than that ..." He stood silent while the setting sun cast an orange glow behind him. "I have training in the martial arts and the military, but even strong men snap," he said so softly I struggled to hear him.

I leaned forward and placed my hands on the smooth bench as the ocean breeze caressed my skin. "Don't, Pierce. If ..." I rubbed my thumb along my brow line, weighing my next words. "Don't do it yourself." There was no need for me to say anything else. Pierce understood exactly what I was implying.

"Sutton made me promise the same thing." His eyes were haunted, and his smile didn't quite touch them. For the first time, Pierce allowed me a glimpse inside of his soul. He was battling his own demons.

I nodded. "Good. I'm glad you have her." My focus drifted across the open field to the cliff.

"Between you and me, Sutton saved me. When I lost my dad, I nearly slipped into the darkness of my past," he said as he continued to search the area.

"Even the strongest people need saving sometimes." I leaned back and tried to relax.

Pierce cleared his throat. "You're one of the strongest people I know."

Shocked, I stared at him.

"My men and Sutton, we've got nothing on you, Gemma." His voice was kind yet firm. "The day I walked into the house in Louisiana and that motherfucker was trying to hurt you ..." He laughed. "You kicked his ass." A wide grin slipped into place. "You were quick and strong. You took down your attacker in broad daylight while the rest of your life was imploding. From that moment on, I respected you."

"That was a fucked-up day, Pierce." I shook my head, the memories barreling at me faster than a bull in heat. "Hendrix was in the hospital, then I walked into our house, and that son of a bitch thought he could rape me again." A harsh, humorless laugh escaped me. "I was bound and determined not to let Carl steal anything else from me. All I could think of was the lamp. If I could reach it, then I could beat the sorry bastard until he got off of me."

"That. Right there. That's what I'm talking about." Pierce knelt on the ground, his expression solemn. "Don't let that determination go, Gemma. I don't care what Brandon throws at you. Dig deep and find your reason for being. Let that flow through your veins. You're here for a reason. You have a purpose. Don't ever let someone else take it from you."

"How do I hold onto that when I'm tired and feeling defeated? How do I find what I need?"

"You don't have to look for it, Gemma. No matter what you're facing, be still inside yourself and help will always find you."

Loud laughter filled the air, and we both glanced up at the house. "Sounds like the festivities have begun." Pierce stood.

"Yeah. I should get back. I know we need to get some sleep tonight, but I can't see that happening. It's our last night together as a family."

"It's only temporary, Gemma."

I got to my feet and stretched. "It better be. My heart can't take much more."

20

Claire took a step away and admired her work. "Gemma, you have the best hair. I'm so jealous." She handed me a mirror, and I admired the gorgeous updo with pearl beads woven through the sides.

Sutton picked up my white high heels and set them next to my chair. "Oh, I almost forgot!" A huge grin spread across her face while she hiked her dress up and darted down the hall.

"Where is she going?" I asked, leaning forward to see if I could get a glimpse of where she'd gone.

"Got it." She entered the room again, carrying a black velvet box. "This was mine and Claire's grandmother's. Claire and I wanted you to wear it today. It will be your something borrowed and something blue." Sutton raised the lid and revealed a sapphire heart pin. "I think it would look perfect between your boobs. It will match all the sapphires on your sash and down the back of your dress as well."

Laughter filled the room. "Can I?" Claire asked.

"Yeah. It's beautiful. Thank you both so much for letting me borrow it."

"It's gorgeous," Mac added, peering at the piece of jewelry.

Claire bent down and fastened the pin in the middle of the sweetheart neckline. All three girls remained speechless as they admired their work.

"Thank you for being here, for being in the wedding, and most of all, for your friendship. I love you guys." I stood and hugged each of them.

Claire glanced at her phone. "Sutton, it's time for us to go. Gemma, we will see you at the altar."

"Okay." My heart pitter-pattered as they left the room.

"Gemma, are you ready to get married?" Mac beamed at me. Her forest-green dress fit her beautifully after the alterations. The cowl neckline dipped and exposed a little bit of her cleavage, and the toe of her silver high heels peeked from beneath the hem as she walked. Her brown hair was in an updo with butterfly hairpins that held it in place.

"Oh my gosh, you're stunning!" Mac's hand moved to her chest, and her eyes misted over. "Let me help with your veil." Mac set her bouquet down on the antique vanity and crossed the room. "I'm all emotional, and I suspect it doesn't have a damned thing to do with the pregnancy. It's just ..." She drew in a shaky breath. "This has been a long time coming, and you're finally walking down the aisle to marry my brother." She stared up at the ceiling. "Don't cry. Don't cry." She laughed, then looked at me again.

"It seems like a dream. All those days I laid in my bedroom, wondering if I would ever have the courage to walk out of the house and make it farther than Ada Lynn's ... I wanted to so much, but I was drowning. Pain and fear had consumed every part of me. I honestly stopped dreaming after a while. Then one bus ride and one incredible roomie changed my entire life." My heart swelled with gratitude that Mac had never given up on me, especially after Mom had died. I sniffled, and a few tears escaped down my cheek.

"Oh, bestie," Mac whispered, and grabbed a box of Kleenex. She handed me a tissue, then took one for herself. "You changed my life too. I was so lost with Asher, and I'd stopped believing in myself. It was as though I was trying to claw my way out of a deep hole, and every time I made headway, I slid back down again." She gently dabbed the moisture from her eyelashes. "Watching you change and having the courage to face the world again ... you gave me hope. Strength. For the first time in my life, I felt as though I belonged. That was you, Gemma. You did that for me, and ..." Mac's lip trembled. "You saved my life in more ways than one."

I sniffled and wiped my nose.

"Fuck it." Mac threw her arms around me. "I love you. My life would be shit without you. Plus I've always wanted a sister."

"Me too," I said softly. "I'm so lucky you're mine." I blinked rapidly in an attempt to not full-on blubber like an idiot.

Mac released me and backed away. Our gazes connected, a sweet silence surrounding us.

"Shit. Welp, that did it." Mac fanned my cheeks and began to blow gently on my skin. "You're all red and blotchy. I'll have to reapply your makeup again. I'll text Pierce and let him know we're running behind schedule. Besides, who gets married on time, anyway?"

We giggled, then I grabbed her and pulled her in for another hug. "I'm so happy you're here with me today."

"Like I'd have it any other way."

After some Visine and reapplication of our makeup, Mac walked backward and assessed her work. "Let's make you a Harrington, Gemma Thompson."

"I'm ready." I inhaled deeply, my legs trembling. It was funny how nerves had made a grand entrance the moment I stepped into my wedding gown. There was no doubt in my heart that Hendrix was the only man for me. *Today and always.*

Mac peered out the window. "Looks like everyone is in place." She beamed at me and picked up the bouquet of flowers from the dresser.

"Can you tell how Hendrix is doing?"

"Girl, my poor brother is pacing back and forth even though he knows you're not going to run away or anything." Mac giggled. "Unless you want to. I'm sure I can find a horse around here, then you can ride off into the sunset like Julia Roberts in the movie *Runaway Bride.*"

I smiled at her attempt to calm my nerves. "I've never ridden a horse, so I don't think that will work out very well."

Mac took one last look around the room. "I think we've got everything we need for now."

"I'll get your train so you don't trip and face plant."

"Oh shit. That would be horrible. I would roll out the door and down the hill and land at Hendrix's feet." I giggled at the mental image of my hair in every direction with sticks and pieces of grass poking out of it.

Mac snickered. "Take your heels off—just don't slide down the stairs. I'm thinking a runner would have been a good idea on those wooden steps to give you some traction. I'll carry them for you."

"Yeah, but with all the other details, it slipped my mind." I shook my arms and blew out a big breath. "Holy crap. I'm nervous."

"I don't think you are. You know you want to be with Hendrix for eternity. I think you're just excited."

I quirked an eyebrow at her and pondered what she'd said. "Huh. I think you're right."

"And you doubted this?" Mac hurried behind me and picked up the long train. "Giddyup!"

We burst into laughter as she made a neighing sound and galloped in place. At this rate, we wouldn't make it downstairs before nightfall if we didn't stop playing around. But I would never forget our time together today. Finally able to contain my giggles, I lifted the front of my dress, then we carefully made our way down the stairs and to the living room.

"Now, remember, Pierce is waiting for you behind the trellis of white and pink roses. Hendrix won't be able to see you until you turn the corner and begin walking the pathway to the altar. Got it?"

"Yeah. Maybe we should have done a real run-through." I licked my lips and instantly regretted the taste and feel of the lip gloss.

"Nah. You've got this."

Mac placed my shoes on the floor, and I slipped them on. I opened the front door and was welcomed by the bright afternoon sunshine and Vaughn, who was dressed to the nines.

"Gemma." He leaned down and kissed my cheek. "You look beautiful." His mismatched eyes twinkled while he adjusted his earpiece. He'd opted for a black suit and white shirt, but his tie matched Claire's dress. This man was smitten to his core, and I melted anytime I saw the love between him and Claire.

"Thanks." I could feel the flush creeping up my neck and cheeks. I took a minute to soak in my peaceful surroundings and will the blush away.

The blades of green grass swayed in the gentle breeze, and we continued down the sidewalk until we reached the top of the pathway. Tree leaves rustled all around us, and I noticed that some of the tips had started to turn red and orange overnight. My heart soared. It was more than I could have ever hoped for.

Mac dropped my train, put her thumb and index finger in her mouth, and let out a high-pitched whistle. A lower one responded within seconds.

"What was that?" I asked, frowning.

"Pierce wanted me to let him know when we were ready. All the guys are taking turns making sure the perimeter is safe. You know how they are." Mac winked at me. "Let's do this, bestie."

Moments later, Pierce appeared, and Vaughn hurried to join the rest of the wedding party.

"You look breathtaking." Pierce bent down and pecked me on the cheek.

"Thank you," I replied shyly. It hadn't ever crossed my mind that I would be the center of attention. At least on stage, I had Hendrix, Cade, and Asa. Today, it was all about me until I joined my fiancé at the altar.

Pierce extended his arm to me, and I slipped mine through it. His large hand covered mine, and he gave my fingers a gentle squeeze. "Are you ready?"

"Yeah." My heart filled with gratitude as I glanced up at my friend. "Thank you for giving me away. It means so much to me."

Pierce offered a sweet smile, respect and brotherly love written all over his face. "Me too, Gemma. Me too." He placed his finger on his earpiece and spoke quietly into the microphone. "Zayne confirmed that everyone is in place." He glanced over his shoulder. "Are you ready back there?"

"Yup," Mac replied.

A long white cloth created a walking path for us, and we followed it in silence. Seagulls flew overhead, riding the wind currents without a care in the world.

"It looks beautiful," I said as we arrived at our places near the seven-foot-tall trellis.

"It does. The floral shop did a great job." Mac smoothed my train out and brushed off her hands. "Okay, that's it. I'm all done here now that we're past the dirt and rocks. I'm off to join the others." She kissed my cheek, then left to join the group.

Pierce poked his head around the trellis. "Don't worry, Vaughn was waiting for her around the corner. We've got you all covered." Pierce had suggested the bodyguards walk the bridesmaids to their places instead of the groomsmen. Hendrix and I had agreed it was a good idea. I hadn't told Hendrix, but it had made Mac's day when she learned that she would be allowed to be on Vaughn's arm for a minute.

"Thank you."

"Now all we need to do is turn the corner. The music will start, and I'll walk you to Hendrix."

"Yeah," I said breathlessly. My ears perked up. "Do you hear that?"

Pierce paused. "I do. There are a lot of helicopters on the coastline. The coastguard was most likely called for a search and rescue. It's a very different ocean here than on the California Coast."

"That makes sense. It fascinates me what happens out there. Lost ships, stranded people, and storms. It's a dark world." I tightened my grip on his arm as I wobbled slightly.

"Are you all right? Don't bend your knees, Gemma." A worry line creased his forehead as he searched my face.

A flutter of excitement erupted in my belly, and I allowed myself to lean into the moment. The moment that I was about to get married. The moment I was surrounded by friends. The moment I'd only recently allowed myself to dream about. And now it had become reality.

"I'm good. Let's do this."

Pierce led me to the entrance on the other side of the trellis, and my attention immediately landed on Hendrix. Cade nudged him, and his head snapped my way, his beautiful face filled with awe. His black tux jacket hugged his broad shoulders, and his cummerbund matched the sapphires in my dress. He'd left his hair down, and strands fluttered in the gentle breeze. My heart stuttered as his mouth gaped open, his eyes filling with so much love it rendered me breathless. I wanted to fall into this memory with him forever. No one and nothing else existed, just him and the depth of my love for a man who had healed my brokenness.

Since we'd kept the ceremony discreet, only a small number of guests were in attendance. Tensley, Layne, Benji, Avery, and her boyfriend Ramsey sat with Michael, Marilyn, and Janice in white folding chairs to the right side of the open field. I imagined Ada Lynn and Mom sitting next to them, smiling and dabbing their tears. A sudden warmth wrapped itself around me, and I knew in my heart they were with me.

The seats on the left of the aisle were occupied by Franklin and Janice's friends who had known Hendrix since he was a little kid. Our music producer was also there with his new girlfriend, along with our agent, assistants, and public relations team.

Cade, Asa, and Franklin stood next to Hendrix, all of them looking incredibly handsome in their tuxes. I'd been elated when Hendrix asked Franklin to be one of his groomsmen. Their relationship had healed so much. I teared up as Franklin emotionally and physically showed up as a supportive and loving father to his son.

My focus drifted to Claire, Sutton, and Mac on the left side of the minister. Sutton and Claire looked stunning. They both wore their hair up with butterfly pins holding it in place. The hems of their mulberry dresses swayed in the breeze.

We'd hired a well-respected minister in the area to perform the ceremony, and he continued to smile at everyone as he waited. The ocean splashed water over the cliff that was directly behind the groomsmen and bridesmaids.

"Your wife and sister are so beautiful." I glanced up at Pierce and smiled.

"I agree." Briefly, Pierce's gaze softened as he looked at Sutton.

"Cade can't take his eyes off of Mac. I suspect they'll be married next."

"The guys and I have a bet on the date." A mischievous grin pulled at the corner of his lips, then the bridal march began to play, and my attention landed on my soon-to-be husband. He smiled the same panty-dropping smile he'd given me the day I met him, and butterflies ran amok inside me. Overwhelmed with love and an urgency to be with him, I took my first step toward our future. Our forever.

Another step. And another. Hendrix faced me, waiting for me to join him at the altar.

Seconds later, a helicopter swooped into view and flew near the cliff. It quickly backed away and hovered over the water.

"Dammit. Is it the press?" I cringed as the red and white flower petals from the archway broke loose and scattered in the wind.

"I don't like this, Gemma." Pierce used his earpiece and ordered his men to get everyone the hell out of there.

A *pop pop pop* overpowered the music, and pockets of dirt in the field began to burst upward as a spray of bullets began. With a quick swoop of his powerful arm, Pierce turned me away from the altar and directed me in the opposite direction of Hendrix.

Terror gripped me, and a scream burst from my throat as I looked over my shoulder. "Hendrix!" Spinning around, I attempted to run to my fiancé, but Pierce tackled me before I gained my footing.

"Get down!" Pierce said, throwing me on the unforgiving ground. He pressed his body over mine, and sheer panic ripped through me.

Struggling to comprehend what had just happened, I gasped for air. I tried to look up, but my head was turned the wrong way. "Pierce! I screamed. "What's happening?"

"God dammit!" His breath grazed my ear as he covered me as best he could. A string of curse words spilled from his mouth, and screams filled the air as the sound of shooting continued.

"Pierce!" Sobs choked off my strangled cries as I envisioned Hendrix lying dead in a pool of blood. "Hendrix. Hendrix. Please tell me that he's okay."

"He's not hit, Gemma. Hendrix isn't hit."

"What's happening?" I clung to his arm, desperate to hear that my loved ones weren't hurt.

"Stay down! Fucking hell. Please stay down."

21

Somehow, through all of the chaos, I was able to detect names being called out. I trembled violently beneath Pierce as I clawed at the ground. Blades of green grass and dirt were packed underneath my freshly manicured nails. Powerlessly, I listened to my entire world being ripped away from me.

Tires screeched near the house. I wasn't sure if the car was coming or going. All I knew was that I had to find my fiancé and best friend.

"Gemma, are you hit?" Pierce rolled off me and hurried to his feet. "The helicopter is gone. Are you hurt?"

I sat up slowly, my vision cloudy. "I don't think so." I glanced down at my torn and dirty wedding gown, then Pierce helped me up. My heart skidded to a stop at the sight of the scene in front of me. "Hendrix!" I screamed.

He hauled ass across the field near the trellis. "Gemma!" Tears flowed down my cheeks as he embraced me. "Are you okay? Were you hit?" His body shook, and moisture clung to his eyelashes as he searched me for any injuries, then he pressed his mouth to mine.

"No. Are you? Oh my God. What happened?"

"Franklin!" Janice screamed.

Horror flooded my senses as she continued to scream Franklin's name.

"Dad!" Hendrix yelled but stayed rooted in place. "What the fuck?"

Blood trickled down Franklin's cheek, and his bottom lip was busted. His eye was quickly swelling shut as he struggled and fought against a guy in a mask who had his arm around Franklin's neck. Everyone halted in their footsteps as the man held a gun to Franklin's head and dragged him away. Pierce and Zayne had their guns trained on the kidnapper, but he used Franklin's body as a shield. No one had a clear shot.

"Don't shoot. Don't even think about it," a voice boomed.

I turned toward the sound and spotted three more men in masks on the hillside above us. They had a clear view and could drop us within seconds. A quick *pop pop* dropped two of them, but I couldn't tell where the shots had come from.

"Stay still, babe." Hendrix moved slowly and stood in front of me, guarding me with his own life.

The man with Franklin scurried backward to a waiting car.

"Franklin," I cried. "They've got Franklin."

I fisted Hendrix's tux jacket in my hands, fully aware that the danger wasn't over. Time stopped as we all remained still, watching the terrifying scene unfold in front of us. As soon as Franklin was in the car, the man on the hill took off running. Pierce and his men opened fire on the vehicle, but the bullets simply pinged off the side and the windows.

"Dad!" Hendrix broke into a run, desperately trying to catch up to the vehicle. He sprinted past Zayne, but Zayne tackled him to the ground before he got too close.

"Man, they'll kill you in front of your fiancée and family. You've got to let him go," Zayne yelled.

A guttural cry shot from Hendrix, and my heart shattered into a million pieces. He sat on his knees, his hands clenched into fists and his body rigid. There was no way I could make this better.

"Baby." I hurried over to him, knelt down, and wrapped my arms around him. Mac and Janice's cries reached my ears as my world continued to crumble around us. I kept my attention focused on Vaughn, Pierce, Sutton, and Zayne as they checked on a few of the bodies in the middle of the field. I wasn't sure if they were hurt or dead, and I couldn't deal with it at the moment.

"Gemma!" Mac barreled toward me. "Are you all right?" Her makeup was streaked with tears as she and Cade joined us.

"Yeah. Are you? Neither of you were hit?" I searched them both but didn't see any wounds.

Mac and Cade knelt down next to me. "No, but they took Dad. Why?" Her petite shoulders shook, and Cade enveloped her in his arms, comforting her as best he could.

Hendrix raised his head and looked at Mac. Suddenly he grabbed her and placed his hands on her cheeks. "You're okay?" His voice was thick and raw.

"Yeah." Mac squeaked out.

"We need to get you and the baby checked, anyway," Hendrix said.

"I agree," Cade said, fear flickering in his expression as he placed his hand on Mac's shoulder. "I need to know they're okay."

Hendrix paused, not letting his sister go. His gaze filled with vengeance. "Whoever took Dad, you have my word I'm going to get him back, then I'm going to kill the motherfuckers and dance on their graves. Do you understand?"

"Promise?" Mac's eyes filled with trust as she stared at her brother. "Yes."

The next hour was a circus as the ambulance and police showed up. Four people were dead—two shooters on top of the hill, our producer's girlfriend, and the minister. According to Sutton, the bullet had nearly hit her, but the minister had shifted his weight and was struck instead.

Blood had soaked the grass and the white flower petals that had landed on the ground. Janice's arm had been grazed, but nothing serious. She'd just lost her husband to a crazed kidnapper, and I didn't even think she noticed her wound.

As the gurneys hauled the bodies away and the EMTs tended to the others that needed to be checked, a strange numbness seeped into me. My attention landed on Hendrix, Claire, Sutton, and the rest of the group, my brain not fully registering that Franklin was gone. I waited to hear him checking on his family, but he didn't. Within minutes, he'd been snatched away from us.

The police questioned us all, and we each gave the account we'd witnessed. Pierce was on the phone with his FBI friend, Brian. I assumed they were issuing alerts for the make and model of the vehicle that Franklin was in. From behind Hendrix, I couldn't even see the color of the car.

"Gemma. Hendrix." Pierce approached us as we were sitting on a large rock. "Why don't you all go inside the house? The temps are dropping, and everyone needs to shower and get cleaned up. The crime scene will be taped off here shortly. There's nothing else you can do tonight."

I stood. "Do you know who took him?" My voice wobbled.

"Not yet. I'm so sorry. They ambushed us from the air and both hills. These weren't amateurs. At least Vaughn took two of them out."

"It was Vaughn that killed two of the men on the hill? He's a sniper?" Hendrix ran his hand through his hair.

"Yeah. I wish he could have taken the knees out on the third—then we would have someone to question—but he couldn't get a clear shot."

"From where?" The air had cooled and elicited a shiver from me. Hendrix slipped off his tux jacket and placed it around my bare shoulders. I pulled it tightly around me. His spicy cologne soothed my overwhelmed senses. We were supposed to be celebrating our marriage right now instead of trying to make sense of the loss.

"After Vaughn walked Mac to the front, he discreetly snuck away. On Friday, he'd scoped out a post where he could keep an eye on the wedding from a distance."

My eyes widened. *Holy shit.* I'd known Vaughn for almost three years, and I'd had no idea.

"It's the special expertise I mentioned the other day. My man can hit a target a half mile away." Pierce's tone was full of pride.

"It sure as hell was useful today." Hendrix glanced around him. "Why couldn't he take out the fucker that got Dad?"

His jaw clenched, and I reached for his hand. He threaded his fingers through mine, warmth seeping into my body from his.

"He tried. He didn't have a direct path since Franklin was used as a human shield." Pierce stared at the angry dark ocean, then looked back at us. "I'd appreciate it if you kept that information to yourself. It's an element of surprise, and I don't want to warn the enemy. I also don't know what he's shared with Claire."

"Of course." Hendrix tightened his hold on me.

"Gemma, I'm so sorry about your wedding." Pierce gave me a quick hug.

"I know. You don't have to …" My words trailed off as grief crashed down on me. I covered my face with my hands. "Do you think it was Brandon?"

Hendrix wrapped his arms around me, and I laid my head against his chest.

"It was too well implemented." Pierce's eyebrows furrowed. "But you mentioned that he said everyone at the prison owed him favors."

We stared at each other, scrambling to put the pieces together.

"If he did this, and we can prove it, the fucker will lose his deal to get out of prison next week." A tug of war between hope and despair began to pull my heart in different directions.

"I'll talk to Brian. First, I need everyone inside. We'll have additional security and police here until we fly home tomorrow."

"Home?" I glanced at Hendrix. "We're not separating?"

Pierce shook his head. "No. Not until we get Franklin back. Mac needs her regular doctor, and Janice needs her own home. We have better protection at our houses. If another attack were to happen while we were there, we'd see it coming."

"What about our place? Can we stay there? Is it safe?" Hendrix's thumb gently stroked the back of my hand.

"I'm beginning to think we should have all relocated sooner and that nowhere is safe," Pierce replied. "You can stop by the house during the day to pick up what you need, but otherwise, we need everyone at Franklin's. Plus, your mom and sister need you guys."

Hendrix nodded. "We have a few handguns at home, so when we're there, we'll keep them loaded and close to us. I'll give Gemma a refresher, but she can shoot now as well."

Pierce quirked an eyebrow at me. "I didn't realize. That's good. Let's get everyone inside. Hendrix, I'll keep you and Janice informed. I'm not sure how to help Mac right now, though."

"I can help with that. Once you've updated us, I can filter the information a bit, but she needs to know what's happening. We also need to get her in to see her OB-GYN to make sure the stress of today hasn't caused any problems. Janice will be a mess, and since I'm the only other one in the group that's had a baby ..." Worrying my bottom lip, I inwardly cringed. Apparently the stress of the events had my mouth moving without my permission.

"Wait. What?" Pierce asked, looking shocked.

A multitude of thoughts scrambled and collided inside my jumbled brain. I looked up at my fiancé. I hadn't meant to say anything.

"You know you can trust him. Tell him if you want to," Hendrix said softly.

"I do trust you, Pierce. And of course I'll keep Vaughn's secret, but you need to keep mine until I'm ready to talk about it."

"Of course."

"When I was raped, I got pregnant. My ..." I gulped. "Kyle wouldn't allow me to have an abortion, and I was forced to carry the baby. Since I was barely fifteen, I gave him up for adoption. His name is Jordan, and he's in Seattle."

"Gemma. Shit, I had no idea." He shook his head, his eyes filling with sympathy. "I won't say anything, so please don't worry about it, but for the record, the day I walked into your house in Louisiana with that son of a bitch attacking you, I should have put a bullet in his skull. The only reason I didn't was because I didn't want to traumatize you any more." He placed his hands on his hips and stared out over the cliff, then his attention drifted back to me. "How are you handling Mac's pregnancy?"

"It's really hard sometimes, but I'm working through it. I'm so happy for her and Cade." I swallowed the lump in my throat. "This is an area I can help my bestie through while you find Franklin and bring him home alive."

A darkness that I'd never seen before appeared in Pierce's eyes, but it didn't scare me. "You have my word you guys. We'll get Franklin back, then we're going after whoever took him. I'm tired of playing by the rules."

"Count me in." Hendrix held his hand out to Pierce.

My heart beat wildly against my rib cage. This was a disaster waiting to get worse.

Pierce reached out and shook hands with Hendrix. "I figured you would be. He's a good man, and more than that, he's my friend."

My gut twisted into knots. I had to figure out what to do before this situation turned even uglier. Pierce's cell rang, and he excused himself to take the call. I hoped like hell it was a lead on Franklin.

"We need to get cleaned up, babe." Hendrix's gaze softened as his focus traveled up and down my wedding gown. "You took my breath away when I saw you in your dress."

Hot angry tears streamed down my face. "We're supposed to be married right now. I'm supposed to be Mrs. Harrington. We should be celebrating instead of swearing revenge." I wiped the moisture from my cheeks. "I think I'm going to lose my shit. I was trying to remain strong until we were alone, but ..." I collected the train of my dress and bundled the dirty and torn fabric in my arms.

"I've got you, babe." Hendrix bent down, slipped his arm behind my knees, and in one powerful swoop, gathered me in his arms. Leaning my head against his shoulder while he carried me to the house, I allowed the sobs and events of the day to consume me. Agony speared my heart, and I muffled a scream against his neck. Peeking behind me, I realized our families were following us. Their hearts were heavy as they trudged up the pathway with tearstained faces and bloodshot eyes.

Hendrix walked into the house and up the stairs without a word. Once in our bedroom, he placed my feet on the floor and closed and locked the door. He removed his tux jacket from my shoulders and tossed it on the bed, then carefully unzipped my ruined wedding gown. I allowed it to crumple in a heap around my feet. It was now a soiled and stained reminder of what would have been the most beautiful day in my life.

I choked on a sob. *Will we be able to get Franklin back? Is he hurt? Are they beating him?* My imagination spun out of control, and I gripped the footboard of the canopy bed in order to ground myself.

Hendrix stripped down to his boxer briefs and helped me step out of my dress. He led me to the bathroom, and I remained silent as he turned on the shower. We both discarded the remainder of our clothing and stepped under the hot spray. I hadn't realized until that moment that my body ached from Pierce throwing me to the ground and lying on top of me.

Hendrix and I looked at each other, our tears mixing with the stream of water. He gently cupped my cheek, his eyes peering into me. "I thought I'd lost you today, Gem. I'm not sure I would have made it through if anything had happened to you."

"You were my first concern when the gunfire started." I chewed on my bottom lip, struggling to keep a rein on my emotions.

"God dammit. We were being so fucking careful." He ran his fingers through my wet hair. "How are we going to win this war? How am I going to protect you?" He leaned his head against mine, then a silent cry shook his shoulders.

I wrapped my arms around him. "I love you, Hendrix. I'm here. We're here together."

He hid his face in my neck and clung to me as he came undone. "I failed Kendra and now Dad. I almost failed you." His words were broken. Haunted.

"Oh, baby, no." This was the first time we'd fallen apart at the same time, and all I wanted to do was love him until his heart healed. Just like he'd done for me. "Those men were trained and came out of nowhere." I held my fiancé as his emotions poured out of him. "No one is to blame."

His body finally stilled, then he looked down at me with red-rimmed eyes. His erection pressed against my belly, and he swallowed visibly. "I need you. I need to touch you and make sure you're all right. I need to lose myself in you. I'm not okay, Gem. For the first time since Kendra, I'm not okay."

"Baby, I'm here." I kissed him gently.

He placed his lips on mine, dominating my mouth. He leaned me against the wall of the shower while his hands roamed every curve of my body. "I love you" he said softly in my ear. "You're my world. My heart." His desperate kisses interrupted my response. Hendrix bent his knees, then lifted me up. I circled my legs around his waist as he gently eased inside of me, and I slid my arms around his neck.

His blue eyes penetrated mine, and my breath hitched in my throat. Suddenly overwhelmed with emotion, I whispered my vows to him.

"No matter what happens, my soul is forever tethered to yours. Hendrix, no matter how lost I might feel, your love continues to be the light in the darkness. Your love set me free, and you taught me how to live. You're the air that I breathe, the song that I sing. You're the reason I found my voice again. It's you that I dream of at night, you that I long for when you're not by my side. Nobody moves me like you, Hendrix Harrington. You're my heaven. You're my always." Tears spilled down my cheeks as he remained inside of me.

Hendrix pressed his mouth against mine, then spoke softly, searching my eyes as he shared his oath to me. "Until I found you behind the library that day, I was in this world alone. I'd faded into the background. You gathered the fragments of my heart and pieced them together. Your courage, your quiet strength, touched a part of me I didn't even realize still existed. Gemma, you're not my other half—you're the fire that burns inside of me. My life has purpose because of you. As long as you're by my side, I'm a whole man. Today and every day, I vow to protect you ..." He swallowed, tears streaming down his face. The world halted, and we were suspended in time, two souls seeking, surging, and becoming one.

"You protected me, Hendrix. You kept your promise."

Silence descended over us, and he shifted inside me. I released a soft moan while we lost ourselves in each other. And for just a few moments, the depth of our bond washed all of the darkness, pain, and fear away.

22

The next day, a heavy-hearted silence blanketed the group as we boarded Franklin's plane without him. I ran my finger-tips over the supple leather of the seats and remembered the first time I'd ever flown. Franklin, Hendrix, Mac, Pierce, Ada Lynn, and I were flying to Spokane from Louisiana unexpectedly after Kyle had been released from jail on a technicality. We all knew that Kyle would be out for revenge since I'd testified against him in court.

Pierce had helped Ada Lynn and me pack clothes and important items, then he drove us to the airport. The most heartbreaking thing about the journey was that Hendrix had amnesia and didn't remember any of us. Mac refused to come home to Spokane because she wanted to stay with Jeremiah, whom she'd dated for a few months while in Louisiana. But once he learned that Franklin was rich, Jeremiah broke things off with Mac. Although she was hurt, he'd done her a huge favor. I was shocked to realize how much our lives had changed since then.

On this flight to Spokane, Hendrix sat next to Janice, and I settled in with Mac and Cade in the back near the conference room. I kept waiting for Franklin to appear and sit next to his wife, but of course he never showed.

Vaughn had a protective arm around Claire, and Sutton snuggled up to Pierce. Asa stared out the window with his headphones on, only speaking if he was spoken to. His face held a fear and sadness I hadn't seen before. The shooting had changed him, and I wasn't sure how to help him deal with what he'd seen. It had changed all of us. A silent scream built inside my chest, and I struggled to shove it back down.

"How are you feeling, Mac? Physically, I mean." I leaned my throbbing head against the seat.

"I'm okay. I have a doctor's appointment tomorrow. Would you go with Cade and me?" Tears brimmed in Mac's eyes. "I don't want to bother Mom with it."

I reached out and squeezed her hand. "Yeah. I'll be there every step of the way."

"Thanks, bestie." She shifted in her seat and placed her head on my shoulder. Less than a minute later, her soft snore reached my ears. My attention landed on Cade in front of me. "You look pale, Cade. Have you eaten?"

He shifted in his seat and stretched his long legs in front of him. "No. I don't have an appetite. I'm too worried about Mac and the baby. It's a given that I'm torn up about Franklin, just so you know."

"I do. You don't have to explain. Where were you and Mac when the gunshots ..." I couldn't finish my sentence.

Cade leaned forward and propped his elbows on his knees. Stubble lined his jaw, and he looked like he hadn't slept in days. "I was close enough to Mac that I was able to grab her, but then—" He stared at the floor and blew out a frustrated breath. "I had to protect her, Gemma. I tried to be gentle, but I threw her on the ground. She landed on her stomach, and I lay over her. What if I ...?" Cade's amber eyes misted over, and my heart dropped like a lead ball. If anything happened to Mac and the baby, Cade would take full responsibility, even if it wasn't his fault.

"You can't think like that, Cade. Of course you protected them. You did everything that you possibly could to save their lives."

"I hope it was enough." His hand clenched into a tight fist. "I just need to know that they're all right. After the appointment tomorrow,

I'll stop worrying, I'm sure." He shook his head. "I need to keep my shit together right now, Gemma. Mac and Hendrix need me. I need to be levelheaded and reassuring. But I'm only human, and yesterday fucked me up. Bad." His leg bounced up and down, and his attention traveled to the window. "Do you think we can get Franklin back alive?"

I hesitated before I spoke. "I refuse to contemplate any other option." Fear whispered in my ear that he was already gone from our lives forever. I gripped the arm of the seat and refused to entertain the thought any longer. Franklin was a fighter. He had to be alive.

"Then I'll think that way too. Maybe between the two of us, we can help Janice, Mac, and Hendrix have some hope."

I attempted a half-hearted smile. "And who's going to be there for you on your dark days, Cade?"

Cade didn't realize it, but that question wasn't just for him. I'd lived through enough hell that I realized I needed someone to help me stay strong, but I had no idea who it might be.

"I don't know yet, but I suspect it will be you." His brown eyes filled with fear. "Is that okay?"

"Of course. We're friends. Family. I'll help in any way I can. Maybe we can be a safe space for each other. When we can't vocalize our fears or thoughts with everyone else, we can talk to each other." I made a mental note to speak with Sutton. She'd helped Claire with counseling, so maybe she could connect me with someone as well. As much as I adored Cade, I knew he wouldn't be enough to help me get through this. Hell, we all needed therapy after what we just lived through. It was a miracle I was walking around with a clear thought in my head.

SEVERAL HOURS LATER, Janice, Mac, Cade, Hendrix, and I stepped into Franklin's house. Vaughn had driven Asa to his place, and Pierce had also quietly assigned another bodyguard to him and his apartment. At least Asa had some protection. My gut told me he would be safe since he wasn't a target, but I couldn't be sure.

Hendrix immediately armed the security system after everyone was inside.

"He should be here," Mac said, a strangled cry escaping her. "Dad should be home with us."

Janice slid her arms around Hendrix and Mac, then kissed them each on their forehead. "I'm not sure how, but he will move heaven and earth to come back to us. I know Franklin. He's strong. A fighter. His love for us will give him the strength he needs."

I bit my bottom lip in an effort to not cry again. My head was already throbbing, and all I wanted to do was crawl into bed and sleep.

Ruby hurried into the foyer and embraced Janice warmly. "I have dinner cooking now. I'm so sorry about Mr. Franklin. I pray he comes home soon." She hugged everyone, then straightened and smoothed her dark hair. "I'll be in the kitchen if anyone needs me." Sniffling, she disappeared around the corner.

"I need a drink," Janice whispered and followed Ruby.

"Mom, why don't you go upstairs and crawl into bed? I'll bring you something to eat and a glass of wine in a few minutes." Hendrix slipped an arm around her shoulders.

Shocked, Janice stared at Hendrix. "You called me Mom."

"What else should I call you?" He kissed the side of her head, and she wrapped her arms around him.

"I'm so scared." Her sobs strangled her words as she and Hendrix held each other.

"We all are, but you're right, Mom. Dad's strong and smart. He's in excellent shape, and he'll find the will to make it through this. Nothing else matters to him more than his wife and family." Mac offered an awkward smile as though she were trying to remind herself as well.

Janice nodded, then stepped away. "I know you're right." She dabbed the tears from her eyes. "I'll be in the bedroom if anyone needs me."

"Get some sleep, Mom," Mac said. "We'll need our energy for when Dad is back."

The rest of us stood in silence as we watched Janice walk down the hall, fragile and exhausted.

IT WAS after seven by the time Hendrix had helped Janice get settled into her room for the night. Mac, Cade, Hendrix, and I reluctantly sat down to eat, but Franklin's empty chair at the head of the table felt dooming, lonely. Mac, Cade, Hendrix, and I picked at our food and pushed it around our plates. None of us had an appetite, but Ruby finally stood over us until we'd eaten some of her lasagna. Afterward, we headed to the family room.

"What next?" Mac asked, flopping into the leather couch.

Hendrix's phone rang, and he grabbed it off the end table. "It's Pierce."

I settled in next to Hendrix while Cade pulled Mac into his lap.

"Hey, Pierce. I've got you on speakerphone. I'm here with Gemma. Mac and Cade are with us as well."

"Hey, guys. Hendrix, I tried to reach Janice, but it went straight to voicemail. I'm assuming she's asleep and didn't hear the phone ring. I would normally contact your dad with updates like this, but I'm going to communicate with you or Gemma until Janice is feeling a little better. I'm hoping she's able to get some rest."

Hendrix rubbed his chin. "Me too. If not, then I'll give her something to help. She needs to be rested and clear minded."

"That goes for everyone." Pierce cleared his throat. "I had a call from Brian, so I thought I'd let you know what they've learned so far."

I sat up, my back ramrod straight. "Do they know where he is?"

"No. I'm sorry. But they found out that a clerk at the office where you applied for your marriage license leaked the information about your wedding."

I frowned. "I thought Franklin had all of that handled. Like, they'd agreed not to divulge the date or state."

"Apparently some guy flashed her some serious money, and it was enough that she shared what she knew. She remembered the bed-and-breakfast selling last year and told the man that it would be a wonderful place to get married. It's public record when a house sells, and the realtor is easy to contact. One thing led to another, and the realtor admitted she'd sold the house to the lead singers of August Clover. Maybe she thought it would boost her sales and publicity for her real estate firm."

I pursed my lips, and my nostrils flared. "Don't people know to keep their fucking mouths shut? First the owner at Mik's and now this."

Hendrix grabbed my hand, rage flickering to life in his dark gaze.

"I felt the same, Gemma," Pierce said. "In fact, I picked up the phone and spoke with the realtor. She said she was horrified when the wedding and kidnapping made the news. She apologized profusely."

"Apologies don't bring Dad back," Mac said.

"I don't think she'll ever share information again after what happened. She's really torn up about it. She wanted to make amends by offering any information that might be helpful. She gave the same description of the guy that talked to the clerk, and her camera system caught his car and license plate."

"That's great, right?" Hendrix's voice held a hint of hope.

"We tracked the car down, and it's a vehicle from Enterprise. We suspected as much, and whoever rented the car covered their tracks. They didn't sign the agreement as an individual. It was rented under the guise of a security company located in Montana."

"Montana?" I asked. "Is it even a real company?"

"No, but I have an old military buddy in Montana. I sent him an image, and he's doing some digging for me." Pierce released a heavy sigh. "We have the FBI, Sutton, and me, and I'm calling in favors across the country. Franklin's face is on every television right now too. He's a high-profile attorney with powerful friends. I've been receiving calls to help all evening. We're going to find him."

Silence filled the room, then Pierce spoke again. "Greyson, Vaughn, Jaxon, Tad, and Zayne are all outside of Franklin's home now.

If any of you leave, then take someone with you. They will drive you, scope out your house, walk you inside, and accompany your every move. Are we clear?"

"Yeah," we all said in unison.

"Keep the alarm system armed at all times," Pierce instructed. His voice was sad, lost.

"I took care of that as soon as we got home." Hendrix ran a hand through his hair.

"I have a doctor's appointment tomorrow. Cade and Gemma will go with me." Mac nervously twirled a strand of hair around her finger.

"What time?" Pierce asked.

"Eleven in the morning."

"I'll talk to Zayne. He and Jaxon will go with you. I'm not sure if you guys have met yet. He's taller than Zayne and has blonde hair. Tad has red, so that will help you know who's who."

"Okay. Thanks." Mac leaned into Cade, and he placed his hands on her flat tummy. I wondered when she would start sporting a baby bump and if she would carry high or low. Hendrix's voice pulled me out of my thoughts and back to the conversation.

"Gemma and I will need to get some things from our place to bring to Dad's house. I'll text you before we go over, and I'll get one of the guys to drive us. I want to get at least one of the guns. I'm kicking myself for not applying for my concealed carry license." Hendrix took my hand. The warmth of his touch soothed my frayed and over-whelmed nerves.

"I can get it pushed through for you. Send me a completed application," Pierce stated.

"Can you help me with that, too?" Cade asked.

I wondered how Mac would feel about the guys carrying, but based on her expression, she seemed comfortable with the idea. At this point, we had to do what was needed to defend ourselves. Whoever had Franklin was highly dangerous and strategic. This wasn't some rookie who got lucky.

"Yeah. I think it's a good idea. What about Gemma and Mac?"

Hendrix arched an inquisitive brow at me, and I nodded. I was on board, but before I could respond, Mac chimed in.

"Hell yeah, but I've got to learn gun safety and how to shoot. Bestie? Wanna use Brandon's face as target practice?"

Without hesitation, I responded, "I'm in on the license, and I have a better idea. Let's use Brandon himself for practice." We all grinned and nodded, then I grew serious again. "If we'd been carrying at the wedding, then ..."

Hendrix squeezed my knee. "It won't do us any good to wish we'd done something different. We'll just waste valuable energy when we need to be focused on bringing Dad home."

"I agree," Pierce said wistfully. "Try to get some sleep. Hendrix, I'll touch base with you tomorrow."

Hendrix ended the call. "I feel as though we have a better chance of finding Dad with Pierce's connections."

"Me too." I stood and stretched. My body was still sore from being thrown on the ground the day before. "After the plane ride, I'm ready to unwind. I'll be in the guest bedroom."

"Hey." Hendrix placed a warm hand on my face and stroked my cheek with his thumb. "Do you want some company or a few minutes alone?"

I leaned into his touch. "Are you okay with Mac and Cade if I take a half hour? Then come join me anytime."

"If you want me to join you before then, just text me." Understanding warmed his expression.

I doubted he'd admit it in front of everyone, but I suspected Hendrix needed a few minutes alone as well. It was difficult to process or fall apart when we were surrounded by people all the time.

"I'll see you guys in the morning." I blew a kiss to Mac and squeezed Cade's shoulder on the way out. I needed to find somewhere safe so I could lose my shit.

I waved my hand in front of the light, and the bedroom I'd lived in while Hendrix had amnesia beckoned to me. The bed had been the first luxurious one I'd ever slept in, not to mention Hendrix and I had plenty of amazing times between the sheets.

The recollection of Hendrix opening my door right after his amnesia had cleared came rushing back to me. There had been weeks of torture not touching him as I allowed him to regain his memory on his own. When he finally did, it was as if the floodgates had opened. The second he recalled us together, he came straight to me. In the middle of the night, he waltzed right in without even knocking, then called me Gem. Nothing sounded sweeter than my nickname on his beautiful lips. After he kissed me more times than I could count, he continued to share memory after amazing memory. I knew then that my baby was back. We'd spent the rest of the evening encompassed in each other's arms, reveling in the time alone that we had together.

Janice had purchased a new black-and-white-striped comforter along with three matching throw pillows. A soft blue blanket was folded at the foot of the bed and matched the accent wall behind the headboard, giving the space a nice splash of color. After Janice's loving touch, it was even more cozy and inviting than it had been previously.

This had also been my room when Ada Lynn died. Grief punched me, then wrenched my heart out of my chest. I couldn't handle it if we lost Franklin. Losing Ada Lynn had been awful, but she'd been elderly. Franklin wasn't. He was in his late forties and had so many good years ahead of him with his family and his career. His grandbaby needed to know its grandpa as well.

Sinking onto the edge of my bed, I located my headphones and iPhone. I slipped my tennis shoes off, then I curled up on top of the comforter while I pulled up a Spotify playlist. "Moved" by Laces filled my ears, and I sank into the pillow. I folded into myself and covered my head, my mind immediately sifting through the memories of the previous day.

Bullets whizzed through the air, and horrified screams rang out across the field. Panicked expressions twisted everyone's faces. Hendrix's eyes connected with mine for a fleeting moment before Pierce threw me to the ground.

As "Break my Broken Heart" filtered through my earbuds, strangled cries burst free from me, and I clutched the pillow to my mouth to muffle the sound. A dark cloud of heartache, along with a windfall of emotions from the past several days, surrounded me like a toxic fog. I sucked in a breath when the bed dipped. A strong yet gentle hand landed on my shoulder. I didn't need to look to see who it was. I knew Hendrix's touch, the scent of his cologne. Without a word, he curled himself around me, then laid his head on the pillow next to mine. I grabbed his fingers and kissed his knuckles. I gave him an earbud, then we lay in each other's arms while we listened to music until we drifted off asleep.

23

The next morning, I slipped out of Hendrix's arms and quietly made my way to the shower. I had an hour to get cleaned up and appear strong before I met with Mac and Cade for her doctor's appointment. The hot water cascaded over me, and I allowed it to run over my swollen and prickly eyes. I hated crying. I always felt like shit the day after.

After washing my hair and body, I stepped out of the shower and dried off. I entered the bedroom and eyed our suitcase. Tiptoeing past a still sleeping Hendrix, I grabbed the luggage and attempted to quietly roll it across the carpet, but it rebelled and toppled over.

Hendrix shot up out of bed, the stark fear in his expression ripping my heart out as he searched the room frantically.

"I'm sorry." I stood in front of him completely naked, feeling guilty for waking him.

He rubbed the sleep from his eyes and stared at me. "You're beautiful." His gaze skimmed over me.

My cheeks warmed. "Did you get some rest?" I knelt down and unzipped the suitcase.

"A little." He rolled over on his side and watched me pull out clean clothes. "Did you?"

I gave a half shrug. "I'm not sure. I woke up a lot, then when I drifted off again, the sound of guns shooting in my dreams woke me." I stood with jeans and a teal shirt in my hands. "I have Mac's appointment to go to. I need to get dressed, but do you want to come down for some breakfast with me?"

"Yeah." He sat up, his bare feet brushing against the carpet. "Maybe Pierce will have something for us today."

"I hope so." I slid my black G-string up my long legs, then stepped into my jeans. "Are you going to stick close to Janice this morning?"

Hendrix stood and stretched, his shirt rising above his waistband and allowing me a glimpse of his muscular stomach. "Yeah. I need to keep an eye on her. Otherwise, she won't eat or take care of herself. I figure when Mac and Cade are back, then you and I can go to our place and get what we need to bring back here."

"Sounds good." I pulled my soft, white shirt over my head, then tugged it down and flipped my hair out from beneath the collar.

Hendrix peeked at the digital clock on my nightstand. "It's been almost forty-eight hours since Dad ..."

"I know," I whispered. "Don't lose hope, babe." I walked over to the bed and sat down next to him. "The first time I met Franklin, he ..." I gave Hendrix a silly grin. "I was nervous because he was your dad, but you and he look so much alike that it threw me for a loop. I'm pretty sure you both saw the flush creep up my neck and cheeks. All I could think of was that I was looking at you in another twenty years, and I liked it. A lot." I glanced at Hendrix and wondered if he understood what I was saying.

He barked out a laugh and fell back on the bed, pulling me with him. I rolled on top of him.

"Were you crushing on Dad for a minute?" He tucked a piece of hair behind my ear.

"No, I wouldn't call it that. It was more like I fell in love with you in the future. I had a glimpse into what you looked like and who you might become." I placed my finger against his hips. "If you recall, that was the night I told you I loved you."

He wrapped his arms around me. "It didn't quite go like that. I told you I was in love with you first."

"I remember. Your confession stole my breath. I wasn't sure what to do with the new feelings, but it was that night I knew without a shadow of a doubt I loved you. It was so deep, so powerful it scared the shit out of me."

He rolled us over until my back was on the mattress and I was looking up into the beautiful blue eyes that had changed my world. "Marry me," he whispered. "As soon as Dad comes back. Let's just do it."

"I'd like that." Although a part of me hated to wait until Franklin had returned, I also couldn't stand the thought of him not with us on that special day. It wouldn't feel right. "I need to get downstairs, babe."

Hendrix kissed me softly, then stood up and held his hand out to me. "Are you going to be okay going with Mac today?" Concern flickered through his serious expression.

"Yeah. I'm good. She needs either Janice or me. We've both had a baby, and since Janice isn't in a position to be there this time, then I will be." I offered him a reassuring smile, even though I didn't feel that great about the situation. Sometimes you just had to suck it up for family, and Mac was worth it.

"I GUESS this is one way to get an ultrasound." Mac hopped up on the table, her feet dangling over the edge.

"Are you worried?" I asked while I sat in one of the chairs along the wall.

"A little, but I think Cade is beside himself." She glanced at him. "If something went wrong, then we'll deal with it. At least Cade is safe, and so am I. We'll make another baby later."

Cade rubbed his forehead. "Mac, I don't think it will be that cut-and-dried."

A light knock on the door interrupted the conversation, then Dr. Whitaker strolled into the room. "Hello again. How are you feeling,

Mac?" He flipped her chart open, the look on his face darkening as he read the update that Mac had provided over the phone when she scheduled the appointment. He leaned against the counter, his concerned gaze landing on my bestie. "I'm sorry about your dad. I have all the faith in the world he'll be home soon."

"Thanks," Mac said. "It sucks. The whole fucking nonwedding sucked." She cringed. "I'm sorry for swearing. I'm a mess."

"From the notes, Cade, you had to protect Mac. What happened exactly?" Dr. Whitaker asked.

Cade shoved his hands in his front pockets, guilt and fear in his eyes. "When the helicopter opened gunfire, I ran to Mac, threw her on the ground, and lay on top of her." Cade gulped and clenched his jaw.

"I would have done the same thing. In fact, I admire that you were fast on your feet and protected Mac and the baby."

"What if I hurt the baby?" Cade ran a hand over his short dark hair. "It would be my fault." His eyes misted over, then he stared at the floor while he regained his composure.

Dr. Whitaker's brows knitted together. "Son, sometimes we have to make hard choices, but in no way would it be your fault if something went wrong. You. Saved. Your. Fiancée. The circumstances were awful. You did the right thing."

Mac kissed Cade's hand gently. "Love you," she whispered.

"Love you too." Cade smoothed Mac's hair.

"All right, let me get a little more information, Mac. Did you land on a rock?" Dr. Whitaker asked.

"I don't think so. It happened so fast that I don't remember everything that happened." She placed her palm on her lower belly.

"I understand. Why don't you lie back, and we'll get some images and see how you and your little one are doing? Let's just make sure the two of you look okay so you have one less thing to worry about." He gave us all a kind smile. "I'm going to put some goop on your tummy again."

Mac nodded, then pulled up her shirt, revealing her stomach. My heart lodged in my throat as my first ultrasound memories haunted me. I gave them a swift kick in the ass and dug my fingernails into my palms. I sucked in a deep breath, forcing myself to remain present.

Dr. Whitaker turned on the machine, applied the gel, then moved the wand around Mac's lower abdomen. The group grew silent as his attention remained on the screen. Mac was squeezing Cade's hand so tightly his fingers had turned white. My pulse kicked into overdrive as we waited for him to say something. Anything.

Dr. Whitaker's face lit up, and he looked at Mac and Cade. "Mac, you can let some blood flow back into Cade's hand. Everything looks great."

The *whoosh, whoosh, whoosh* of the baby's heartbeat filled the room. I released the breath I hadn't realized I was holding, and my hand flew over my mouth. Relief washed over me, and I looked at Mac. Tears were streaming down her cheeks. "Oh my gosh." She placed her hand on her forehead. "See, babe? I told you it would be all right."

Cade bent down and kissed her gently.

Dr. Whitaker patiently waited for everyone to compose themselves. "Would you like the first pictures of the baby?"

Cade frowned as he leaned toward the screen, squinting. "What are we looking at?"

I stood, hoping to learn along with them. I'd never wanted to see Jordan or have any images. In fact, I'd looked the other direction during the ultrasound. But this time was different, and I wanted to understand what we were looking at. I wanted to see my niece or nephew, then tell Hendrix all about it.

Mac held her hand out to me, and I approached the table as Dr. Whitaker explained the images. My chest squeezed tight, but not from fear. Suddenly, I wondered what it would be like if this were me and Hendrix was by my side. A jolt of anxiety shot through me, and I swiftly shut it down. Inwardly I smiled, because it was huge progress to even consider what that scenario might be like.

LATER THAT DAY, Zayne drove us to our house. It was strange to watch as he and Jaxon checked the property and inside the home before we were allowed in.

"It's clear." Jaxon opened the back door of the Mercedes for us. Pierce had neglected to mention that Jaxon had eyes the color of honey. He was almost as wonderfully distracting as Vaughn. If Mac had been with us, I was pretty sure she would have a difficult time choosing who was hotter, Vaughn or Jaxon. If I were honest, I wasn't sure I would be able to help her decide either.

Once we were safely in the house, my emotions flip-flopped like a fish on dry land. I missed our home. I missed Franklin. I ran my fingertips along the top of the leather couch and inhaled deeply.

"I miss it, too, babe." Hendrix took my hand in his. "The music studio is also a safe room. Guys, why don't you come on back, and I'll show you what we've got in case you have more recommendations."

I followed the men back to the studio and listened to their conversation and suggestions for additional safety. "Gemma, if you were here by yourself, then this is where you would need to go," Zayne said.

"Yup, I got that." I nudged Zayne in the side with my elbow and laughed.

His chuckle filled the room. "I guess I didn't need to say that, but I have to cover my ass."

"I know." I smiled at him. "I'll let Hendrix explain everything to you now."

Hendrix winked at me, then continued. "Gem and I have this room equipped with enough to survive for over a month. Canned food, a bathroom, drinking water, a gun, ammo. I think we did well planning for the worst." Hendrix's face fell. "For some dumb reason, I thought the worst was over and we were moving forward." His eyes filled with sadness as he looked at me.

"Pierce is working around the clock with the police and FBI to find your dad, man. Try to stay positive, but if you need to box or spar, let me know. I'm happy to help." Zayne patted Hendrix on the back. Maybe some raw guy time was what Hendrix needed.

My phone screen lit up with a call from Sutton, and I excused myself. "Hey," I said while I entered my office. "Any news on Franklin?"

"We're following a few leads, but nothing solid yet. How are you holding up?" Sutton asked.

"Okay." I sank into my chair and propped my feet up on the cluttered desk. "I was hoping the reason you were calling was that you had some good news. I have some, though. Mac had her appointment today. The baby is fine."

"That's really good to hear. But how are *you*?"

I fiddled with the drawer handle, struggling to find something to say, but there were no words to describe the despair and fear I felt about Franklin.

"Your silence speaks volumes."

I rubbed my temples. "I'm trying to keep my shit together so I can be there for Hendrix and Mac."

"Who's there for you?"

"Hendrix. Plus Cade and I talk to each other a lot. We don't want to bring up certain concerns or worries in front of Mac and Hendrix, so we've agreed to speak to each other privately."

"Good. What we all went through was fucked-up, Gemma. Don't stuff your feelings or not deal with them. It will only come back to bite you in that cute little ass of yours."

"Babe." Hendrix leaned into the office. "We're going outside. Jaxon will be out front while I show Zayne where I think some additional cameras might work."

"Okay. Sutton says hi."

"Hey, Sutton," Hendrix called out, then gave me a little wave before he disappeared down the hall.

"Did I hear him say cameras?" Sutton asked.

"Yeah, the guys are looking to add some more or something like that. I'm not sure exactly. I thought we were here to grab our guns and some more clothes."

I could almost hear Sutton smile through the phone. "He called Pierce today. He wants to take you home. He feels it would be healthier for you and him to have your normal environment than spend time at Franklin's."

My forehead knitted together in confusion. "He hasn't said anything to me."

"He probably didn't want to get your hopes up. Pierce has to sign off on the plan before he agrees."

"I would love to be here for even part of the evening. Don't get me wrong, I'll stay with Janice all day long if I need to, but having a little bit of a sanctuary would help me recharge so I could help everyone else."

"That's why Hendrix talked to Pierce about it, Gemma. He's seen you slip into take-care-of-everyone mode, and he's concerned you're not processing or taking care of yourself."

I nearly rolled my eyes. "He's doing the same thing."

"I know. Everyone is turning it off and on to help the other person. It's how we work, but he's trying to take care of you both. I admire him for it. And it's okay to say that you want to sleep at your own home, have the privacy to cry, or yell and throw something."

"No, it's not. I'm being selfish." I stared at the ceiling and chastised myself for wanting a little bit of separation from the chaos.

"I've never shared this with you, but after graduation, I found out I was pregnant with Pierce's baby."

I nearly shot out of my chair. "Holy shit." Sutton didn't have any kids, so obviously something had happened.

"Pierce had left for the military. I hadn't found out before he left, so he didn't know. Anyway, I finally got up the courage to knock on his mom's door to tell her. To make a long story short, she was terminally ill."

"Oh my God. I'm so sorry."

"It's okay. I'm glad that I showed up to spend those last days with her. Pierce was gone, and his mom was trying to wait until he was home for a visit to tell him, but she didn't make it."

My hand flew over my mouth, and my heart broke for Pierce. "I had no idea. That had to have broken his heart."

Sutton released a sigh. "It devastated him. She was a tough little cookie, and he loved her so much."

"Like you. I mean, you're a tough little cookie too."

"Some days I am. Others, not so much. One afternoon when I was with his mom, she told me the story of a father walking his daughter home from school when it began to rain. He opened the umbrella and held it over his daughter's head so she wouldn't get sick. Instead, he got sick and was barely able to take care of his daughter for the next several days."

A smile tugged at the corner of my mouth. "Is this your way of telling me if I don't take care of myself a little bit, I can't give my best to Hendrix and his family?"

"Exactly. You're not being selfish. You're practicing very healthy self-care. If that doesn't absolve your guilt, maybe this will: I give you, Gemma Thompson, permission to live in your own home with your fiancé, even during this shitstorm."

I allowed her words to soak in. If I was quiet and still enough inside myself, I could hear Ada Lynn agreeing with Sutton.

"Okay. I won't say anything to Hendrix about our conversation, but it would be really nice to at least come home and sleep in our own bed."

"Excellent. What are you doing tomorrow?"

I mentally searched my schedule. "No plans. I'll just hang out with Mac and help Hendrix with Janice."

"Excellent. I'll pick you up at Franklin's, then we're going to hang out. I have some errands to run, so we'll put a hat on you along with some sunglasses to hide your identity. Then we'll blast some music, sing at the top of our lungs, and do whatever else feels good in the moment. On the way home, we'll grab some sushi and eat on the back patio."

"That sounds amazing. It would be nice to see you for a while and not have a male bodyguard around. I'm surrounded by testosterone twenty-four-seven."

"Sometimes, it just needs to be the girls. Oh, hang on."

I could hear Pierce talking in the background but couldn't make out what he was saying.

"I'm back. Sounds like your additional cameras will be in place by tomorrow night."

"You mean we might be able to sleep in our own bed soon?"

"I would say yes, but you'll have to see when Hendrix talks to you."

The men's voices carried down the hall. "It sounds like the guys are back," I said. "I'm going to see if Hendrix will tell me or not. Regardless, thank you for calling, and it will be nice to hang out tomorrow."

I disconnected the call and hurried into the living room.

24

"How does everything look?" I asked, joining the guys.

"Well, after tomorrow, we should have additional cameras, and Pierce is comfortable with us coming home." Hendrix crossed the room and slid his arms around me.

"Really? We can sleep in our own bed and use the studio?" Even though Sutton had just talked to me about the possibility, I hadn't gotten my hopes up.

"Gem, we need a little bit of space to recharge. I don't know what the future looks like, but I want us to be able to process without upsetting Mom and Mac."

I peered up at him. "I think we need that too." I pushed up onto my tiptoes and kissed him.

"We've got a few more things to do, babe, then we'll head back over to Mom's."

"I'll be paying bills, then." I squeezed his hand. Although he was acting a bit more upbeat, I knew he was in turmoil. We all were. Each hour that passed without hearing about Franklin left a bigger hole inside of me.

Rubbing my arms in order to comfort myself, I returned to the office and shut the door. I sat at the desk and flipped open my laptop.

The old appointment reminder for the wedding flashed in the upper right-hand corner, and I angrily closed it out. "Fuck you," I mumbled. I rubbed my face with my hands and sighed. I rarely had a minute alone anymore, and I needed it.

My phone rang and I pulled it out of my back pocket. Someone was attempting to facetime. Lydia was the only one who contacted me that way. *Shit.* I hadn't reached out to her since the bachelorette party.

I answered. "Hey, Ly—"

"Hello, beautiful." Brandon's sneer lit up the screen.

My hand hovered over the end-call button, but my intuition nudged me not to hang up. "How did you get my number?"

"I told you every person in that prison owes me a favor." He leaned back in a chair and propped his military boots on the top of an old scuffed-up desk.

"Where are you?"

Brandon wagged his finger at me. "Have you lost track of the days without dear ol' Franklin to keep the family straight? I was released yesterday."

"Early."

"Just a few days, but yeah. It's good to be free again." A malicious grin slipped over his face, then he placed his hands behind his head. "I have something you want."

I leaned in closer, my heart skipping a beat. "Franklin? Do you have Franklin?" My pitch climbed with each word.

"If anyone comes running because you're being too loud, I will end him right now."

I nodded and covered my hand with my mouth. "I need to see him."

"Not so fast." He smoothed his black polo shirt, then stood. "You can have him back."

I remained silent, trying to emotionally disengage as much as I could. Brandon was up to something, and the more fear I showed, the worse this could go. "What do you want?"

He ran his fingertips along the back of a black leather chair, appearing as though he were thinking through his request.

"Cut the shit, Brandon. You and I both know you have an agenda. What is it? I'll get you anything you want."

"That's my girl."

My nostrils flared with disgust. "I'll never be your girl. Don't call me that again."

Brandon rubbed his stubbled chin. "If you want Franklin back, then you will be. I want *you*. Plain and simple."

I closed my eyes while my heart thudded wildly. "I need proof of life." My voice was soft as I scrambled for a plan to bring Franklin home.

Brandon tapped the screen and the camera flipped around. Franklin sat in a chair in the corner of the room, gagged and tied up. Dried blood was caked under his nose, and one eye was swollen shut. His tux shirt was torn and ripped open, exposing his bruised stomach. He looked like hell.

"Franklin," I whisper-yelled. "Brandon, you get me close enough to talk to him, remove the gag so he can speak to me, then we'll negotiate." Fear flooded my system, and my adrenaline kicked into high gear.

Brandon roughly tugged the dirty fabric from Franklin's mouth, and he smacked Franklin's cheek. "Someone wants to say a few words to you, old man."

"Franklin, it's Gemma. Are you okay? Are your injuries bad?"

"Gemma." Franklin swallowed. "Don't do it. Don't ..."

Brandon jerked the phone away, the camera landing on his evil smile.

I smacked my desk with both hands and seethed. "You cock-sucking son of a bitch, you let him go. If you hurt him anymore, there's no deal. I'll make the trade, but when I see him, if there are any fresh wounds, I'll fucking end you."

Brandon tipped his head back and laughed. "I like this new you. My dick is rock hard just thinking about how much fun we're going to have together."

Bile swam up my throat, and I forced it back down. He couldn't see any signs of weakness.

192

"You have twenty-four hours, Gemma. Say goodbye to everyone tonight, and figure out how you can slip out without being followed. If I even *think* someone is with you or that you've told Hendrix, Pierce, or anyone else, I'll slice Franklin's throat open in front of you. Am I clear? Make sure you come alone."

I nodded in agreement.

"No bullshit, Gemma. If you do this, you're willingly mine."

I would never be his, but it wasn't the time to tell him that. I had to get Franklin back first. "I promise, but you have to leave my family alone. You can't ever mess with them again. If we make the exchange, then you're finished with them forever. Don't send other people to harm them either. It's over, Brandon."

"When you're by my side, Gemma, they'll no longer have anything I want. You have my word that no one will fucking mess with them."

I narrowed my eyes, searching for any signs he was lying. It was irrelevant, because I knew he was a liar. I couldn't trust anything that came out of his mouth.

"Where should I meet you?"

Brandon's lips pursed. "Leave by four tomorrow afternoon, and head to Idaho. I'll be in touch."

With that, he disconnected the call. I slumped in my chair, trembling. Franklin was alive. He was hurt but alive. That was what I had to focus on, not that I'd just made a deal with the devil.

I picked up my bottle of water and downed it. A multitude of thoughts scrambled and collided inside my jumbled brain, and I dug my fingernails into the palms of my hands. How was I going to get out of this predicament? I was about to come face-to-face with a disgusting, sick bastard who was holding Franklin hostage.

A soft knock on the door startled me, and I jumped out of the chair. "Yeah?" My voice sounded foreign to my own ears.

"Hey, babe. Are you ready to go?" Hendrix strolled across the room to me, and my heart skidded to a stop.

Can he tell something is wrong? "Yeah. Let me grab my purse."

"Are you feeling all right? You're really pale." Concern filled his expression as he pulled me to him.

I laid my head on his chest and slid my arms around him. I had less than twenty-four hours to capture as many memories of him as possible. It was the only way I'd be able to go through with the exchange. I would do this for Hendrix. For Franklin. For my family.

"Yeah. I'm just worried about Franklin. Sutton and I are going to hang out tomorrow. I'm hoping a change of scenery will help." I tightened my hold on him, inhaling his musky scent.

"Me too. I'm trying not to think about Dad every waking minute, but I can't help it. A part of me is beginning to wonder if he's going to make it home." Hendrix's chest heaved.

"Don't say that." I shook my head. "I have to believe that he's going to be all right and make it back to us." I wanted to tell him Franklin was alive, but I couldn't risk it. If Franklin died, it would be my fault.

"You're right." Hendrix leaned down and pressed a warm kiss on my forehead. "I need to spend some time with Mom tonight, then tomorrow evening, we should be able to sleep here." He ran his thumb along my lower lip. "I thought once we were here, we could figure out where we should get married."

"I'd like that."

Tears pricked my eyes. Unable to contain the rush of fear and grief over my decision to save Franklin, I fell apart. Hendrix sat in the chair, then pulled me into his lap.

"I'm sorry," I said. "I love you so much, baby." I wasn't sure if I could let him go. I wasn't sure I had the strength to go through with the exchange, but I had no other ideas of how to get Franklin back.

Hendrix rubbed my neck until I quieted. "I love you, too, Gemma."

His words wrapped themselves around my heart, and I tucked them away for the darker times ahead. Brandon might be able to take me, but he would never steal the memories I had with Hendrix, Mac, and my family.

I sat up, and Hendrix smoothed the hair from my face. "Let's go so we can get some rest tonight."

I nodded, then stood. He might be able to sleep, but there was no way I would be able to.

25

Once we'd settled in at Franklin's, I finally had the opportunity to make a plan for the next day. I chewed my fingernail as I shoved the fear away and forced myself to focus on a strategy. Franklin's life depended on it.

I flopped back on the bed and massaged my temples. "Think, Gemma," I whispered to myself.

My blue Beemer would be easily detected by the cops once Hendrix realized I was missing. I located my phone, hopped online, and rented a black Camry. I would have to swap cars before I crossed the border into Idaho. It wouldn't give me much time, but the police would be looking for the BMW, which would allow me to move undetected.

I would have Sutton drop me off at my place after our brunch, then I'd pull my car into the driveway. Zayne would ask questions, but I'd have to figure it out later. Maybe I'd tell him the dealership was going to pick it up for some maintenance. That left me with getting out of the house.

The realization that, by this time the next day, I would be face-to-face with Brandon sent a chill rippling down my spine. At least Franklin would be home if it all went well. A part of me understood that Brandon might not let him go, but my gut instinct said that the sick bastard didn't want Franklin. He never had. Franklin was a means to an end.

"Hey, bestie." Mac poked her head into the bedroom. She looked adorable in her pink-and-black pajama shorts and white tank. Soon, she wouldn't be able to fit into them.

"Hey." I offered her a tired smile. "How are you feeling?" I patted the bed next to me.

She crawled into the California king with me. "Just like the college days." She grinned. "We had some great conversations in that tiny dorm room."

"We did. I'll never forget them either." Little did she know that I was cementing in my mind every word, the way she looked, and her smile. My chest tightened with grief, and I struggled to hold the heartache at bay. This would be our last night together.

"Hendrix said you guys are going home tomorrow evening." Mac stuck her lower lip out, then gave a half-hearted laugh. "I wish we could."

"It's only because Pierce signed off on the additional security cameras. I guess they'll be put in place before we go back."

"You'll still be over every day, though, right?"

My words lodged in my throat. I hated lying to her, but I had no other choice. "Of course. It just means that I can pay the bills and take care of things at the house. Hendrix just wants to make sure— I'm not sure exactly, Mac."

She frowned. "What do you mean?"

I shifted on the bed. "I think he's struggling, and the only way he can manage is to not have it in his face every second of the day. At times, I'm worried he's going to crack. If anything happens to Franklin—" I couldn't finish the sentence.

"He did this after Kendra." Mac stared at the bedspread. "He pulled away and shut down. I know he's grown, but I can see the signs. If …" Mac hesitated. "Gemma, if Dad doesn't—if he …" Tears slipped down her cheeks, and she wiped them away. "If Dad doesn't come back, promise me that you won't allow Hendrix to disappear on us."

"What? Mac, he wouldn't do that. There's no way that he'd let you all go. You're his sister. He just started calling Janice 'Mom.'"

"I hope you're right, but promise me that if we lose Dad, that we won't lose him too." Mac hopped off the bed and grabbed a tissue. "I'm so tired of crying. All I want is Dad back safe and sound. I would do anything to bring him home."

There it was—my reason for my decision. Mac needed Franklin, and so did the grandbaby.

"It's going to be okay." I stood, then gave her a long hug. "I'm not sure how, but it's going to be okay."

"I hope you're right." Mac laid her head on my shoulder and continued to cry.

"Love ya, Mac." I released her and gave her a playful tug on her braided pigtail.

"Love you, too, bestie."

We sat back down and fluffed the pillows before we leaned back.

"Hey." Hendrix entered the bedroom and plopped down on the bed. "How are you feeling, Mac?" He leaned over and kissed my cheek.

"Tired. Hormonal. Freaked-out. Worried sick. Hungry. I think that sums it all up, but if you give me a minute, I'm sure I can add more."

"I get it. I'm not hormonal, but all the other shit fits." Hendrix crawled in between us, leaned back against the headboard, straightened his legs in front of him, then patted the space between them.

I settled myself between his parted thighs and leaned against his chest. His arms circled around me, and I melted into him. He was my safe place, but only for one more night. This was my last evening with him, and I couldn't tell him. *God dammit. There has to be a way to take Brandon down.*

My thoughts shifted, and I began to replay all of my self-defense and karate training. My stomach knotted as I started to form a game plan that would allow Franklin, and eventually me, to return home. If I had an opportunity to get that close to Brandon, I was going to use it to bury the motherfucker.

Hope rose inside me. I could do this. I could join Brandon in the underbelly of Hell, then dismantle him bit by bit. Maybe even bring down the organization.

Cade joined us a few minutes later, and we spent the rest of the evening talking about the band and touring. We weren't sure when we would be able to hit the road again, but it helped to plan. We kept the conversation light and even had a few laughs. Although I was paying attention to what everyone was saying, my brain was multitasking as I formulated a strategy to finally end Brandon Montgomery and take our lives back. I just hoped like hell it would work.

At nearly midnight, I hugged Mac and Cade goodnight. I changed into one of Hendrix's shirts to sleep in, then snuggled against him. I placed my palm over his heart and focused on the rhythmic beat.

"You seem distracted tonight, but I guess we all are." Hendrix smoothed the hair on the top of my head.

Unable to trust myself not to blab all about my plans, I nodded. I hated that I was keeping this from him, but I couldn't risk having Franklin's blood on my hands.

"I keep waiting for Pierce to call me and say that they've found Dad. Waiting is killing me. I would give anything to have him home."

I slammed my eyes closed. "Mac said the same thing."

His hand gently massaged my back, and I traced his muscular bicep with my fingertips. "Maybe we'll hear something tomorrow." If the plan went well, Franklin would be back soon. Based on the injuries I'd seen earlier, I suspected the hospital would be the first place he needed to go.

"I miss making love to you in our own bed," Hendrix said softly.

I glanced up at him through my eyelashes. "Then I say we just be quiet and enjoy one more time together in this room."

Hendrix slid down under the blankets and placed a warm hand on my cheek. "You're my forever, Gemma."

"And you're my always," I replied. He kissed me gently and for the next half hour, nothing in this world existed except for us.

26

After telling Hendrix goodbye the next morning, I slipped into the back of the Mercedes. Zayne eased down the winding driveway, and I stared out the window. There were still a few more pieces of my plan I had to put together, but I was feeling more confident. I was no longer the scared little girl who Brandon had threatened. I'd trained with Pierce, Hendrix, and Sutton for the last few years.

My brain told me I should talk to Sutton that day, but I couldn't risk her telling Pierce. It could blow the entire thing wide open, and I would never forgive myself if anything happened to Franklin. Even if she did swear not to tell, Pierce would be furious with her. I chewed my bottom lip, desperate to make the right decision about whether to include her or not.

"You're quiet this morning," Zayne said from the driver's seat.

"I've got a lot on my mind." I shifted uneasily.

"I know, but I wanted to check in with you anyway."

"You're a good guy, Zayne. I'm glad we're friends." I offered him a genuine smile when he peered into the rearview mirror, his green eyes hidden behind his Ray-Bans.

Zayne pulled up to the gated security system at the entrance of Pierce and Sutton's log home.

"I never get tired of visiting here. It's so peaceful."

Zayne chuckled. "It can get a little wild when we're all here drinking."

"I'd love to see that." I laughed softly.

Once Zayne had been identified by the scanner and the gate had opened, he parked the car, then opened the back door for me. We walked to the entrance, and Zayne strolled in as though he owned the place. "We're here," he called out.

"In the kitchen," Sutton replied.

"Not sure you could be any safer than in this house, so I'll let you have some space for a change." Zayne removed his sunglasses and smiled.

"Thanks." Pierce and Sutton had built the log home almost a year before, and the more time I spent there, the more I fell in love with it. I walked through the living room, eyeing the large beams in the ceiling. The hardwood floors had enough contrast to the logs that it blended together beautifully. Even though the house was huge, it always felt homey and lived in.

"Hey," I said before I entered. I never wanted to sneak up on Sutton.

"Hey!" She hurried around the island and gave me a huge hug. "I'm so glad to see you." Her eyes searched mine. "I'm not going to ask you a ton of questions, like 'How are you doing?' or 'How's Hendrix coping?' None of that." She picked up her purse from the black granite counter and slung the strap over her shoulder. "Before I forget, I went back to Mik's and collected your gifts from the party. They're in the living room, so before you leave today, I'll help you put them in the car."

"Oh wow. Thank you. With all of the crap that went down, I completely forgot about the presents."

"I didn't." She grinned at me. "I got an unexpected call this morning, so I need to drop by someone's house, but it won't be long. On the way back, we can grab some food and come back here. It's a gorgeous day, the guys will be gone, and we can hang out on the back patio and eat. How does that sound?"

"Wonderful. And just for a few hours, I'm going to pretend that you're not a bodyguard."

Sutton laughed. "Nope, just some girl time. But if anyone fucks with you, I'm dropping them to the ground. I'll ask questions later."

We chatted as we walked to the back door and into the garage. "Has Pierce learned anything new about Franklin?" I slid into the passenger seat of her Audi, buckled my seat belt, and slipped my sunglasses on.

"There've been some leads, but nothing has panned out yet. He doesn't mention those because he's afraid to get everyone's hopes up. Honestly, between us, Pierce has been on an emotional roller coaster. He blames himself for this happening. He and Franklin are really close." She opened the garage, then backed out. "Since Pierce's dad passed away, Franklin has offered my husband some stability and parental wisdom. We all need someone like that in our lives."

"I hadn't thought about how awful it would be to think you've got a lead, then it fizzles out. That would suck. Like for us, we just don't have any news, which tells us that we're not any closer." My pulse pounded in my ears. I didn't know where Franklin was, but I knew he was alive. "What have the tips been? I mean have they seen Franklin?" I needed to gauge where Sutton was about the information, to see if I could trust her to help me. My insides were in a tug of war about whether to involve her or not.

"Always, but the one that got our attention was a tip in Montana."

I stared out the window, trying to remember if anything in Brandon's FaceTime might fit with that state, but I came up blank. There was no way of telling if he'd contacted me from a house or a warehouse.

"Montana is only a four-hour drive from Spokane. I mean parts of it."

"Right, which means when they took him from Maine, they didn't stay in the area." Sutton flipped her turn signal on, then merged onto Highway 395.

"Does anyone have any clue of who kidnapped Franklin?" I slipped my trembling hands under my legs to still them. I couldn't let her see my nerves.

"We think it was Brandon and his men."

Bingo. But I couldn't confirm it yet. Alarm bells went off inside me. I was about to dive into the lion's den.

"Why would Brandon want Franklin?" Maybe if I asked leading questions, she would realize she and Pierce were on the right path.

Sutton fell silent. "We're not sure."

I narrowed my eyes behind my sunglasses. There was something she wasn't telling me, but I wasn't sure how to encourage her to keep talking.

"So the guy's house that we're going to, he's one of Pierce's ex-military buddies. He's pretty rough around the edges, but he's a good guy. I just didn't want you to be startled by him. His place is disgusting, and there are beer cans everywhere, but he's a fucking genius. He and Pierce have been working on a new device for the FBI, CIA, cops, and military."

"What does it do?"

"Right now, it looks like a little toy gun. People would inject themselves with this serum before they go undercover. If it works right, then it travels into their bloodstream, and they can be tracked for up to a year."

I gasped. "What? Is it ready? Has it been tested?"

Sutton eyed me suspiciously. "The guys are still working the kinks out of it. The last injection lasted a few weeks, but they weren't able to pick up the tracking signal all of the time. They're trying to identify under what conditions the signal can't be detected. Pierce has offered to try the newest serum."

"Is it dangerous?"

"We're still studying the long-term side effects. I'm not thrilled that Pierce wants to take it, but my husband can be hardheaded. He said if he can experience it, he can help streamline the fixes faster."

"That actually makes sense." I leaned back against the headrest, weighing the possibilities of getting my hands on the serum.

"We're here. Again, try to ignore the mess. He's a good guy, and one you definitely want on your side."

I followed Sutton to the house. White paint had begun to peel, and a funky odor assaulted my nose. A junked-out car was in the small yard with the hood up. It was too rusted to actually run. Maybe this guy liked to tinker or got his ideas from engine parts. Hell, creativity worked in strange ways, so, I wasn't going to judge.

The door was wide-open already, but Sutton used the brass knocker anyway. She probably didn't think it was smart to sneak up on people either.

"Who is it?" a gruff and grumpy voice asked.

"Abe, it's Sutton. I have a friend with me."

"Hang on." The sound of a chair scraping across the floor reached my ears. A few grunts later, a heavyset man with a beer belly came into view. His short dark hair stuck up in every direction, and his brown eyes were bloodshot. He limped as he walked toward us.

"Here it is." Abe handed Sutton a black case no bigger than a cigar box. His gaze narrowed when they landed on me. "Who's she?" He asked as though I weren't standing right there.

"Abe, this is Gemma. She's the lead singer of a famous band, and I'm her bodyguard today."

He snorted, then leaned in closer to me. I stifled the desire to pull back and wrinkle my nose. My eyes watered from the atrocious body odor and smell of stale beer. Apparently, Sutton had left out the detail that he didn't bathe. At least, not often enough.

I gave him a half-hearted wave. "Hi."

"Not sure I like you bringing someone that I don't know to my doorstep." He smacked his lips and pinned me with an intense look.

"Don't worry, Abe. I never would have brought her if she were a concern. I promise. She's one of us," Sutton said.

He grunted again, then stepped back. "Have Pierce call me." Then he walked away without saying goodbye.

I turned away from the entrance, bit my bottom lip, and inhaled deeply, pulling the fresh outdoor air into my lungs. Once we were in the car and backing out of the driveway, I snickered. "Holy shit,

Sutton. You could have warned me that taking a shower and using soap were against his religion."

A lopsided grin tugged at the corner of her mouth. "I didn't know. It's hit or miss with Abe. I swear, every time I see him, there's something different. One time, his hair was gray and longer. It looked like it hadn't been brushed in a year. Another time, he wore these little round glasses. Pierce said he's never known Abe not to have twenty-twenty vision. He's quirky, but once you get to know him, he's a really good guy. I swear." Sutton giggled.

"Wow. I've heard highly intelligent people don't always have good social skills."

Sutton snorted, then laughed again. "He definitely doesn't."

After we picked up some sushi from Wasabi, Sutton and I headed back to her place. I glanced at the car clock. It was already eleven. My time until I was face-to-face with Brandon was growing shorter. Fire squeezed my lungs and burned up the back of my throat. I couldn't breathe. Grinding my molars together, I forced myself to settle down. When my pulse calmed a little bit, I reminded myself that I couldn't risk falling apart in front of Brandon. Somewhere inside me, I had to switch off my emotions and remember why I was doing this. Franklin. When I'd needed a safe place the most, he'd opened up his home to Ada Lynn and me. He'd watched over us, protected us, and welcomed us as his own family. The least I could do for him was return the favor. I loved him like he was my own flesh and blood.

Sutton continued to chat as we arrived back at her place and prepared to eat. She placed the takeout bag and the box with the serum on the counter. I eyed it, then her. "Can I look at it?"

"I don't see why not, but Gemma, all of what I've shared with you today is confidential. You can't talk to anyone about it other than me."

I nodded. She had no idea how good I was at keeping secrets. "I understand."

She flipped the latches, then opened the box. "We're hoping that this round will last at least six months."

My attention landed on a little black toy gun. I could see a small glass vial inside of it. "How does it work?"

Sutton picked it up and held it. "You inject it into the side of your neck, then in twenty-four hours, it activates in your system."

"Does it hurt?" If I could get my hands on it without her around, then I'd find out myself, but I wasn't sure if she'd leave me alone with it.

"I'll be sure and ask Pierce after he uses it." She grinned and replaced the serum in the box and closed the case.

She turned around and gathered plates for us to use on the back patio. I stared at the container that might have the ability to save me. At one point, I would have chastised myself for figuring out how to steal something, but this was life and death—not only Franklin's, but mine as well if things went to shit.

I helped Sutton gather glasses and ice water while she took the bag of food onto the patio.

"Yeah, give me just a minute," Sutton said into her phone as she came back inside. She held her finger up, then excused herself from the room.

I listened as her voice grew farther and farther away. Nearly spilling my drink, I set it down and opened the box. Before I could talk myself out of it, I removed the gun, placed it against my neck, and squeezed the trigger. A sharp sting pierced my skin, and I gasped as the serum entered my system. *Holy shit, it hurts.* My head spun as I reached for the counter and held on.

"What the fuck?" Sutton stared at the hand that still held the dispenser.

27

I placed the gadget on the counter and grabbed my neck. "I know this looks bad, but you have to trust me." My stomach churned as the room tilted on its axis, the injection making me feel like shit. I staggered backward and propped myself up against the refrigerator. A trickle of blood seeped through my fingers.

Sutton darted around the island. "You're bleeding. Dammit, Gemma, what the hell?"

"I need your help." I wobbled over to the little table nestled near the bay windows. "But you have to swear you won't tell anyone."

"Gemma, you just went behind my back and shot a tracker system into your body that hasn't been fully tested. You'd better start singing like a canary, girlfriend." She pulled the chair out for me as I collapsed into it.

"Swear to me, Sutton. Not Pierce, not Hendrix, not a fucking soul."

Sutton pinned me with her angry and intense stare, but I refused to look away. I held my ground. She either got on board, or I'd figure this out on my own.

"Oh shit." Her mouth opened and closed, then she shared her suspicions. "Brandon got in touch with you." Her voice barely hovered above a whisper.

"He did. Sutton, please, I need your help."

Silence hung in the air between us, then she nodded. "What can I do?"

Realizing she'd just agreed, I experienced a moment of relief. "I'm sorry I went behind your back with the serum. I couldn't take the chance of you stopping me." I wiped the moisture from my cheeks. "I'm trading myself for Franklin tonight. He's alive."

"Oh God." Sutton balled her hands into fists, tears brimming in her eyes. "You can't, Gemma. As much as I want Franklin back, it's too risky. Brandon has no conscience. No." She shook her head adamantly and grabbed my hand.

"This isn't up for discussion. I'm not asking your permission. I'm going. Will you help me or not?" I clenched my jaw, readying myself for her to say no.

Realization dawned on Sutton. "You're willing to risk your life for Franklin's?"

"Hendrix and Mac need their dad. Janice needs her husband. He's been more like a father to me than mine ever was. So yes, but I'm also hoping we can take care of Brandon once and for all." A lump formed in my throat, and I swallowed it down.

"I underestimated you."

"I underestimated myself." I looked at the clock on the stove. "I have to leave my house by four this afternoon, then drive to Idaho. That's all I know at this point. He will contact me once I'm on the road."

"Gemma, the tracker takes twenty-four hours to get into your system. By the time I can locate you, it might be too late." She placed her hand on her forehead and closed her blue eyes briefly. I could almost see the wheels turning inside of her brilliant mind.

"Sutton, I've wrestled with this since yesterday afternoon. He said if I told anyone, he would slit Franklin's throat in front of me. Please, help me come up with a plan. Let me help bring Franklin home, then use the tracking serum to find me and take Brandon down for good."

"Pierce and Hendrix are going to be furious at me, but I don't have a choice. I love you, Gemma. Not only are you my friend—you're part of my extended family too. As pissed as the guys are going to be with me, they would never forgive me if I didn't do all I could to help you. Shit, I would never forgive myself if I didn't do everything possible to bring you back to us." She blew out a big breath. "So here I am, doing something." Sutton stood and held her hand out to me. "Let's eat. We have a lot of work to do in a short amount of time."

Over the next hour, we talked strategy, and she told me the fastest ways to kill Brandon if it came down to it, like stabbing him in the neck with a fork. I cringed, but it was good information to have.

The closer four o'clock got, the more terrified I became. Once we were finished at her place, and she'd picked up a few additional tools, she drove me to my house. I texted Hendrix that I was still with Sutton and checked on how Janice and Mac were doing.

"I hate that the first time you're at my place it's because …" I allowed the system to scan my fingerprint and waited for the door to unlock.

"Yeah, I was just thinking the same thing, Gemma."

"How were you planning on slipping past Zayne?" she asked as she followed me inside.

I closed and flipped the deadbolt into place behind us. I tossed my purse on the couch. "Make yourself comfortable or check out the house if you need to."

Sutton glanced around the living room, then strolled over to the slider. "Wow. You have a gorgeous view of the river."

"It's one of my favorite things about the property. To answer your question, the original plan was that I'd be home, then I would tell Zayne I saw someone outside that looked suspicious. It's already been established that if there's a threat, Hendrix and I have to stay in the studio. We have supplies, guns, ammo, you name it. We could live in there for a month if we had to. Anyway, Zayne would think that I was in there when I'd actually snuck away."

"Remind me to keep two bodyguards on you at all times moving forward." Sutton placed her hands on her hips, then frowned.

I folded my arms over my chest. "I want to make Hendrix a video so he knows where I am. I'm going to use the studio. I'll need some privacy to tell him goodbye in case I don't ..." A horrible pang shot through my heart at the thought that I would never again touch his gorgeous face, kiss his soft lips, hear his laugh, or make love to him again. Most of all, I regretted not making it final and becoming Hendrix's wife, but that alone would drive me to make it through hell and back and into his arms again.

Sutton quirked an eyebrow at me. "I'll be right here, so you can't sneak out."

"I wouldn't have told you all of that if I were going to try and slip past you." I nervously tucked my hair behind my ear. "I'm sorry I brought you into all of this. I wasn't going to, but then you started talking about the tracking serum, and I knew it was my best hope for coming home."

Sutton crossed the room and threw her arms around me. "You'd better. You'd better fucking come back to us." We hugged each other in silence, then she let me go and dabbed the tears from her eyes.

"The studio is this way." I motioned for her to follow me down the hall.

Once I was situated at the soundboard, I removed my phone from my pocket. I blew out a big breath and rolled my shoulders, attempting to relieve some of the tightness. I loved Hendrix so deeply that I would do anything to protect him, including sacrificing myself.

Tapping the screen, I set the video to begin recording and mounted it on the control panel.

"Hi, baby." I looked away, tears clouding my vision. *Stay strong. Stay strong.* "I'm not sure where to start, but I love you. No matter what happens, please know that my heart will always find its way back to you." I paused and tucked my hair behind my ear in a nervous gesture.

"Brandon contacted me and offered an exchange for Franklin, and I accepted. I don't have any idea when Franklin will return home, but from what I saw, he needs medical care. He's alive, though." I briefly stared at the floor, trying to maintain my composure. It wouldn't help the situation if I cried, and it wasn't the time for it.

"Brandon said if I told anyone about the trade that he would slit Franklin's throat in front of me, so I couldn't take any chances. Plus you would have stopped me." I shook my head. "You and your family have loved me and taken me in, baby. I had to do everything I possibly could to bring Franklin home. Please know that I did this because I love you more than my own life." I chewed on my lower lip.

"I can't say anything else, but you need to reach out to Sutton immediately. She can help you track me down." My chin trembled, and I glanced at the clock. It was time to go. "Baby, if this fails ... just know that you gave me wings to fly. I love you so much. Please—come find me." I kissed my fingertips, then touched the screen before I stopped the video. I emailed it to Sutton, who had agreed to forward it to Hendrix after I was gone. I allowed myself one last cry, then shoved my emotions into a little box and threw away the key.

I opened the door, my attention landing on Sutton, who'd remained in the hallway. "I'm ready."

2 8

Sutton took me to pick up the rental, then planted three tiny trackers on the car. Her reasoning was that if one was discovered or fell off, then there were still two more. I drove the Camry to the nearest gas station while Sutton followed and made sure the devices were working correctly. After I fueled up, I parked in the parking lot, but left it running.

Sutton hopped out of her Audi and offered to give me any last bits of advice I needed. "My guess is that Brandon will have you leave your car somewhere, but at least it will give me some information about where you are."

"Okay." My heart was hammering so hard I thought it might burst out of my chest. "I have to go. He said he'd call me after I was on the road but to leave at four."

Sutton grabbed my hands, her chin trembling. "Stay strong. I know you're not trained for undercover work, but that's what you're doing." She squeezed my fingers. "When you're alone and scared, remember all of the wonderful things you love about Hendrix. His touch, his kiss, his voice. Tuck those special moments away and rely on them to get you through the tough times."

"He's going to be really pissed at me." I attempted a smile, my heart splintering.

"Hendrix will be mad that you did this—that you selflessly risked your own life to bring Franklin home and take down Brandon. You're one of the bravest people I know, Gemma."

"I don't feel brave." I ground my molars together to contain my emotions. "If I don't see you again, then thank you, and please take care of Hendrix for me. Let him know that he's not responsible for my choice and that I love him so much." I pulled Sutton in for a hug goodbye.

"It's not goodbye, Gemma. It's 'I'll see you later.'" Tears streamed down her cheeks and landed on my shoulder.

I hoped like hell she was right. I gave her a little wave, then settled into the Camry. I didn't have time to connect my phone to the rental's Bluetooth system, but I knew Brandon or one of his men would contact me, and I needed to keep my cell close. Making sure I had my phone on the seat next to me, I pulled out of the parking lot and headed down the highway toward Idaho with my heart in my fucking throat.

AN HOUR INTO THE DRIVE, my phone rang. I tapped the green answer button, then the speaker.

"Hello?" My hands shook so hard I wasn't sure if I could continue to drive.

"Stay on I-90, then follow the exits to St. Regis, Montana. Do you understand?"

"I want to talk to Franklin!" I forced myself to clamp my emotions down. I couldn't mess this up.

"I'll call back in an hour."

I slammed the palm of my hand against the dashboard. What if Brandon had reneged on the deal and Franklin wasn't alive? Fuming and terrified, I selected a Spotify playlist in hopes that some music would soothe my frazzled nerves. "Run" by James Gillespie blared through the iPhone's speaker.

"Dammit. Not fucking funny, universe!" I tapped the screen to change the song.

Nightfall descended, and my mind wandered to Hendrix. It had been nearly two hours since I'd left. *Does he think I'm still with Sutton?* I wasn't sure when she'd planned on sending the video to his email, but I trusted her to take care of him.

The miles stretched on forever as I continued to follow the directions I'd been given. Once I reached St. Regis, I located a gas station and a restroom. Maybe I was ahead of schedule since I hadn't received a call back. *Did Brandon change his mind?* Multiple dreadful scenarios assaulted my overactive brain while I sat in the car, waiting.

My phone rang, and I snatched it up. It was Hendrix calling. I couldn't talk to him. I would turn around and run to the safety of his arms if I did. I sent the call to voicemail, and seconds later, a text message from him lit up my screen.

Don't! Gemma, please!

Oh. God. It was Hendrix. I stared at the phone, my heart racing and my throat constricting.

Baby, please. Come home. I can't lose you. I love you, Gem.

My cell rang, saving me from the heartbroken pleas of my fiancé. "Hello."

"Pull onto the highway, then take the Big Timber exit. You'll drive a mile down a country road. Pull your vehicle over to the side and wait for my instructions."

Click. The motherfucker hung up on me.

It was almost time. I stared at the phone, then texted Hendrix back.

I love you, Hendrix. My God, you're the beat of my heart. This decision wasn't made lightly. I have to believe that this is the right thing, and if all goes well, Franklin will be home soon. Find me, baby, and send the devil back to Hell so we can finally be free. So our family can live in peace and we can finally have a future together.

My heart plummeted to my toes and I hit the send button.

"I love you, Hendrix. You'll be in my memories every second." I blocked his number, then tossed the phone onto the seat next to me. It was time to get Franklin.

Ten minutes later, I parked the Camry on the side of the road. My pulse hammered so loudly I was afraid I would pass out. I took several deep breaths, then identified headlights growing closer. The rumbling of an engine vibrated through the air, and my heart rattled.

My phone rang. "Get out of the car and don't hang up," a male voice ordered. My eyes slammed shut, and I offered a silent prayer to anyone who might hear me.

I got out of the Camry and leaned against it. My legs were heavy with fear, and I wiggled my toes in my shoes. My breathing came in short bursts as a van stopped on the other side of the road.

"Stay where you are," the man ordered.

The side door slid open and several armed men jumped out. They quickly dispersed across the road and in front of the vehicle, guns raised and aiming at me.

My legs trembled beneath me and I leaned on the car for support. Images of Hendrix flashed before me. "I love you, baby. Oh God. I love you so much."

A man toppled from the vehicle and fell to his knees. *Franklin!*

Adrenaline pumped through my body, and my only focus was to reach him.

He slowly got to his feet, and I blinked to see him more clearly, but the headlights were blinding my view. I shielded my eyes with my hands.

Franklin staggered forward, and a cry escaped me. Four men had trained guns on him. I wasn't sure we were going to make it out alive. Once the bastards and Franklin were halfway to me, the guy on my phone spoke again.

"Walk slowly to Franklin. Once you're there, drop your phone on the ground and raise your hands in the air."

"I want to make sure he's okay." My voice sounded confident.

"Do as you're told or he's a dead man."

I stopped in my tracks. "You listen to me, you little coward. I get to

214

hug Franklin before I join Satan in Hell, or you can tell Brandon he can suck his own dick."

Silence filled the line, then the man said, "Five seconds. Make it count."

I sped up, keeping my attention on Franklin while my hands were in the air so the idiots could see I wasn't armed. Only a few yards away, my feet argued with my brain and picked up the pace. My logic told me to fucking run, but love wasn't always logical.

"Franklin!" I hurried in his direction.

"Gemma." He walked to me, nearly falling to the ground.

"Oh my God." I threw my arms around his neck, tears streaming down my cheeks. My emotions overflowed, churning through me like a storm over the sea. The push and pull were chaotic and uncontrollable. I knew saving Franklin was the right thing to do, but I was terrified and wanted to return to the safety of my fiancé's arms.

Franklin embraced me as I sobbed against him. "Get the hell out of here, Franklin." I pulled away from him, our eyes locking. I gasped. Although I didn't see any new injuries on his face, they were worse in person than on FaceTime.

"No, Gemma, I can't let you do this. I won't allow it. He's a fucking monster." He gripped my arm.

I pushed up on my tiptoes and put my mouth close to his ear so no one could hear what I was saying. "You have to, Franklin. Sutton knows how to find me. I'm going in to take this bastard down. You need medical care too. Your kids and grandbaby need you. Janice is worried sick. Not only that, but if we try to run, they'll gun us both down. We'll be dead before we take three steps toward the car. In order to save us both, you have to go, Franklin. Please."

Fear and regret twisted his facial features. "I don't like this, and I'm not sure how I'm going to live with this, but if they gunned you down, I would never forgive myself. Neither option is what I want. I'll call the police the minute I find a phone. Then I'll call Sutton. Please be careful, Gemma. He's dangerous." Franklin kissed my forehead and clutched his side, doubling over in pain.

"Get moving!" one of the men barked.

"I'll see you soon." I looked up into his pain-filled expression.

Tears clung to his eyelashes. "I love you, Gemma. I swear we'll find you."

One of the guys jabbed Franklin in the back with the barrel of his gun and he lurched forward. I caught him before we both went down.

"God dammit, stop!" I screamed. "Leave him alone." I placed myself between Brandon's men and Franklin. "Tell Brandon he made a promise. I'm here. I've done everything that he asked me, so stop hurting Franklin and let him go!" I raised my arms in surrender, then glanced over my shoulder at Franklin. Internally, I sighed with relief. He'd made it to the car.

"Someone has really grown some balls." Brandon got out of the vehicle. "Let him go and bring her to me."

The headlights from the Camry changed directions, and I turned and watched as Franklin drove away. A large man to the right of me grabbed my arm and jerked me forward, my toes barely touching the ground.

He halted in front of Brandon. With a wicked grin and a glint in his eye, Brandon squared his shoulders and approached me. He stopped only a few feet away from me. The atmosphere heated like Satan himself had come to visit. I clenched my hands into fists as our gazes locked.

"You're more beautiful than I remembered. Your tits and ass are bigger." His tongue flicked across his lower lip, and he leaned down to my ear. "I can't wait to have that smart little mouth of yours around my cock."

Rage sizzled beneath the surface, battling with my sorrow. Before I realized it, I snapped my head back and spat in his face. "See you in hell, motherfucker."

He wiped his cheek, pinned me with a bored stare, and made a gesture with his hand. A sharp sting pierced my neck, then I tumbled into darkness.

My head throbbed like a son of a bitch. I reached up to rub my blurry eyes and struggled to piece together what had happened. Brandon. Franklin. I sat up gradually, taking in my surroundings. The oversized black T-shirt hung off my frame. Someone had changed my clothes. Terror spiked inside of me, sending my heart racing. I'd been unconscious. *Did Brandon touch me?*

I continued to survey the room. A lone beige blanket and pillow were the only items on the small bed. Placing my feet on the floor, I stared at the gray cinderblock walls. The chilly air was stale and musty. One little window allowed the moonlight into the tiny space. A toilet was mounted to the wall to the left of my cot. I continued to survey the space. Bars. A tremor wracked my body, and my blood chilled. What had I done?

I stood on shaky legs and dragged my numb feet to the entrance. I wrapped my fingers around the cold metal, and a scream gathered in my throat.

"Brandon!" I yelled. "Brandon!" Pulling on the door of the cell, I called out his name again, but my cries were only met with silence.

A band squeezed tighter and tighter around my chest until I could barely breathe. Then it snapped, and I crumbled. Everything I'd held together broke free and spun around inside me like a roaring tornado that I couldn't escape. An anguished cry pricked my eardrums. Mine. My pain was evident in my strangled sobs as I struggled to pull myself off the floor.

"What have I done?" I whispered. I hadn't even begun to understand how fucked-up Brandon really was. I wasn't the same girl he'd held at gunpoint in the warehouse, but he wasn't the same man who'd held the gun.

I gritted my teeth as despair consumed me. Brandon had lost any trace of humanity he might have had left. He wasn't human. Brandon Montgomery was a monster.

29

T hin rays of golden sunshine filtered through the window and into my cell the next morning. I'd spent hours berating myself for agreeing to the exchange with Brandon, but at least Franklin was free. I hoped. The mere thought that he might not have made it home safely sent a chill rippling down my spine. He had to be all right, or my attempts to help him would be futile.

My thoughts bounced around like an uncontained rubber ball on a tennis court. One second, I was calm and ready to do anything I had to in order to take Brandon down. The next, fear slithered into my thoughts and played me like a puppet master. I held my hands against the sides of my head and forced myself to breathe. Sutton and Hendrix would find me. My baby would move heaven and earth to bring me home again, and I had to trust that they were already looking for me. Sutton had a tracker on the car, and although Franklin drove it back to Spokane, she should have been able to pinpoint the place of the exchange and work from there.

As my mind drifted to Hendrix, I imagined that his strong arms were around me. I continued to build myself a safe haven with memories of his smile and touch. The thought of his laughter calmed my frantic heart rate and renewed my hope that I would make it out of there alive.

I'D LOST all track of the time while I was locked away. All I knew was that I'd been in the cell since the previous night without any food or water for what felt like an eternity. I suspected the serum had reached the twenty-four-hour mark, or it was close. I continually reminded myself that Sutton would be working around the clock to pick up the signal. Hopefully, there wasn't anything blocking my location.

Desperation clawed its way through my body while dark scenarios once again began to play through my mind. *What if the serum didn't work?* A small whimper slipped through my lips, and I slapped my hands over my mouth. I stared at the ceiling, and a glint caught my attention. I searched the walls with my eyes, keeping my head still until I could confirm my suspicions. A camera. *Why didn't I think to look for it before?*

My gaze narrowed while I wondered if it was angled toward or away from the toilet. Away. I stood and stretched my achy body, then faced the little green light in the ceiling. "Brandon. I came to you willingly. Please let me out." Obviously spitting in his face had landed me here, so I needed to try a different approach. "I'm hungry and thirsty. Please."

Nothing. I tried to reason with him again to no avail. I sank down onto the edge of the bed and rubbed my temples while I scrambled for a way to reach Brandon, but how could you reason with insanity?

EXHAUSTED but too scared to sleep, I finally lay down while the last bit of the sunset lit my cell. My eyes fluttered closed, and I continued to listen for any indication that Brandon had decided to visit me. For the moment, it was deathly quiet. A heavy weight settled on my shoulders, nearly smothering me. I began to sing Dua Lipa's "Homesick" softly to myself. Music and Hendrix's love had saved me before, and maybe they would again.

"HELLO, GEMMA."

My mind swam with dreams as a voice chased away the illusion of Ada Lynn. I bolted upright in my bed and realized that I wasn't sitting in Ada Lynn's rocking chair on her porch in Louisiana. *Shit.* I'd drifted off to sleep.

"I trust you slept well." Brandon ran his fingers across the bars, then stared at me as though he wasn't sure I was really there.

I glared at him. "This bed fucking sucks."

"If I can trust you to behave, I'll let you come upstairs. You can eat breakfast with me."

Maybe this was my chance to see where I was and form an escape plan, but in order to do that, Brandon had to see that he could trust me.

"That would be nice." I rubbed my arms as goosebumps dotted my skin. I was about to spend time alone with the devil himself.

Brandon slipped a key in place, then slid the door open. I stood and anxiously walked toward him. *Is this a joke, or is he really letting me out?*

He held his hand out to me. "As I said, if you behave, you can join me."

Inwardly, I cringed as I tentatively touched his fingers. Stepping out of the cell, I immediately noticed two armed guards and gulped. Brandon wasn't fucking around, but I hadn't expected so much heavily armed security. This fucked up my plan.

Without another word, Brandon led me up the stairs and through a hall that entered into the upstairs of the house. Fresh air filled the main floor, and I breathed in as deeply as my lungs would allow. I hadn't realized how stifling the cell was.

Brandon continued to hold my hand while we walked through a large living area with an expensive brown leather couch and matching recliner. A flat screen television hung over a fireplace. A beautiful chestnut-and-beige rug covered most of the hardwood floor, and pictures of mountains lined the opposite wall. The house was gorgeous and had been well maintained. Windows took up the far wall, allowing me to see parts of the wooded property. We turned left into the dining area, which had a long table that could easily accommodate eight people.

"Take a seat." He nodded to the chair at the end, and I silently sat down.

Two different armed men joined us in the corners of the room. I wondered if they were the same ones who had kidnapped Franklin as the metal of their guns glinted in the sunlight. I imagined Pierce, Vaughn, and Zayne bursting through the door at any minute and ending the shit show. More than anything, I wanted to see what Brandon's game was and why he wanted me there with him.

Brandon sat at the other end and scooted his chair up, resting his elbows on the table. "You can shower after you eat. You look like shit."

"Huh, I wonder why?" I mumbled.

He leaned back, his intense gaze never leaving me. "There are three bedrooms upstairs, including mine. How you choose to speak to me, or act, will decide where you'll sleep tonight."

"Where am I, Brandon? And why? Why did you take Franklin?" I shook my head and rubbed my face. Never in a million years had I imagined that I would be having any type of conversation with Brandon, much less this one.

"This is one of my father's homes the FBI never learned about. I have a few others as well."

My nostrils flared at the mention of his father. I bit my lower lip in order to keep from spewing profanities at the bastard. It would only land me back in the cell.

"Breakfast, sir."

My mouth gaped as a scantily dressed young lady brought

221

Brandon a plate of food, then plunked another in front of me. She was around eighteen—maybe younger, but I couldn't handle entertaining that idea. She wore a short dress that skimmed the lower part of her ass cheeks, and her full breasts bulged out at the top. Her nipples were barely contained in the red-and-white fabric. Her brown eyes assessed me, glaring.

"Why is she here?" she squeaked and looked at Brandon, her lower lip jutting out.

"That's none of your business." Brandon stabbed his scrambled eggs with his fork. He shoved a bite into his mouth.

Since he was eating, I assumed the meal would be safe. I hoped I wasn't wrong. After moving my food around on my plate, I finally took a small bite. They tasted normal, and I prayed like hell my water wasn't drugged. I needed to stay alert in case an opportunity to run presented itself.

"I don't like her." She stomped her foot like a spoiled schoolgirl. Her eyes widened, then her mouth opened while she dropped to her knees. Her fingers tugged at a collar I hadn't noticed before.

"I didn't fucking ask you," he growled. "You will always show Gemma respect. Get over here."

Terror wrecked me as I realized Brandon had placed a shock collar around her neck. Gripping the edge of the table, I stared at my food and inhaled deeply several times.

"Master, I'm sorry," she whined while she crawled on the floor toward him.

"You won't be able to say anything when your mouth is full of my cock." The sound of his zipper filled the room. She removed his dick and began to suck him off.

"You'll be here soon, Gemma. I have so many things planned for us."

I grimaced and looked away. Any calm I'd gathered through my breathing exercise vanished when my heart jumped so hard it almost leaped out of my throat.

Brandon grunted. The sound of his chair moving startled me, and my eyes flew open. I'd fight him with everything I had if he tried to hurt me.

He stood and bent the girl over the table and began to fuck her. His fingers tugged on her collar and her face was red. She attempted to pull it away from her skin, but it was too tight. *What is his fascination with strangling women while he screws them?*

Bile rose up my throat. I clutched my chest and tried to get my thundering heartbeat under control. He was sick.

Once they were finished and the girl left the room, I shot him a *Go to hell* look. "That was fucked-up. What's the point, Brandon? What's this all about?" I motioned to him and the guards.

Brandon sat back down and continued to eat as though he hadn't just had sex with some possibly underage girl in front of me. "Franklin was a means to an end. You." He took a drink of his orange juice. "I've learned things in prison I never even dreamed were possible. Control. Manipulation. Strategy. Basically, how to rebuild my father's empire."

Maybe he didn't have the balls I thought he did if he still answered to daddy. "He betrayed you, Brandon. He left you and your brother to get arrested while he ran and hid. Why would you want to restore the Dark Circle Society for him?" I crumpled my paper napkin in my hand and wished it was his head instead.

"It's not for him. He's no longer involved in the society. I've taken it over. It will be stronger, larger, and more dangerous than ever before." He wiped the corners of his mouth with his thumb and relaxed in his chair. "As for why you're here, you understand what the Dark Circle Society is about, or have a basic understanding at least. Also, your father betrayed you. You've experienced what it feels like to be discarded as though you're not a human being. I have the opportunity to prove him wrong, and while dear ol' Dad is behind bars, I'll be running the family business. I'm already worth millions, which unfortunately makes me an easy target, and I had to hire guards." He took a bite of his bacon and smirked.

"Are you sure it's the money that makes you an easy target, or could it possibly be your winning personality?" Internally, I cringed. If

I kept provoking him, I'd end up back in the cell. At least here I was able to learn more about what he was up to, then I could testify in court against him.

Brandon stood and walked toward me slowly as he peered straight into my soul, peeling away my protective layers and exposing my fear. He positioned himself behind my chair and placed both of his filthy hands on my shoulders. Leaning forward, he whispered in my ear. "Careful, beautiful, or you'll find yourself with a collar around your neck just like Cara." He traced my neck and collarbone and slipped his hand into my shirt. He cupped my breast and nipped at my earlobe. I ground my teeth, afraid to make a sudden move. "I have big plans for you." His promise was coated with evil so slick it could slip through my fingers. He removed his hand and straightened up. "For now, you need to get cleaned up."

A fresh sprinkle of hate for him crawled over my skin. He strolled past me and out of the room, leaving me shaking uncontrollably in my seat. Before I could move, another young girl entered, dressed the same way that Cara was.

"Come with me, Gemma."

At least this one didn't seem to care that I was here, but she wasn't friendly either. Maybe I could talk to her and find out how she'd ended up in this house with Brandon. Was she here willingly, or had she been taken from a family who was still frantically searching for her?

I followed her up a curved set of stairs and down a long hallway. She inserted a key into a door, then pushed it open. "You'll find clothes in the closet that will fit you. Toiletries, shampoo, and conditioner, along with towels, are in the adjoining bathroom. Brandon wants you clean and dressed in an hour. I'll be back to get you when it's time."

Before I could utter a word, she left. A loud click rang in my ears. I darted across the room and wiggled the doorknob. It was locked. I leaned against the wall while my heart raced. My breathing was erratic and labored as I clutched my chest. Salty tears burned a trail down my cheeks, and I struggled to keep myself together, but that fucker had touched me. I swallowed excessively. *What does he mean by "big plans"? And is he really not going to hurt me for now?*

My attention swept the well-lit area. The sun was overhead, and I wondered if it was almost noon. The windows were barred. There was no chance that I could fit between them. A queen-sized bed with a dark-blue comforter sat against the wall, and the matching dresser was on the other side. I hurried across the room and yanked open a drawer—G-strings and thongs in a variety of colors. I removed one and glanced at the tag. They would fit. I pursed my lips as I continued to rifle through the clothing. A wide range of bras, lingerie, tops, shirts, and pajamas were all in my size.

Shit. He'd been planning this for a while. I flung open the closet door and gasped. Jeans, dresses, shoes, and handbags filled the large space. Anger radiated off me. Whatever he'd planned, it was long-term in his eyes. I couldn't wait to disappoint him.

After selecting clean clothes, I hurried to what I thought was the bathroom and flipped on the light. The room had white walls, dual sinks, and black granite countertops. At that point, I couldn't care less what it looked like.

I eyed the ceiling and walls, but I didn't see any tiny cameras. Desperately needing to pee, I clutched the new set of clothes in front of me in hopes it would conceal me below the waist in case there were video cameras in the lights.

Once I was finished, I tugged my jeans up with one hand, deposited the stack of clean clothes on the counter, located a towel inside the cabinet, and headed for the shower. I pulled the curtain back and turned on the water. Steam filled the room, and I took in a slow, deep breath. After removing my tennis shoes and socks, I tilted the water away from me, dropped the towel onto the floor where I could reach it, and stepped in with my clothes on. Since the oversized black T-shirt grew damp quickly, I struggled to remove it.

I adjusted the water and stood under it. My stomach did flip-flops as despair and anger seeped into my thoughts. "Hendrix."

My chin shook as a rush of emotion hit me all at once. I placed my palm on the wall as my breathing came fast and hard. Images of

Hendrix, Mac, Franklin, and Janice filled my mind, and once again, I remembered why I was here. Brandon had promised he would leave them alone. None of them would be hurt again. Mac could stop living in fear, Janice had her husband back, and Hendrix could sing and tour again. I'd agreed to the exchange because I loved them. They deserved a better life than to constantly look over their shoulders, wondering when the monster would strike next. My family deserved to be free.

30

I looked at the digital clock on the nightstand. It had been more than an hour since I'd cleaned up and dressed. I rubbed my sweaty palm along my jeaned thigh. The new clothes creeped me out. How had he learned what size I was? Every pair of jeans fit a woman differently, but these were like a second skin. I wasn't sure I could have picked out a better pair. The long-sleeved, plum-colored shirt was soft to the touch. I found myself mindlessly rubbing my arms.

I stared out the window and drummed my fingers against the pane. Although the back of the house had seemed heavily wooded, this side of the property was vast and open. Large mountains weren't too far away either. I strained to get a better view, but the bars blocked my progress. From what I could tell, there was a good possibility we were in Montana. I'd watched enough *Yellowstone* to understand the landscape. I wondered where Rip and John Dutton were, then I released a maniacal laugh. I was losing my shit if I was hoping that fictional characters would burst into the house and rescue me.

The door opened and I nearly screamed. I clutched the collar of my shirt and tried to stop shaking as Brandon crossed the room to me.

"These fucking bars remind me of prison. Let's go." He tugged on my hand, and I fell in behind him.

"Where are we going?" I asked, noting an armed man following us. Apparently Brandon didn't trust me to be alone with him. He shouldn't. The second I had an opportunity, I would attack him, then haul ass out of here.

We hurried down the stairs and into the living room. From what I could tell, this was my third day. Sutton should know where I was by now. Panic-stricken at the possibility that the serum hadn't worked, I stumbled and collided into Brandon's muscular back. He lurched forward, then we tumbled to the hardwood floor. I attempted to jump off him, but he was faster. He wrapped his arms around me, then his strong leg came up between mine, blocking me from moving.

"Feel that?" He shifted his hips, his erection pressing into me.

My breath hitched in my throat as my pulse skyrocketed. "If you think I'll willingly have sex with you, you're sadly mistaken. Your dick is probably diseased and ready to fall off after all the girls you've raped."

Brandon gaped at me as if I'd just cut his black heart out of his chest. He released me, and I scrambled backward. He shuffled to his feet, his eyes narrowing. "I like this side of you. It will make it a lot more fun when I claim you as mine once and for all." He grabbed my arm and jerked me forward. "Try to stay upright this time."

"You're hurting me." I rubbed my wrist, then dug my nails into his skin. "Let go. I'll walk with you. Seriously. You have a man with a gun trained on me. I'm not stupid enough to run or attack you."

Unless I'm ready to die, I thought. But I wasn't, and I refused to give up on the idea that Sutton would find me.

He burst through the front door and onto the porch, then let me go when his security joined us. Without a word, he descended the steps. The trees had begun to change to a glorious orange and red. Some had already fallen on the landscaped lawn. The afternoon sun was bright, burning off some of the autumn chill. I welcomed the soft caress of the golden rays on my face.

Brandon turned right and followed a trail into the wooded area. Sticks and pinecones crunched under my feet as I ducked beneath low-hanging branches on the pine and fir trees. Aspens were intermingled with the conifers, and their yellow leaves rustled in the breeze.

We continued down an overgrown path, then reached a small clearing. If I'd been here with Hendrix, I would have gasped. The mountain peaks were already covered with snow. They were so close that I wondered if I could reach out and touch them. The fresh air tickled my nose, and I inhaled deeply. I had no idea if Brandon would toss me into the cell again or not, so I would take every opportunity I could to taste freedom.

"Enjoy it. In a few more days, we'll relocate, and the view isn't as magnificent. Until then, if you consider making a run for it—" He made a sweeping motion with his hand. "As you can see, you're in the middle of fucking nowhere. Besides, I would have you hunted and killed before you were able to find anyone to help." Brandon crossed his arms over his broad chest, his biceps bulging beneath his T-shirt. He'd packed on a lot of muscle while in prison. "I realize I could have told you all of this from inside the house, but words rarely teach. Experiences do. I doubt you would have believed me unless you saw it yourself. I would rather not kill you unless I have no other choice." He sneered, a slight wobble to his voice.

A shudder worked its way up my spine. I wasn't interested in a game of cat and mouse either. "Where are we?" I wasn't expecting an answer, but I figured I would ask anyway.

He eyed me suspiciously. "Central Montana near White Sulphur Springs."

"You seem to like it here. Why are we moving somewhere else?" I wasn't sure if this was good or not. Maybe there was interference here with the serum, and if we changed places …

"I've had a new headquarters built for the society. You of course will join me as my right-hand … woman." Brandon flashed a devious smile. "You'll definitely be my right hand."

"If you want me so bad, why haven't you already raped me?" The question escaped me without permission, but a part of me needed to know what the fucker was up to.

He closed the gap between us and placed his palm on my cheek. He leaned down near my ear and whispered, "Because I want our wedding night to be special."

My mouth gaped in horror, then a blistering rage licked through me. "Why in God's name do you think I would marry you? You sick, twisted, fuck. I love Hendrix and no one else."

Brandon's tongue darted over his bottom lip in a salacious manner as he moved closer to me. His hand wrapped around my neck, and he shoved me against a tree and lifted my feet off the ground. I clawed at his fingers while I attempted to suck in much needed air.

"Listen, bitch. You'll do what I tell you to. When I want you to sit on my cock, you do it. When I tell you to say, 'I do,' you do it. When I want to fuck your tight little pussy, you'll spread your legs for me. You'll run this organization with me, or I'll slit Hendrix's throat in his sleep. I'll fucking kill everyone you love, then dance in their blood."

Spittle sprayed on my cheek as he talked. I almost passed out, but seconds before that could happen, he dropped his hand, and I slumped to the unforgiving hard ground. I sputtered and coughed while I pulled air into my lungs. My tears fell on the leaves at the thought that he would hurt my family, but I should have known he'd found a way to keep me prisoner. Franklin had tried to warn me, but prison had changed Brandon. He was cunning, manipulative, and smarter than before.

I picked myself off the ground as Hendrix's beautiful smile flashed across my mind. My heart stuttered while I wondered if I would ever see him again. The only reason I refused to think I'd fucked up by turning myself over to this monster was that I'd been able to send Franklin home.

Squaring my shoulders, I stared Satan straight in the eye. "I want a white dress."

Shock flashed in Brandon's eyes. "That's more like it. Now, let's get down to business."

THE REST of the afternoon moved by in a blur. My brain refused to engage or admit where I really was. After he'd choked me, I'd shut down. Maybe the lack of oxygen had messed me up, but I couldn't focus. Brandon and I sat at the kitchen table, and he rolled out the plans for headquarters that were located near the mountains in the Midwest. He wouldn't tell me the location, but I wondered if it was in Colorado.

Apparently, my cell downstairs was a test of what Brandon wanted for the girls he planned on selling to the highest bidder. He referred to the females as "the elite" since they earned top dollar. Bile swam up my throat as he showed me the changes he'd made to the cages. Thick glass walls, a drain in the center of the floor, and air holes at the top. There was no escaping unless someone helped them. I clenched my jaw in order to keep my fury at bay. There had to be some way I could kill Brandon, even if it meant I died with him. He couldn't get away with this. These girls were human beings, not cattle. Even then, I'd seen animals receive better treatment than what he had in store for them.

"Consider yourself my queen."

I blinked rapidly, my brain not grasping what he was saying to me. "What?"

"My wife, my right hand, my business partner. You'll be my confidant. Every great king has a great queen."

My thoughts were discombobulated, and I struggled to find the correct reply. Fire squeezed my lungs and burned up the back of my throat. I couldn't breathe. I was in the underbelly of the Dark Circle Society.

"Water!" Brandon yelled.

In seconds, a glass was sat in front of me, and I gulped it greedily. I wiped the droplets off my mouth with the back of my hand and stared at him in disbelief. "You can't expect me to digest all of this"—I motioned to the plans and information that were scattered all over the table—"at once."

He stood and paced. "I suppose you're right. I grew up in the society and this way of thinking. You were a victim, so I can see where you might need a day or so to chew on it."

I knitted my brows together. "Why? Why do you think that selling girls is okay? I mean, does your moral meter not scream at you?"

Brandon chuckled and sat down. "What's a moral meter?"

A tiny flicker of hope surged through me. I was surprised that he was actually engaging with me in this conversation. Maybe there was a chance that I could use his feelings for me against him and gain the upper hand. My thoughts churned out multiple possibilities of how to play this, but I couldn't grab a hold of one long enough to make sense of it.

I slid my hand across the table and placed it on his. His fingers intertwined with mine, and his expression softened. "Why me? Why me, when we both know there are so many girls who would be more than eager to be with you? What makes me so special? Do you love me?" I whispered, trying not to gag on my words before he answered.

He looked away and stared out the living room windows. "Yes." His attention traveled back to me. "Ever since I saw you that day on the college campus in that fucked-up hat and glasses, I knew. I knew you were the one for me. All I've ever wanted was to have you next to me as we ran the society. When you traded yourself for Mac at the warehouse, it just confirmed what I already knew. You were smart, lethal, courageous. You'd been betrayed just like I had. We're kindred spirits."

Holy shit.

"But then you chose Hendrix. He stole you from me. He took what I wanted. Again." Brandon slammed his fist on the table, making the pen and pencil jump.

"It's obviously over now." I had to calm him down before he attacked me again.

He seethed, his cheeks burning bright red.

"Why do you two hate each other so much?" I asked. "Even before me, there were issues. What happened?" This definitely wouldn't settle him down, but my need to know overpowered my logic.

Brandon scrubbed his face with his hands, then leaned back in the chair. "When Hendrix and I were in middle school, my dad asked Franklin for help. Dad had lost a ton of money in a bad investment, and we were about to lose the house and cars. Basically everything. What I didn't know was that along with the shitty business deal, he was also trying to keep my sorry piece-of-shit brother out of jail, which cost a lot of money. Matthew was a total jack wad and confessed that he'd raped a girl at a party. Her family said that if he paid them a bunch of money, then they wouldn't report it to the police. My brother was always getting into trouble. I stopped counting the times he almost landed in jail." Brandon paused and blew out a heavy breath. "Franklin said no. It wasn't that he didn't have the funds—he just refused to help."

"Did Dillon tell Franklin what it was for?"

Brandon laughed. "He wasn't stupid, Gemma."

"Is that why you took Franklin at the wedding?" A lump lodged in my throat. I missed Franklin so much.

"I took him for two reasons. The first was because he didn't help my father and we ended up homeless for a few weeks. He needed to be taught a lesson for fucking my family over. Second, I knew you and your bleeding heart would want to save him." He gestured to me. "And I was right. I got exactly what I wanted. Gemma Thompson in my house, next to me, while we plan the next level of the society."

"You beat the shit out of Franklin," I whisper-yelled. My hands clenched into fists and I placed them in my lap in order to hide them from Brandon.

"It was just an added perk for me."

His wicked grin sent shivers down my spine. I shook my head and tried to listen to my breathing in order to ground myself. "So why blame Hendrix for Franklin's choices?"

He gave a half shrug. "Because he was the one within reach. I was too young to seek revenge on Franklin, so I went after Hendrix. The fucker is just like his father, though. He gets anything he wants." The simmering rage that always lurked inside him flickered in his gaze. "The boxing trophies, the career, the girl, and the perfect family."

"You're jealous of him? That's what this is all about?"

Brandon scoffed at me. "I was willing to let it go until you showed up."

I flinched as though he'd just hit me. "This is *my* fault?" I choked out, my words thick with guilt and remorse. *I should have stayed in Louisiana.*

"Pretty much. There was no way I was going to lose you to him." He smirked. "And I didn't. You're sitting here with me, not him."

I barked out a laugh. "You're fucking crazy. You. Will. Never. Own. My. Heart." I slapped the table with the palm of my hand.

Before I realized it, Brandon flew across the table at me, knocking me and the chair backward. He pinned my shoulders to the floor as he straddled me. "I don't have to have your heart, but make no mistake that I do *own* you." He got to his feet, then motioned to his guard.

Minutes later, I found myself back in the cold dark cell.

3 1

The sun set and rose a few more times before I lost count. Food and water came once a day, but other than the person who brought it to me, I never saw anyone. To the best of my recollection, I'd been with Brandon for nearly five days. Hope had tied my hands behind my back. Something had gone terribly wrong. I knew in my heart that Sutton would have already found me otherwise.

The ache that never stopped throbbing in my chest intensified to an earth-shattering roar. I curled into a ball on my bed and sobbed as a memory of Hendrix softly whispered my name.

Eventually, he lifted me off him, and we crawled under the covers. He slid his arm around me while I snuggled up to him, the steady thrum of his heartbeat in my ear.

"I'm afraid for you to go to sleep. What if you wake up tomorrow and your memories are gone again?" I asked, attempting to shut down my panic. I looked up at him, and his blue eyes held mine.

"If I lose my memories again, Gem, then you hold onto tonight with everything you have inside of yourself, and know I'll always find my way back to you."

Loneliness clawed at my heart, pulling me into the darkness. After a while, I cried myself out, then exhaustion settled in. My soul longed to be at home, laughing with Mac and helping her shop for items for the baby. The only comfort I could draw on was that she had her dad back. The baby had its grandpa. Hendrix had his family. A tear slipped down my cheek, and my breath shuddered as I inhaled deeply. I couldn't wait for anyone to find me. I was on my own. If I was going to make it out alive, I would have to change my plan. At this point, I could try to connect with one of the girls who catered to Brandon's every whim. Surely one of them wanted out of this way of life like I did. I hoped.

THE CREAK of the cell opening woke me the next morning. I bolted upright, immediately on guard.

Brandon closed the door but didn't lock it. "Even when you look like hell, you're still beautiful."

He sat on the edge of the bed, studying me. I remained quiet. If there was any chance of me getting out, I didn't want to screw it up.

He placed a finger beneath my chin and tilted it up. "I'm not a monster, Gemma. I have my crazy moments, but I'm just a man."

I snorted. "Brandon, something broke up here." I pointed to my head. "You don't think like normal people. Do you know that?" I made sure the tone of my voice was gentle and not accusatory. If he was in a different place mentally for a few minutes, I needed to try to break through to him.

"Hendrix and I weren't always enemies. We used to hang out sometimes."

"You did?" Hendrix had never said much about his past with Brandon, so this was news to me.

"Our first year in high school, I stayed the night at his place before a boxing match."

"Wait, you both boxed?"

Brandon nodded. "Yeah. He took the trophy every time too." A hint of anger twisted his expression, then disappeared. "Janice was super sweet. She was caring and attentive to Hendrix and Mackenzie. I didn't have that at home. Mom hadn't been around in years. It was just Dad, Matthew, and me."

"I'm sorry." I hoped he thought my sympathy was real. "What was your mom like?"

Silence filled the small space. "As I got older and heard the stories about Franklin being a drunk, I understood a little bit better that Hendrix had some tough years, but not like mine." He swallowed audibly, a faraway look on his face. "When I was seven, I came home from school. I called out for Mom, but she didn't answer. After searching the house for her, I went upstairs. Her and Dad's bedroom door was open. Some guy that wasn't Dad had his head between her legs. She was naked and totally oblivious to me standing there. I had no idea what I was looking at, so I just stood there with my mouth open. The guy got off the floor, pulled her to the edge, and started fucking her. Her old-lady tits bounced as he slammed into her. I finally left and just went downstairs."

"Did you ever find out who the man was?" I hoped he would continue to open up to me and I could find his soft spot. With his mood changes, I knew it was risky territory, though.

"Later that night, when Dad got home. I asked him who Mom's friend was and told him I'd seen them playing in the bedroom. To this day, I've never seen his cheeks turn that red. It was terrifying. He stomped up the stairs to the master bathroom where Mom was in the shower. He jerked her out, naked and wet. Dad dragged Mom by the hair through the house while she was kicking at him and desperately clawing at the furniture for leverage. Her screams still haunt my dreams."

I covered my mouth with my hands as he continued to talk. "Dad opened the door to the basement and tossed her down the stairs, then locked it so she couldn't get out. I never saw her again. Later, I learned that he sold her." He looked at me, his eyes full of hatred. "After I turned twelve, Dad took me to one of his clubs for my birthday. I had no idea they even existed, but there I was, my mouth hanging open as men openly fucked women of all ages."

"A sex club," I whispered. "Your dad owned a sex club?" This information wasn't a shock to me, but the fact that he'd taken a twelve-year-old kid was. Talk about a way to fuck him up for the rest of his life. Brandon had never experienced a normal, healthy sexual relationship. The concept was completely foreign to him.

"He and a few other men in the society opened it to fund their lifestyles and the organization. The clubs are all over the world now. That night, Dad sat me in a chair, then had a girl that barely looked eighteen sit on his lap. She leaned back against him, and he flipped up her short dress, exposing her pussy to me. He finger fucked her and played with her clit while I watched. The bitch was soaking wet. She begged for more. After a few minutes, he lifted her off of him, unzipped his pants, then screwed her." Brandon shifted on the seat and adjusted the bulge in his jeans. "The next thing I knew, he motioned for me to come over, get on my knees, and lick her wet pussy. I did and she came all over me. A few minutes later, Dad brought in a girl that was younger, and I couldn't wait to get my hands on her. Maybe it was because she was closer to my age, although I never asked. All I knew was that she was my reward for being the son that Dad had wanted me to be. She made my dick harder than anyone I'd ever seen too."

My stomach churned at the idea of young girls working as sex slaves. Dillon had made millions and catered to sick men across the world. The organization was even larger than I'd thought.

"Since then, I've preferred younger girls. Several nights a week, Dad would take Matthew and me to the club, and we had free rein to pick any age and any fantasy that we could dream up. A college girl opened me up to the world of bondage, and I liked it for years, but I always felt empty afterward. Nothing was working anymore. It wasn't long after that when my desires shifted again, and I wanted some chick I'd never met at a party. She was pretty tipsy, so it was super easy to talk her into going to a bedroom with me. Once I had her away from everyone, I did what I wanted. She clawed and kicked me, just like Mom had with Dad, but I covered her mouth with my hand." Brandon paused as if recalling more memories. "Dad brought me into the society and began to set the girls up for me. Some as young as fourteen. He fed my demons, I guess."

I frowned, confused. "I'm legal, though. I'm twenty-two."

"Except you. You were the exception. Maybe it's because you looked so young the first time I saw you. You were terrified of your own shadow. I liked your fear."

Lucky me.

"Eventually, I fell head over heels for Stephanie Johnson. We were freshmen. She seemed so normal, and I was desperate to feel something real. I asked her out, and she laughed in my face. Two weeks later, she was hanging on Hendrix's arm. I snapped."

I sat quietly and tried to wrap my head around all of the details that he'd just shared with me. He'd been horribly abused by Dillon, and so had his mother. No wonder something inside him was broken. Regardless, it didn't excuse his actions and behavior, but it might help me walk out of here alive.

"Do you want to fix me now?" Maniacal brown eyes bore a hole into me.

"No. I'm just trying to understand you better." That wasn't a lie. However, I wanted to watch him die a slow painful death for what he and his family had done to innocent women and girls, including me.

His smile turned devious and he stood. "I have a surprise for you." He held his hand out to me, and I took it. He tugged me to a standing position, his minty breath fanning across my cheek as he stared at me. Brandon whirled around, then led me out of the cell and to the main floor. My stomach growled as we passed the kitchen.

"I'll get you some food in a little bit. You'll need your strength."

His words hummed in my brain and created a haze of fear inside me as he continued up the stairs toward the bedroom where my clothes were kept. At the end of the hall, he stopped in front of another door. He swung it open, then flipped on the lights. A beautiful four-poster bed with two matching dressers filled the room. A ceiling fan circulated the air, and the metal chain pinged off the light.

"Whose room is this?"

"Mine." He tugged on my arm until we reached the bathroom.

White marble countertops with dual sinks ran along one side of the large room. A soaking tub and separate shower took up the other, and the toilet was against the opposite wall. I began to tremble. What is he up to?

He leaned over and turned on the water to the bathtub. He remained silent as he tested the temperature, then poured bubble bath in. "Get undressed."

I froze, shaking harder beneath his heated stare.

"Now!" he ordered, his patience obviously running out.

I turned my back to him and fumbled with the buttons of my shirt. If I couldn't get my fingers to work, he'd help me, and I didn't want his hands to touch my skin again. I glanced over my shoulder, but as usual, security was standing near the bathroom entrance. If I ran, it would be a death sentence.

I tossed my shirt on the floor as he sighed impatiently. "Hurry up or I'll tear your clothes off of you."

Slipping out of my jeans, I stood with my back to him, in my bra and thong.

"Turn around," he barked.

I covered myself with my hands as best I could and looked at him.

"Amy!" Brandon's voice boomed off the walls.

I cringed and backed away from him as a girl our age entered the bathroom. "Wash her hair, exfoliate her skin, then wax her legs." He raised a finger. "Also, a Brazilian wax. Get Agatha for a massage afterward. I want her pampered and relaxed. Audrey will be here shortly to help." Brandon peered at me, then back at Amy. "If she gives you any trouble, she can be pampered and naked in front of two of my men while you continue. I'm sure they would love to see her get her pussy waxed."

"Yes, master." She bowed quickly while she kept her attention on the floor.

Brandon quirked an eyebrow at me as he raked his heated gaze over my body, then he left the room and took his goon with him.

"Is anyone else with you?" I asked, my legs finally buckling beneath me.

"No. It's just you and me. Finish undressing, then get into the bath before your water gets cold."

I removed the last articles of clothing and stuck my foot into the tub.

"Is it too hot? Too cold?" she asked.

I frowned at her. "Why do you care? You're just doing what master tells you to do. It's not like you look at me as a human being held against my will."

"Do you know why I'm here?" Amy's chocolate-brown eyes narrowed at me as she placed her hands on her slender hips.

"No." I sank into the tub, the bubbles popping as I moved.

"Then shut up and do as you're told."

"For the record, you're not giving me a Brazilian wax." I cocked an eyebrow at her. She was small, and I could easily take her down. The tricky part would be getting past Brandon's goons afterward.

"It's up to you. I do it or Sam does." She smirked and slipped on a pair of long gloves. She picked up a container, filled it, and poured water over my head.

"Who's Sam?" I sputtered, spitting bubbles out of my mouth.

"He's the hot security guard that's been with you most of the time. He's walked around with a major boner since you've been here. I'm sure he'd love to get his hands on you."

"Brandon would kill him if he touched me without permission." I wasn't sure if he would or not, but as possessive as Brandon was, I figured it was a realistic scenario.

Amy poured shampoo into her hands, then lathered my hair. "I highly recommend that you get out of your head for a minute and relax."

"I'm in a psycho's bathtub. How do you suggest I do that?"

She responded with silence as she began to massage my scalp. A soft sigh slipped from my lips as she continued.

"See, it's not so hard is it?" She rinsed my long strands, then grabbed the conditioner. "Master likes strawberries and vanilla." She rubbed the product into my long hair and piled it on top of my head. Her fingers skimmed the back of my neck. "Sit up."

I did as she told me. Her dexterous hands dug into my shoulders. Between the hot water and her expertise at releasing the knots, I began to unwind. All my fear and thoughts about my surroundings seemed to slip away.

After I was dried off, Amy handed me a thick, plush robe. I snuggled into it and sat in the recliner that was nestled into the corner of the room. Vegetable soup and a roast-beef-and-cheese sandwich were brought up for me, and I stuffed my face like it was my last meal. After my belly was satisfied, I stifled a big yawn.

Hopefully, Brandon would allow me to sleep in a real bed that night instead of the one in the cell. Thoughts of Hendrix tickled the back of my mind, and I smiled. I missed my baby.

Audrey finally arrived and began trimming my hair and styling it. I struggled to keep my head still. My neck felt too heavy to hold up. By the time she was finished, I was too tired to fight her when she gave me a Brazilian wax. It stung, but not as much as I'd imagined it would. In the back of my mind, I wondered what Hendrix would think if he could see me.

Thirty minutes later, my head lolled to the side while Amy finished my manicure and pedicure. Next would be a full-body massage, but I wasn't sure I could stay awake. I was emotionally, mentally, and physically drained.

"You'll feel better after a little nap," Amy said, jerking me out of my haze. "Maybe we should skip the massage and just get you dressed."

She hopped off her stool and hurried to the closet. She flung open the door and briefly disappeared. I wasn't sure for how long because I couldn't keep my eyes from closing.

As I forced my eyelids open, the room spun, and I grabbed onto the arm of the chair. "I don't feel so good."

"It will pass in a minute, but I won't get you dressed yet, just in case." She hurried into the bathroom and returned with the trash can.

"Do you know who I am?" My words sounded slurred.

"You're one of the lead singers for August Clover, and you're engaged to Hendrix. I love your music."

"If you know who I am, why aren't you helping me run?"

A blush crept up her neck and fair skin. "He'll kill my little brother if I don't help him." Fear twisted her expression, and my heart broke for her.

"Same, except he'll kill Hendrix. Do you really think he could? Kill another person, I mean?" My fingers played with the belt of my robe while my brain struggled to break through the fog.

"There's no doubt in my mind that he's capable of such cruel and sick things."

I narrowed my eyes at her. "Why are you being nicer to me now?"

"Because you're not a threat. You can't overpower me right now. The drug is in your system."

"I don't understand." I furrowed my brows together.

"I'm not sure what he did. All he said was the bath water had something to help you become more compliant."

"Why? Amy, please."

"Don't ask questions, Gemma."

I wasn't sure how much more time passed before Amy decided it was time to get me dressed. "Be careful not to mess up your hair."

I patted my long strands. How had I forgotten that Audrey had already been here and left? Amy guided me to the bedpost and wrapped my fingers around it. The rustling of a plastic bag caught my attention. "What's that?"

"Your dress. Hold onto my shoulder and step in carefully."

"Okay." I attempted to lift my leg, but it weighed a hundred pounds. "I can't move it."

"I don't have much time left, then." Amy worked furiously and finally slid the dress up over my hips. My arms felt like limp noodles as she guided them into the sleeves. She hurried behind me and pulled up the zipper.

A loud knock broke through my jumbled thoughts, and I slowly turned my head toward the sound.

"Master." Amy knelt and fluffed the fabric on the floor.

Brandon's eyes widened as he walked around me as though I were on display. "You look more beautiful than I ever dreamed."

"Why am I wearing a dress? Amy won't tell me." I peered at him through heavy eyelids.

"Because tonight, you're going to become my wife."

"No." I thought I screamed, but the words came out so softly I wasn't sure anyone could hear me. "No. I won't do it."

"You need to sleep, but when I get back from my errands, we'll have a quick ceremony. And afterward—" He leaned down, his breath grazing my ear. "I will take you to my bed."

Inwardly, I shouted at him and clawed his cheeks with my newly manicured nails. I would never marry him. He couldn't force me too.

"It's all worked out, Gemma. In a few hours you'll sign the license. Even if you try to annul the marriage, no judge will allow it. Well, none on my payroll anyway. Plus, we consummated the marriage as far as they know. We were in a relationship. You visited me in jail and fucked my brains out for the world to see. Remember the video?" His laugh filled the room. He lowered his face to mine. "I. Own. You."

In a quick movement, he swept me off my feet and carried me to his bed. My muscles refused to obey me, and I remained limp and unable to fight him. "Sweet dreams." Brandon pressed his mouth against mine, then I slipped into a peaceful oblivion.

Don't miss the continuation of Hendrix and Gemma's story in **Love & Retaliation from Hendrix's point of view**! Universal link: https://readerlinks.com/l/1777497

Need to catch up on the International bestselling series before June? https://readerlinks.com/l/1604424/love-and-ruin-series-page

ALSO BY J.A. OWENBY

Where I'll Find You

READ MY BOOKS EARLY!

Want to read my books before they release? Join my review team. Email me at jenowenby@frontier.com for details.

I appreciate your help in spreading the word online as well as telling a friend. Reviews help readers find books they love, so please leave a review on your favorite book site.

You can also join my Facebook group, J.A. Owenby's One Page At A Time, for exclusive giveaways and sneak peeks of future books.

A NOTE FROM THE AUTHOR:

Dear Readers,

If you have experienced sexual assault or physical abuse, there is free confidential help. Please visit:

Website: https://www.rainn.org/
Phone: 800-656-4673

ABOUT THE AUTHOR

International bestselling author J.A. Owenby grew up in a small backwoods town in Arkansas where she learned how to swear like a sailor and spot water moccasins skimming across the lake.

She finally ditched the south and headed to Oregon. The first winter there, she was literally blown away a few times by ninety mile an hour winds and storms that rolled in off the ocean.

Eventually, she longed for quiet and headed up to snowier pastures. She now resides in Washington state with her hot nerdy husband and cat, Chloe (who frequently encourages her to drink). She spends her days coming up with ways to torture characters in a way that either makes you want to throw your book down a flight of stairs or sob hysterically into a pillow.

J.A. Owenby writes new adult and romantic thriller novels. Her books ooze with emotion, angst, and twists that will leave you breathless. Having battled her own demons, she's not afraid to tackle the secrets women are forced to hide. After all, the road to love is paved in the dark.

Her friends describe her as delightfully twisted. She loves fan mail and wine. Please send her all the wine.

You can follow the progress of her upcoming novel on Facebook at Author J.A. Owenby and on Twitter @jaowenby.

Sign up for J.A. Owenby's Newsletter:
https://www.authorjaowenby.com/newsletter

J.A. Owenby's One Page At A Time reader group:
https://www.facebook.com/groups/JAOwenby

CPSIA information can be obtained
at www.ICGtesting.com
Printed in the USA
FSHW010744040521
81000FS